STRAWBERRY RHUBARB PIE

A Family Gathering Mystery

David Marshall Hunt

Copyright

CONTENTS

THE BEST PLACE
TO HIDE A FAMILY
SECRET IS IN
PLAIN SIGHT.

CHAPTER 1

*3:15 am SAST, March 21,
1992, Witwatersrand,
Johannesburg, South Africa*

The persistent ringing of a telephone is disturbing my sleep. I am not sure if it's real or part of a dream. I live in a rented cottage thousands of miles from where I was born. My life is that of a wanderer, never developing a feeling that where I rest my head is home. It's been my experience late-night calls are from someone who forgets to check the time zone difference before calling or heaven forbid; they foreshadow disaster.

A disturbing nightmare invades my restless sleep and mingles with the persistent ringing.

The figure appears of a handsome yet ghostly white-haired, grey-eyed woman in her seventies, dressed in a threadbare cotton nightgown. She struggles to reach the telephone on the nightstand next to her bed. Her withered left arm reaches for the receiver, her trembling fingers miss, and it tumbles to the floor.

She sighs in frustration and moves to turn on the lamp. It falls, entangling with the cord. She attempts to rise and put on her slippers. She untangles the phone and is dialing the numbers to call someone.

Her lips are mouthing the words, "Daniel Matthew, it's mom!"

Twisting my bedsheets into a knot, I'm sweating as the ringing persists.

Some sounds are comforting to me. The gong of the great Silla bell in South Korea, the rhythmic calls to prayer from the minarets of mosques in the Emirates and Karachi, church bells from St. James Cathedral in Seattle, all are familiar. But I sense that the unrelenting sound I'm hearing or dreaming about is a harbinger of distressing news.

Calls from overseas don't always come through to South Africa during the monsoon season. My habit is to let my phone ring several times before picking it up. Besides, I'm renting this place, and I get a dozen calls a day for the previous tenant.

This morning, my dream-state couples with a hangover, magnifying the volume and annoyance of the rings.

I attempt to mute the sound by covering my head with a pillow, hiding from the disturbing images of mom's struggles.

The ringing intensifies and awakens me at 3:20 am SAST. I struggle out of bed, grab the receiver from the night-table, and admonish the caller.

"Do you know what the time is?"

"Little brother... sad news... mom died... sleep last night," a familiar voice says as static crackles between Yuma and Johannesburg disrupting the call.

"Daniel, are you there?"

"Yes, I'm here," I say. "I spoke with mom last Friday. She apologized for missing my birthday by a day, but she seemed fine."

He reports that the Yuma County medical examiner gave a preliminary determination of a heart attack, cardio something or other.

More static breaks up his words, then he says, "The landlord called the police about an hour ago, and they found mom laying on the floor with the receiver buzzing."

I struggle to distinguish dream from reality.

"They will cremate her remains as she wished," Jer says, "There are no plans for a memorial of any kind."

I'm relieved that I won't need to be at the service. But upset at not having a role in the last act of my mother's existence.

"I'll check with my secretary about catching a flight back from Joburg to Seattle, then shuttle over to Spokane."

"That'll put you at the Jonson farm in a few days," he says. "I'll meet you there, and we'll bury mom's ashes in the cemetery next to Grandpa and Grandma, daughter Esther, and brother Paul."

After Jer hangs up, I continue to muse over my disturbing dream. It occurred only moments before my brother's call. Was my nightmare the last communication between my mother and me, her youngest son?

Once a month I have dutifully called mom, but that's the extent of my connecting with relatives. I have distanced myself from family responsibilities as I drift around the globe. It's a year since I spoke to my older brother and longer since I went stateside. The lure of overseas experience is intoxicating and the work fulfilling.

Huckleberry Finn ran away from home to find adventure. As did I. The challenge of finding the road back is hard for a wanderer. Ask my mom. Change that, ask any expatriate, they'll explain what I mean.

I haven't thought of family to this extent for years, but my first recall is troubling. Mom's death triggers a disturbing childhood memory that rattles around in my head. Near the end of the War in the Pacific, we paid our last respects to Paul, my favorite storytelling uncle. It was the earliest death of a beloved one that I experienced. At 13, I took it hard as I was Uncle Paul's apprentice. Every day I completed my chores about the farm as a child, but my most meaningful role was apprentice storyteller.

Jer thinks of me as a hermit, and perhaps he's right, I am narcissistic. My focus on self is troubling me, a product of my career and my three decades of living abroad. I'm disturbed by my dodging of family responsibilities.

I'm Daniel Matthew Jonson, a 61-year-old American of Swedish ancestry. My lifelong passion for running and mountain biking keeps me lean and fit. My hair and beard are grey as befits my station and stage in life. I'm a Visiting Professor of International Business History at the University of the Witwatersrand (WITS) Graduate School at the Parktown Campus in Johannesburg (Joburg).

South Africa is suffering from debilitating global

trade sanctions, internal political turmoil, and a staggering 60 percent unemployment rate. Mine work is a primary source of employment. It's hazardous. Lung disease is common among laborers in gold and diamond mines over a mile beneath the earth's surface. Living in stark barracks, far from families, is a sorry fate. I focus my research on these working conditions and the miner's compensation and morale.

Traveling and pursuing adventure in exotic lands is an essential aspect of my profession as an international business scholar. I meet people of varied cultural backgrounds and values and assist them in improving their employment practices. To travel is to learn, and as I expand my knowledge, I share what I have experienced.

My university salary is adequate, but I pay a price in terms of infrequent returns to the states and the home of my childhood. I limit my family visits to Christmas holidays or summers between academic semesters.

Devoting my past 25 years to lecturing and researching at universities around the world has taken me far from the center of my upbringing in Spokane's River Valley in eastern Washington. On the rare occasions of my stateside visits, my mom often reminds me I possess the look of a wanderer in my blue-gray eyes. She is the only one who calls me Daniel Matthew.

Two months of monsoon rains just ended, and it's time to leave the gymnasium and resume my outdoor running routine. Yesterday I ran in a 15-kilometer race with a group of my graduate students. It exhausted me. We celebrated a bit too much at the pub in the rear of Mike's Kitchen. Carling's Black Label Lager has done me in more than once.

From time to time, I assess where I am and where I come from, and why am I doing whatever I'm doing. As the details of the sad and shocking nightmare and the pursuant reality set in, I sense that it's necessary for me to step back and take stock. It's been some while since my last deep introspection. I'll need some help in doing this.

7:05 am SAST, March 22, 1992, Johannesburg, South Africa

My thoughts of the dream and death of mom and memories of my childhood and Uncle Paul are haunting me when a second call comes from Yuma the next morning. The ringing is less persistent, and the hour doesn't matter because I haven't slept since the nightmare.

"Jonson, Stanhope, & Houseman attorneys at law, Mary here, is this Daniel?"

"Hi Mary, yes, it's me, good to hear your voice," I say, recalling that Mary has been Jer's legal secretary for two decades.

"You too, Daniel," Mary says, "hold for Jerry, please."

"There's no urgent reason for you to return, stateside," Jer says. "I believe mom is at peace. There isn't anything you can do here until we get together with Sara Swenson, mom's lawyer up in Spokane."

Again, I feel a twinge of disappointment at not having a role to play at mom's interment.

"I remember Sara," I say, "the lady who wears the big sunhats, even in the winter."

"That's her, and she wants us to determine what happens next at the auction of the Jonson homestead."

"Auction!" I say, startled at the thought of selling the hub of our childhood to strangers.

"Sara said that mom left packages with her and instructed that you and I open them together at the farm."

"What's that about?"

"Your guess is as good as mine."

Reflecting on family is filling my head with events and relatives I haven't thought of for years. We once numbered over fifty members of varied ethnicities living in the Pacific Northwest. Since WWII we scattered far and wide. I left the home of my childhood and gradually became a loner and a wanderer during my decades of international adventures.

Mom worked hard over the years to stay in communication with our scattered relatives. Jer is a year older than me, and we shared many an adventure as children on the farm. Before the War, we used to have Christmas gatherings for the entire clan. Mom, Jer, and I were present at our last family gathering during December 1941 when the Japanese attacked Pearl Harbor. We lost Paul and three adopted members, Charlee Sang, Franklin Yoshino, and Tinya Yoshino, vanished between 1941 and 1945. I've not spoken these names for fifty years, but they come into my thoughts, in a manner that is unnerving.

Jer has shouldered most of the responsibility while raising children of his own. Perhaps it's my turn to do something for the family, but what?

The more I think about family, the more I feel guilt. This perception of guilt seems rooted in my childhood. Spent mostly at the Jonson's farm in the Spokane River Valley. Fragments of stories have popped into my dreams, but not for years. Family gatherings at the homestead for Christmas were special events.

My brother and I stealing one of grandma's pies. Can't forget Grandpa's willow switch. Paul made the university rowing team. Paul was the family storyteller and I recall that he loved to tell scary stories from atop Big Black Rock. I try to make sense of it all, but details escape my grasp.

My childhood recollections of home lie buried beneath layers of my adventures abroad. Exotic sights and career relocations to many countries in Africa, the middle east, and Southeast Asia are my resume. Kenya's lush tea and coffee lands in Kericho and the splendors of the Masai Mara. The escarpments of South Africa and the waterfalls known in Afrikaans as the Witwatersrand. The city of Johannesburg grew during a late 19th-century gold rush. Mountainous piles of yellow slag bear testimony to the waste, perhaps serving as monuments to the difference in wealth and poverty.

All these contemporary memories are of people and places in distant lands, not part of an auction or my childhood. But the images that haunt me are not only about mom's death, but about the man I admired most as a boy. I loved my Uncle Paul, the rower, the sailor, the adventurer, the storyteller who took me under his wing as his apprentice, he was my mom Connie's youngest brother. I haven't thought about him for decades.

An hour after Jer's second call, I stuff some student papers I've been grading into my backpack and lock up my rental cottage. I live on a quiet residential side street between the Technikon and Hillbrow Tower in Johannesburg's Parktown district. It's the first week after the rainy season, and I start out the front door on my trek to the campus. My lecture in the Bert Wessels Building starts in two hours.

As I latch the gate, the phone rings again. I wish someone would invent a way to block unwanted calls.

The ringing seems less persistent, but the devastating news of the previous call prompts me to turn around and reenter the cottage.

A fourth ring sounds. Before going to bed last night, I reset the answering machine to take over after the fourth ring with a recorded message.

"You reached the party you dialed, if urgent, leave your name and number and I'll call back, if not, enjoy your day."

"It's me," I say as I recognize the caller's resonant tone.

"Hi, Daniel!" Claire says, "Jer just called me with the news about your mom. I'm so sad. How are you holding up?"

Earlier I said that I'd turned into a loner, that's not accurate. I have a select few compatriots. Claire Parsons is more than a close friend and colleague; she's my main squeeze.

She is a professor in the Department of Anthropology at Washington University in Seattle. A brilliant researcher and a sought-after speaker on topics of vanished civilizations and lost persons. She also has a doctorate in clinical psychology and maintains a small private practice. When I'm confronted by personal challenges help often comes in the form of this gorgeous and insightful woman.

"Sometimes, a journey to the past reveals why you behave the way you do in the present," Claire says.

I have lived abroad most of my life, and I recognize that I see things from a changed perspective whenever I return home. An example being how I see elements of the ghetto suburb of Soweto in America's cities.

Homeless persons on park benches and living under sheets of cardboard or beneath highway overpasses. Piles of garbage and a lack of medical clinics. Schools with their windows broken. These are the attributes of sections of Pacific coast cities from San Diego to Seattle. My lens changes with every overseas experience and adventure. Poverty and wealth, beauty and waste often are separated by a single street or railroad track or lake.

When I'm stateside in the summers, Claire and I run through the grounds of Washington Park Arboretum near her hilltop home in Seattle's Parkside district. It is an example of the beauty and wealth that exists. Not far to the south is Nickelsville, an unauthorized tent city on the Duwamish Waterway.

Geographic distance has long been a challenge to our relationship. Our careers and 8,000 miles separate us. It isn't the most intimate arrangement to have with one's main squeeze. We remain close despite geographic distance. Her fiery love of life matches her flaming red hair, unless it's blonde or brunette depending on her mood and her matching outfit.

"I wish I could be with you," Claire says, her soft, gravelly voice a soothing balm.

"I know how much you and your brother loved and respected your mom," she says. "Jer conveyed that you plan to finish your stint at WITS and said something about a marathon with someone named Dawselle. He also asked me to persuade you that there is no need to rush home."

I'm finishing the story about my terrifying dream when we lose our Seattle to Joburg connection. A thunderstorm drenches the city, and me thinking the stormy season is over. The phone crackles back on, and they restore the line.

"That nightmare has me wrestling with fragments of memories of Uncle Paul, who returned from The Philippines in 1945 and died shortly before the fighting ended."

"That must have been a painful experience," Claire says, "the death of someone you loved."

"Resurrecting events of my childhood is adding to my feelings of guilt," I say. "Could it be the shock of auctioning off our family home?"

"I understand the grief, but why the guilt?"

"Because I've been running away from family responsibility for decades."

Claire lets this pass without comment.

The lights in my Joburg cottage flicker and go out, and our call gets cut off. I grab a flashlight and check the utility room behind the kitchen and flip and reset the circuit breakers.
Ten minutes later, the storm has blown past, and they reconnect us.

"Let's take stock before we discuss more about the fragments of your heritage," Claire says.

My grasp of home and love of family has changed

over the times, and the way back to them, in distance and time, requires me to return.

She senses that my depression runs deeper than the nightmare of mom's death, mingling with the demise of Uncle Paul. There is a greater connection. The auction is upsetting; but she suspects there's something buried deep in my memory-attic that exaggerates my sense of guilt.

"We must get to the source of the guilt," she says, "and determine why it dates to your childhood, then we need a treatment plan."

If it were anyone other than Claire, I would have hung up, but I respect her professional skills and I listen to her excellent advice.

The Journal of Ancient Cultures and Antiquities published her research into the disappearance in the islands of the South Pacific Ocean of the famous aviatrix Amelia Earhart. Now she's doing research that involves the 50th anniversary of EO9066. The executive order that incarcerated over 100,000 Japanese during WWII.

President Bush just issued a public apology to these American citizens of Japanese heritage for the nation's folly. That apology sparked her investigation into the fate of imprisoned Japanese Americans, many from the Seattle/Tacoma area where she works and lives. Their land and property are not being restored to them since their release from the camps in 1945. Compensation is being considered.

"This week, I'm putting the finishing touches to the first part of my latest investigation project."

"I have a proposal for you, Daniel," she says. "I'll get a colleague to cover my last two weeks of classes. Then I'll fly to Johannesburg. We'll work on finding some answers together?"

"You can join our running team," I say. "Our favorite trail takes in some local sights including the planetarium and the zoo."

"Can we take one of those hot-air balloon rides over Kruger National Park?" she says. "You'll break my heart if you say no."

"You're teasing," I say, sensing and visualizing a twinkle in the emerald flecks of her slate-grey eyes.

All I hear is her laughter, then comes another power failure. The line goes dead. I wait for it to ring. I'm thinking, how can the phone company call to tell me the lines are down?

I'm also thinking about how much Claire means to me.

Her call has sent a breath of fresh air sweeping through the cottage. For a moment, I feel I won't have to make it through this guilt and grief on my own. She is right about my distress, but I have my research, lecturing, and classes, and my training with Dawselle for the Comrades to take my mind off my miseries. Meanwhile, I need to get to WITS for the morning run and my lecture.

CHAPTER 2

Running is a passion of mine and over the next two weeks, I average 50 miles a week. To run is to feel free, a time to think creatively.

I run daily with a small group of my students, led by Dawselle Webber, my graduate assistant, and an accomplished distance runner. My days begin with a brisk run with team Dawselle. She has her team doing fartlek runs, intervals and sprints, mixed in with lots of hills, aimed at getting us into the best condition of our lives. She is in the last stages of training for the forthcoming Olympics in Barcelona.

The Comrades is an ultra marathon race that attracts a field of thousands of runners to South Africa. She is running to further establish her qualifications with the RSA Olympic committee. She waves at a group of four runners as they glide past us near the zoo; they are world caliber athletes.

"That's Bruce Fordyce, he's won the Comrades nine times," Dawselle says, "he'll be one of the favorites for the men this year."

"I need two runners to keep me company and pace me for the initial quarter of the race, 13 miles from Pietermaritzburg to Camperdown," she says.

While I'm still stuck on the 13 miles, she explains that I only need to run the first leg. Then her other pacer takes over and I can drop out and catch a ride to the finish line in Durban. We'll have a drink together with the team at one of the beachfront hotels on the Indian Ocean and celebrate after the race.

A beer and lolling about on the beaches at Durban, how can I resist.

Despite my lectures and the distractions of a rigorous running routine, buoyed by an end to the rainy season, I'm unable to shake my depression and feelings of responsibility. The nightmare of mom's last call returns. Fragments of memories of the family farm and my favorite storytelling Uncle are emerging day and night. I recall visiting the Montlake Cut to see the skull races; but I'm puzzled about why I have repressed the details of these childhood memories. I soon learn that I can't force them. I need to discuss this with Claire.

This morning, I awake to a nagging sense that I have forgotten to do something. I ignore the feeling and continue to prep for my lecture. I'm giving my last lecture to my WITS graduate class for the Spring semester. The title is "Mentoring: Formal vs. Informal."

After my presentation, the students head for their next classes. Trekking across St. David's Street in Parktown, I follow the aroma of bread baking in the huge brick ovens at Mike's Kitchen. My favorite table is outside beneath a pergola overgrown with vines and under the fragrant sweet purple lavender blooms of rows of Jacaranda trees. I bask in the lavender's essence and the aroma of bread baking, sipping on a Carling lager. To eat was my goal for coming here, but I'm satiated and order a three-bean salad. My heavenly bliss conflicts with a nagging feeling that I have forgotten something important.

When I return to my office, it's past noon. My secretary has left a fluorescent green post-it stuck on the wall. She posted it behind my desk, next to a female lioness poster downing a frantic gazelle in Kruger National Park.

The symbolism suggests urgency.

To Prof Daniel:
April 14: Professor Claire arriving on South Africa Air flight #735 at 12:45 noon local time, 9:45 Greenwich time, Johannesburg International Airport in Kempton Park.

The nagging was for real, I had forgotten something. Claire wasn't teasing, she's arriving in 40 minutes. The nagging feeling goes away.

It's 12:05 and it takes 40 minutes to get to Kempton Park in lunch hour traffic. I shower and change into my favorite white linen slacks and shirt and rush out to the parking lot, shouting for my driver. Major is in the driveway next to the cottage polishing his old Benz. He's been my reliable driver since I decided I do not wish to die driving at 140 kph on the highways on the wrong side.

"We need to meet a flight at Kempton Airport at 12:45, can we make it?"

"No problem, Sahib," Major says.

He used to call me boss. I prefer Sahib.

Rolling to the taxiway from the runway, scattering several leaping Grant's gazelles, is a white, red, and blue South African Air Boeing 747 with its distinct gold tail. The animals move with righteous indignation across the runway as the tires screech, and puffs of smoke rise on touchdown. The big jet taxies for ten minutes, as if it's reluctant to end its graceful flight before rolling to a stop at the terminal.

The door behind the pilot's cabin swings open and a flight attendant pokes her head out. She gazes left, then right, and disappears back into the aircraft. Then she locks the opened door in place. A ramp rolls up, with a set of debarking stairs. A graceful form glides down the ramp from the jet. She tucks her long reddish-brown locks under her sunbonnet and ties it down with a white scarf flowing in the breeze.

This elegant Ingrid Bergman look-alike is experienced at theatrical entrances. I half expect to see an entourage descending the stairs behind her, a Hollywood movie crew arriving to do a Bogart and Bergman remake of *Casablanca*.

She squints in the bright sunlight, adjusts a pair of sunglasses as she descends royally. The sun reflects off the huge, mirrored lenses. She pauses midway down the stairs to lower the shades halfway down her nose. Peering over the rims, she searches for someone in the crowd that lines the fence near the terminal entrance.

"Hi Daniel Jonson!" she calls out with a queenly wave, "You beautiful man!"

"Hello to you too gorgeous," I call back, "that's our ride."

I point at the well-polished vintage black Benz, with a VIP flag flying from the radio antennae.

"Meet you at baggage claim," I say, "ask for Major, he'll help you with customs and your luggage."

My mistake I'm thinking, I told Major to put the VIP flag up, and that was what drew the crowd, that, and the dramatic entrance. Did I mention that Claire always travels first class?

After she clears customs, she repeats her condolences over my mom's recent demise, and gives me a hug that lasts for several minutes. To my way of thinking, she's irresistible. I admit to Claire that I lust after her, and she smiles back at me; then, when she is ready, she ravishes me. It works for me.

Major holds the passenger door open with a tip of his hat to Claire, and we slide into the backseat of the Benz. There are paparazzi gathering, enticed by Claire's flamboyant entrance. The VIP flag gets us through the traffic and guardhouse at the exit without a hitch.

Major drops Claire and I off in the Auckland Park District at the Bistro Coffee House.

"We'll walk home from here, Major," I say. "Thanks for the lift."

"I thought a lift is an elevator over here," Claire says.

"Is a boot a glove box or the trunk?" I say.

"And is a 'Benz' a Mercedes or a 'Merc' a Ford Mercury?" she says.

"When I hired Major as my driver, I owned a 10-year-old Nissan that needed some repairs. I couldn't find an auto body shop listing in the yellow pages to repair the dents. Major recommended that I take the car to the panel beaters on Fourth Street by the SA Bank."

"What's a panel beater?"

"That's what I said," I say. "It's a shop where you get the dents knocked out of your car and then get it repainted."

"Very intuitive!" she says with a laugh. "What would I find in Seattle if I checked the yellow pages for a panel beater?"

Hugging and laughing, we enter The Bistro and order French press coffee for two. For the next several minutes, I stare into her hypnotic steely eyes, and she looks back into my blue-grey orbs, smiling all the while.

"Miss me?" she murmurs, laughing with a most appealing girlish laugh.

"Uh, huh!" I say, "And I love your do."

Learning to compliment her changes in hairstyle is a major element in our continuing relationship.

After catching up on her latest research, we chat about some local stuff, and the forthcoming Comrades double marathon that Dawselle plans to run next month.

"I can't wait to meet Dawselle," Claire says, "she sounds like someone I need to know so's I can catch up on what you've been up to."

"We're running several miles through the park and past the zoo tomorrow at 6 am rain or shine, care to join us?" I say.

"After a night's rest."

As we sip our French press coffees, I introduce Claire to the waitress who brings us a bag of bagels and cream cheese to go.

"This terrific young lady who is serving us is Flo," I say. "She's the Co-owner of The Bistro, and she's a friend and regular running partner of Dawselle's and mine."

"Welcome to The Bistro, my brother Dirk and I own this establishment," Flo says, "the coffee and bagels are on us."

"It's so nice to see a couple who enjoy each other's company," Flo says, adding, "Besides, you solved an enigma for Dirk and me about Professor Doctor Jonson."

We walk in silence, arm in arm, back to my two-bedroom white rental cottage.

"What did Flo mean about my solving an enigma about you?" Claire asks.

"She's just happy that I have such a beautiful lady as you in my life,"

"That's nice!" she says as I hug her and kiss her full on the mouth.

"Did I know you were coming to Joburg?" I say with a grin.

Claire's luggage blocks the front door to the cottage. Major had left them in the foyer in case it rained. I go behind the cottage and enter through the kitchen; then, I haul all seven bags inside. Each one must weigh over the limit at the airport.

While Claire unpacks, which seems to take hours, I run around the house cleaning up a bit. After cleaning the dishes, I brew a pot of hojicha tea. I carry it with a plate of oven warmed sliced bagels and a bowl of cream cheese covered in wax paper to keep the flies away. We can enjoy the sunset from the porch swing. As I set the scene, I'm thinking to myself, I too have a flair for theatrics. No, make that the romantic.

Claire floats out onto the porch, backlit by the kitchen light.

"Have you got any extra hangers?"

Her long reddish-brown hair hangs down over her shoulders, glistening from her shower. She's wearing an alluring sheer beige nightdress that distracts me and has me gawking.

She laughs, having attained the desired effect.

"The hangers can wait," she says.

Sitting on the back-porch swing, we watch in silence as a masterpiece gets drawn in front of us by mother nature.

Claire smiles and curls up next to me.

"You have missed me, haven't you?"

An unbelievable cast of planets and twinkling lights decorates the night sky along with several shooting stars streaking by. We miss most of the show.

After an hour of delighting each other, we do a second hour of cuddling. Claire gets out of bed, a lithe leopard stretching in a manner that has me enthralled.

A hearty, deep-throated laugh trails behind her as she retrieves an envelope from her spacious handbag and hands it to me.

"Later big boy!" she says. "Let's attend to business, if you're up to it?"

"I'm hoping that this news article will trigger more of your childhood memories of your storytelling uncle."

She hands me a copy of a Seattle-Times newspaper with a feature on the 50th anniversary of Pearl Harbor. The article also reprints a presidential apology letter to the Japanese American survivors and families of the internment camps. A part of Claire's latest research into lost and separated family members because of EO9066.

"Sara Swenson, your mom's lawyer, called me and

asked for your address in Africa," Claire says.

Sara apologizes for failing to reach you in person and sends her condolences. She sets forth the tentative schedule for the sale of the Jonson farm at auction this Autumn. Scribbled on the top of the page is a note: Jer and Daniel: Please notify me soon of a specific auction date best for you; the first to respond sets the date.

Details of family gatherings from back in 1940 and 1941, creep into my consciousness.

The first to arrive is a mental image of the farm, the geographic hub for the Jonson and Nordling clans.

I take a sip of hojicha tea and pick up the Seattle-Times. A column on page eight catches my eye. It's an editorial advocating building a second bridge across the Montlake Cut in Seattle. The plan is to accommodate foot and bicycle traffic and reduce crowding and congestion at Opening Day ceremonies.

At the bottom of the editorial, there's a plug for Opening Day of Seattle's Boating Spectacle for 1992. There is a photograph of the Montlake Cut Bridge. In the first week of May each year, the Bridge is the site of Opening Day. It marks the start of the boating season and festivities on the lakes and tributaries of the Puget Sound that surround Seattle.

"We visited the Montlake Cut on Opening Day with Uncle Paul in 1940."

"Tell me more."

"We arrived here to honor Uncle Paul's making the prestigious UW Huskies freshman rowing team and see his first race," I say, "it was a special day with a picnic."

"That's significant detail," she says, "we need detail in each childhood memory that comes to you."

Then Claire lays an unexpected bomb on me.

"I'm sorry, I almost forgot," she says as she digs around in her handbag, which I swear contains enough stuff to equip an army platoon.

"Sara Swenson sent another envelope with me," she says, "one I'm to give to you if I see you before Jer."

I open the envelope. It contains a note from Uncle Paul addressed to Connie back in 1940. It has a page of directions on how to get from Seattle's King Street train station to Montlake Cut Bridge.

"Go figure!" Claire says. "Put those directions together with the Opening Day news article, and I bet you can guess where we'll be on May 4."

"Seattle for the Opening Day festivities at the Montlake Cut Bridge," I say. "That's only a week from now."

"Eerie isn't it," she says. "Do you sense some force is leading you back to Seattle?"

"Could be family ghosts."

Uncle Paul's letter with directions for Connie to get to the bridge sparks my optimism. The log jam unravels in my memory attic, but it's only the start of what Claire is planning for me.

"I have a therapeutic plan for you to consider. How to deal with all the cobwebs and break up at least some log jams and confusion in your memory-attic," Claire says. "Want to hear it?"

"Are you suggesting that my memory-attic is log jam and needs organizing?"

"Your words, not mine," Claire says, "My early prognosis is that you are suffering from repressed memories caused by a traumatic event during your childhood."

Uncle Paul's map and directions lead us to the bridge, where the Opening Day celebration starts on May 4, 1992.

"We will reenact your family celebration and picnic trip of 1940 with a visit to the Montlake Bridge," Claire says. "Sounds exciting."

"Let me guess," I say, "the next step is to make a list of the key places and events that link to my childhood and Uncle Paul."

"You grasp things quickly for someone with only one PhD," Claire says with a wry smile. "We'll start with events, people, and places which already are invading your consciousness."

"A picnic, Uncle Paul's return from the War, and family gatherings for Christmas at the Jonson farm in Spokane in 1940 and 1941 before the raids on Pearl Harbor," I say. "Those are high on the list. I believe we have a plan."

"I'll start a file in my notepad, you do the same."

"Okay, if I get some rest first?"

"You can try, but you're so wound up, it's not likely."

She's betting that I won't be able to sleep with all the logs rushing down the sluice and into the open water. She's right. More logs slide down the sluice and reveal details in my dreams, and I get no sleep.

After Opening Day, it's on to log step two, then step three, and so forth, careful so's I don't slip off the rolling logs. Her plan calls for slight steps until we turn over the log that uncovers the event and reason behind my trauma, repressed memories, and feelings of guilt.

We discuss why I'm stressing over mom's passing. Why is it coupled with the demise of my uncle?

"No wonder nothing else seems to matter," Claire says. "All you say makes sense, but I suspect there is something else that is bothering you. An event hidden deep in the childhood years of the log jam in your memory-attic."

"It's coming back a log at a time," I say, "but it may turn into a flood of logs at some point?"

"That's why I'm here," Claire says with a warm smile.

After a morning run, at a breakfast of hot oatmeal, topped with slices of golden delicious apples and brown sugar, we discuss the news that is the context for my childhood.

The attacks on Pearl Harbor were all the motivation Uncle Paul needed to enlist in the Navy. Three months later, President Roosevelt issued Executive Order #9066, evacuating, and incarcerating thousands of Japanese Americans from the Pacific coast. My extended family was soon scattered all over the globe.

"Is it possible to recover enough fragments of one's old memories to uncover a single secret lost fifty years ago?"

"Slow down," Claire says, "what's this 50-year-old secret about?"

"That's my dilemma," I say, "I don't remember. I'm not sure if I ever knew the secret reason behind my Uncle Paul's last story."

"What story is that?"

"Uncle Paul made up a scary story about a Chinaman," I say. "He made me promise to spread the tale all over the neighborhood while he was away."

"You were his apprentice storyteller?"

"I reveled in the role of his apprentice, but I've repressed most of my memories of Uncle Paul," I say. "His story about a Chinaman is starting to come back to me and I think I kept my promise."

I attempt to recall our extended family members at Big Black Rock when Uncle Paul first told his scary tale and secured my promise to spread it to the children in the neighborhood while he is away.

Claire sees my distress and says, "Don't force it, Daniel."

"With mom gone," I say, "Jer's the only family member left who heard Uncle Paul's stories."

"You can't force these memories," Claire says, "your pain keeps them buried deep in the agony of losing Uncle Paul and other extended family members to the war."

She's right, and their loss is painful to recall.

"We'll open the sluice more when we get to Opening Day," she says. "You can ask Jer what he remembers about your uncle's storytelling when you meet at the farm to inter Connie's ashes."

"Meanwhile, do you recall who else was there?" Claire asks.

"That's the problem," I say. "I can't remember individual names. But I'm certain some of them were with mom, Jer, and I at the Montlake Cut."

"Details," Claire says, "that's what we're looking for, and you're already breaking through the barrier."

"After he secured my solemn declaration to retell the story, he made me swear to a second promise," I say, "But, for the life of me, I can't recall what it was."

"Let me get this straight," Claire says. "What we are looking for is a forgotten commitment to your favorite storytelling uncle. Hidden amongst the cobwebs of your memory-attic. And your uncle had a secret reason for devising a story and making you promise to spread it throughout the neighborhood. Then he wanted you to do something else?"

"That's the gist of it."

"How simple can it get," Claire says. "I get the scary part of his story, he wanted to ward off trespassers while he's away, makes sense, but why are you full of feelings of guilt?"

"I sense that you are grappling with something," Claire says, "but you're not making it clear my love."

"You suggested that some traumatic event occurred in my childhood, and it is blocking or repressing my memories."

"Can Jer verify whether you kept your pledge to Uncle Paul?" she says, "Do you want to call him or wait until the two of you are at the farm?"

It becomes noticeable that exhaustion is setting in for both of us. I suggest that we take a fresh look at the issue in the morning.

"There's a secret hidden somewhere deep in your memory-attic, but why guilt?" Claire says as she falls asleep before finishing her thought.

In seconds she's sawing wood. I don't dare wake her, and I'll never tell her she snores like a lumberjack.

CHAPTER 3

The quaint rental cottage is owned by a WITS faculty member on sabbatical. They left the shutters locked. I need to open them to let in a cool morning breeze. Hanging over the kitchen sink is a ring of keys, problem solved. Claire and I snuggle under the feather comforter, reluctant to leave our cozy nest.

"Care to join Dawselle and me for this morning's run?" I say.

She yawns and does her leopard stretch.

Smiling in her familiar satisfied way, she shifts gears and answers my question from before our distraction.

"Shaking my jet lag is today's goal, and meeting Dalisay," she says. "With the caveat that I can drop out if Joburg's thin air gets to me."

She knows that she'll be sucking for oxygen in the high-altitude. I still do, and I've been here for months. Running at high altitude is something one is born into. I get dressed in my running gear, lace up my shoes, heading for the kitchen for orange juice and a banana, a low carb snack before our run. I'm not sure if I'm disappointed or pleased. At least she caught the gist of what I was telling her before we got sidetracked.

Several of my graduate students are at the parking area behind the WITS campus when we arrive, waiting under a plexiglass canopy while a shower passes. Dawselle Webber doffs her rain suit and adjusts her white singlet, revealing a powerful, slender bronze body. She tucks her flaxen ponytail into a UW baseball cap. She's 26, with green eyes that sparkle with flecks of gold when the sunlight is at the right angle. Traci, her 4-year-old adopted daughter, is a handful. She is a diligent parent. She, too, began life as an orphan.

When Claire and Dawselle first meet it appears cordial, but cool. Am I sensing jealousy?

Stretching and warming up ends as the rain stops.

"Let's start our run through the park and head for the zoo," Dawselle says. "We'll take a brief rest there so our guest can visit with the lions, then we'll return up the hill to the campus."

Claire keeps up with the pack fine until we hit the upgrade on the second leg of the course, a strenuous 12% grade that lasts for three kilometers. This morning's route weaves through the suburbs, past some enormous blue-gum trees that line the street between the zoo and WITS. I love the refreshing smell of blue-gums, eucalyptus to me. I snap off a leaf, break it, and share the scent with Claire.

"It's my drug of choice," I say.

Dawselle makes a friend for life and a fan forever when we reach the midpoint at the Johannesburg Zoo as we pass the giraffes. She suggests that the rest of the runners continue while she introduces Claire to the lions and the two of them get acquainted. They have been girlfriends ever since. They utter nothing but praise for each other. She soon realizes it's Dawselle's team, not mine. Somehow that seems to signal to her it's okay for me to be a boss and friend of this beautiful, talented young lady.

"I'm headed for the office," Dawselle says as the team takes off for classes. "I'll finish that report grading today."

Claire and I settle in at a corner table at the Bistro after our morning run. Flo brings a fresh pot of Kenya AA in a stainless-steel and plexiglass French coffee press and two savory, buttery croissants. She tells us to wait three minutes then push the plunger down, hence the name cafetière à piston.

"Sorry I couldn't make this dawn's run," Flo says. "Did Dawselle mention whether she's coming by later?"

"I met Dawselle," Claire says, taking in a deep breath and letting it out with a whew. "Now I understand what you said yesterday about Rick and you and an enigma. No, Daniel isn't gay, and she's stunning."

Touring is an art form. Avoiding being ugly Americans is as critical as appreciating the local sights. We only have ten days left in Joburg to play tourists. Time goes by swiftly and my childhood memories never breakthrough. I'm finding it a pleasant distraction, but it doesn't last long.

If we are to get back to Seattle by May 4th, I won't be able to keep my agreement with Dawselle to pace her at the Comrades.

Triggering a memory of another promise, made

to my Uncle Paul. It's my first recall of my years as Uncle Paul's apprentice storyteller. Did I ever tell him I had kept my commitment?

I must have said this aloud.

"What promise would that be?"

"One I made to Uncle Paul to spread one of his scary stories throughout the neighborhood."

"Tell me more."

"That's it for now," I say. "I don't recall more."

Procrastinating is not my way; I call Dawselle.

"Hi Dawselle, how's Tracy?"

"Tracy's playing with the neighbor's Rhodesian Ridgeback puppy out in the yard."

"Claire and I will need to depart Joburg sooner than expected," I say. "We just learned that May 4 is 'Opening Day' for the boat races in Seattle and that the Jonson family farm is being put up for auction."

The memory of my vow to Uncle Paul is making an appearance. I tell her of my storytelling apprenticeship with my Uncle Paul, emphasis on keeping one's promise, and here I am breaking mine to her.

"Trading off one promise for another," Dawselle says. "I understand. I'll miss your support at the Comrades. Meanwhile, take care of that lovely lady of yours."

"Good luck at the Comrades and making the SA Olympic squad," I say. "Tell Tracy hi, and I'll get her a souvenir from the Opening Day boat races if she brings me back something from Barcelona."

CHAPTER 4

May 1, 1992

We bid adieux to Johannesburg. At the Bistro we say totsiens and sala kahuhle to our team of runners, my graduate students, and Dawselle and Traci. At Kempton Airport we check in Claire's seven matching pale blue suitcases she purchased at Parktown Mall. I say enkosi to Major. My luggage comprises, a scruffy Navy duffle and a backpack. The clerk tells her the airline charges for excess baggage; I cringe. On my professor's salary I can't afford premium airfares, but Claire always insists on paying for me so we can travel together.

I swear this woman gets special attention wherever we go. Captain De Klerk, the SAA pilot for our flight, stops by to ask if she needs anything, and a waitress brings two glasses of champagne. Maybe all first-class patrons get this same treatment?

After an hour in the VIP lounge, a voice announces over the loudspeaker, "Premium and passengers in need of assistance on SAA 359 for London, now boarding at gate 3."

At London's Heathrow Airport, we change from SAA to American Airlines for the leg to Chicago and on to Seattle. We land at Boeing International Airport around six p.m. Pacific Standard Time. After crossing eleven time zones flying east to west, it's still May 1st. The jet lag hasn't hit yet. Forty minutes later, the limousine driver drops us off in the driveway to Claire's home in Seattle's Parkside district.

Her two-story brick house is second from the top on an incredibly steep slope on Hillside Drive. The only drawback is that we must climb with her matching luggage while trying not to trip on the narrow steps at the front door.

Without the driver's help, I'd have strained my lower back hauling her baggage. I tipped him my last twenty.

"I saw a For Sale sign, when did the Halverson's move out of the house at the bottom of the hill?"

"They moved over to a place on the Oregon coast about a month ago."

We sit on the swing on her back porch and sip some dry white wine. Gazing at a fantastic view of the city and suburban lights shimmering and reflecting off Lake Washington. We have two full days at her pad to recover from jet lag before Opening Day. I recall the picnic Uncle Paul mentioned in his directions.

These initial memories have me hoping that we are on the right track to discovering the source of my guilt and distress. But I have an uncomfortable feeling, I'm uncertain I want to remember everything from my past.

"Tell me more about the origins of Opening Day and why it centers on the Montlake Cut Bridge," Claire says.

We cuddle up on her big four-poster bed, but before I get started on my telling, body contact takes control, and we are otherwise engaged.

"You can finish the history lesson tomorrow," she says as she kisses my neck.

CHAPTER 5

May 4, 1992, Seattle,
Opening Day

The next morning, we wake up still spooning. Being with Claire has a way of freeing the logs stuck in my memory-attic. After breakfast we jog from her hillside home through the Washington Park Arboretum to the Montlake Cut for the Opening Day festivities. Fragments of memories are coming down the sluice at a rapid pace.

Relaxing usually helps my recall but does not ensure what I remember will be pleasant. I've deluded myself all my life by thinking I'm pursuing adventure, whereas I've been running from my past and responsibility. But I'm gaining optimism that Claire's plan to reenact events of my childhood just might lead to the source of my depression and guilt. The first reenactment begins this morning.

"Let's resume where you left off before last night's beautiful interlude," Claire says as we warm-up for a run through a light mist as dawn breaks. "Tell me about the origins of Opening Day."

"That bit of history is best told from the bridge," I say.

It's a picturesque route, starting on Lake Washington Blvd, past the Botanic Gardens and the Japanese Gardens with ponds full of colorful coy. The smell of spring flowers is intoxicating. The run ends on 24th Avenue, where we pick up the trolley car's bell clanging before we see it crossing the Montlake Cut Bridge. We pause at the path along the Montlake District side of The Cut. It's a typical misty Seattle morning. The rain gives everything an elfin golden-green, freshness.

She unfolds and reads Uncle Paul's directions aloud.

"Catch a taxi at the old King Street Train Station in Pioneer Square. Ask the driver to drop you off on the Montlake side of the bridge, on 24th Avenue," she says. "OK we're at the bridge, even if Uncle Paul's directions didn't include the constant Seattle rain, and we flew into Seattle's Boeing Airport, a slight deviation from the correct starting point."

"Walk up the footpath to the bridge; you can't miss it," Claire reads on. "See you all at 9 am, the race starts at noon, and we'll picnic after. PS: The boys may enjoy a trip on a ferryboat after we tour the campus."

Walking and reflecting, a deep sadness comes over me.

"The last time I saw and spoke with my favorite uncle was when mom, Jer, and I took the MV Kalakala to Bremerton. We visited Paul at the Naval Hospital when he came home from the war in the Pacific."

"After we visit the Opening Day festivities, we must add a ferryboat ride to Bremerton to our reenactment list," I say. "Then, I'll tell you what I recall about the history of the Kalakala."

Although I'm struggling with recalling details of the Kalakala, I'm not sure why. Relaxing is one way of restoring the ferryboat's story to my consciousness.

While we slow to a walk on the path beside The Cut, some things are both familiar and different. Paved sidewalks and trees have grown over the trails. Fifty years have brought on a lot of changes in the area. New, taller buildings stretch along the banks on the Montlake District side.

"One of my colleagues lives in that spite house," Claire says, pointing at a three-story grey stone structure on the east bank.

"Spite, I get it," I say. "Folks add a third floor to get a better view, which annoys neighbors behind them."

"I always wanted to own a house on The Cut, love these gorgeous views."

"You don't think my place has a magnificent view?"

"No, I love your home, and it has a fabulous view of Lake Washington."

Mental note to myself, make a positive comment about the view when we return to her place.

We next pause at the bridge. I stand with my arms outstretched, signaling victory. We look up as the fog lifts and the sun's early rays ignite the tops of the twin Gothic towers that support the drawbridge. Turning them into huge copper candles.

"That fiery image has stayed with me since I was ten years old."

"Daniel, come back!" Claire says, shaking my shoulders and staring at me.

"Sorry, I got lost in the past for a moment."

I'm fortunate to have her to remind me we are in 1992, not 1940.

After Uncle Paul's directions to Connie lead us to Seattle's Montlake District, Opening Day is about to explode. We are among the first to arrive, but soon we are standing amidst a crowd of onlookers on the Montlake side of the bridge. A cacophony of boat whistles, sirens, horns, and bells provides a musical overture. It's the signal to open the drawbridge. Seattle's boating season is underway.

"Meanwhile, living and working here at UW for going on five years," Claire says, "I've meant to discover the story of the Montlake Cut and this fabulous bridge."

Because we got sidetracked last night. Now, it's time to fill her in on the history of this event and place. But I do wonder why she assumes that I know this history.

"I wish Mom and Uncle Paul were here," I say. "She was the family historian, and most of what I learned about the bridge came from stories she and Paul told."

"I'll give it my best shot."

Collecting my thoughts and recalling all I can of the story of the drawbridge and what surrounds it.

"It might come in a torrent or one log at a time, so stay with me."

"We'll organize the logs later," Claire says.

The Montlake Cut Bridge is a historical landmark built in the 1920s. Seattle's Opening Day festivities; boating season starts here each May. The drawbridge has two control towers. They are of same medieval architecture as many of the buildings on the UW campus.

My recall seems dull. I'm reciting from a history

book. I take a deep breath to relax. I need to act the part of ten-year-old Danny to spark the recall of my childhood.

"On my first visit, I thought this place was magic and eerie," I say, "a Medieval European castle surrounded by a moat with a drawbridge entrance."

"Appropriate for a 10-year-old," Claire says, encouraging my attempt to get in character.

Paul and Connie described the area around Seattle as a connection of lakes, bridges, and access to the many islands of the Puget Sound. Those connections include ferry boats to the Naval Base in Bremerton.

Before the logging industry and the sluice, the Duwamish named this strip of land 'Carry a Canoe'; now, the waterway is The Montlake Cut or The Cut for short. Native people portaged between Lake Union and the big lake by carrying their canoes or sometimes floating them in a creek that flowed between the lakes when Lake Washington overflowed. The indigenous tribes of the Puget Sound area used this route. They have lived here for ten thousand years.

I recall mom saying, "That would be back to the glacial era. You boys learned the story of Big Black Rock from Paul."

It was a rhetorical question since Uncle Paul told many of his scary stories from Big Black Rock, but we knew it well. But at this moment, my memory fails me.

"Japanese warships and aircraft did not attack Hawaii until the following December," Claire says.

She's trying to help me set the timing in my mind. I struggle to recall anything but remain blocked.

"Something happened that day in May 1940 before the war, we'll figure it out," Claire says.

I point while standing in front of the bridge on the Montlake district side. To my left is Lake Union and to the right Lake Washington. Another log tumbles into my consciousness.

"The tribe descended from separate tribes; what they call the 'people of the inside', Lake Union, and the 'people of the big lake', Lake Washington."

In the 1920s, the engineers dredged between the two lakes, forming The Cut. It replaced the sluice that connects Portage Bay with Lake Washington. The Cut facilitated the transport of logs felled on the forested islands in the Puget Sound. They floated logs across Lake Union to The Cut. Loggers gathered them into large log mats and continued the journey across Lake Washington to the cedar and lumber mills of Seattle. The timber industry and sawmills were significant employers in these parts.

"At last," Claire says, with an exaggerated sigh, "the inspiration and source of your log jam metaphor."

"Sorry," I say, "I'm getting signals from my memory-attic in whatever order they appear."

I'm also slipping in and out of character, I'll do better.

It's Opening Day in Seattle back in 1940.

There are hundreds of onlookers and passersby on the bridge when we arrive.

Three lads are running down the path towards

us. The lanky young man in the middle is my Uncle Paul. Jer and I wave back while Connie snaps a picture with her Leica.

Mom, Jer, and I arrived at the bridge from King Street Station, gawking at the twin towers in all their flaming copper and gold glory. A slender scull passes beneath, gliding towards Lake Washington to the sound of "pull, pull, pull."

"That large sailboat is waiting for the raising of the bascule drawbridge on the half hour," Uncle Paul said, pointing at his wristwatch.

"I know what bascule means," Claire says. "It's French for balance scale, and this drawbridge has spans that open on either side. Castle moats are raised and lowered on one side."

I ignore her interruption and continue my story.

The wailing tone of a siren fills the air. The bridge is evacuated. I take it as a warning.

"Watch out!" I say.

"See the spans rising," Uncle Paul says. "Two giant steel jaws are opening to let that sailboat pass through to open water."

I stare in awe as the spans of the bridge rise. I imagine an ancient monstrous shark.

"What if someone gets caught in the shark's jaws as they open and close?"

To his credit, Uncle Paul did not laugh; he put an arm across my shoulders and said, "You have a good heart, Danny."

The two lads with Uncle Paul are convulsing with laughter as they gather around us. Uncle Paul gives mom, Jer, and I bear hugs, he is the only man in the Jonson clan that embraces anyone.

Uncle Paul and the two lads point at the schooner that glides towards the bridge as it clears a cloud bank to the west. The boat's sails are furled, making it invisible until it gets through the fog. It's a ghostly pirate ship slipping quietly past the castle turrets into Lake Washington's inland waters.

The vessel passes under the drawbridge and is soon 100 yards down The Cut when the siren wails again. Soon the trolley car is clanging, and foot traffic are scurrying back and forth across the bridge as people jockey for better vantage places for the Opening Day festivities and races. Students are everywhere as cancel classes are cancelled at UW for the day.

Thirty minutes after the schooner passes, the siren wails again but only a single 8+ shell comes beneath the bridge.

"Why open the bridge for such a small boat?"

"It opens on the hour and half-hour," Uncle Paul said, "and on-demand for larger vessels at other times."

"Seat 4 focus straight ahead", a voice calls out as the scull's crew strokes their way down The Cut and out of sight into Lake Washington.

"The Cal Bears varsity team, getting in some extra practice."

Paul's two companions are laughing. Uncle Paul gives them a stern glare.

"That's the coxswain at the rear of the shell," he said. "That's why they call it an 8 +, he's the +. He calls out the cadence and instructions on a bullhorn to the eight oarsmen."

The cox sits facing forward, so he can see where the shell is going, while the rowers get their backs into each stroke. He is shouting an order to the oarsman in the fourth seat to focus on his direction.

"Which one's the 4th seat?"

"Count from the coxswain forward in the direction the scull is moving."

I'm tiring as I end my version of the history of The Montlake Cut Bridge. I've been performing two roles and at times I'm uncertain who is remembering what.

"Thanks, Uncle Paul," Claire says, "most informative. And thank you too, young Danny."

"Uncle Paul, so good to meet you at last," Claire says. "I'm looking forward to your telling us one of your stories at Big Black Rock. Can you explain why you wrote them?"

"Nice try!" I say, "But that's a family secret."

"Can't blame a girl for trying."

"Nice to meet you too, Doctor Claire," I say, getting in the spirit of her game. "This lad's my nephew Danny, he's my apprentice storyteller, I'll get him to tell you a scary story when we get to Big Black Rock at the farm in Spokane."

"Danny, is it?" she says, unable to contain a laugh, "In our future I will know you as Daniel."

The 1940 visit and today are juxtaposing a bit too much for me; I'm struggling to handle the time lapses.

"Do you or Jer still have any of your mom's photos from that day?" Claire says, returning us to the present.

I blink a few times to clear the images that are jamming up in my head and bring myself back to reality. Claire is snapping pictures while we stand at the base of the bridge. For one moment, I think of Connie and her Leica. I laugh as I look up and down The Cut.

"Uncle Paul is not here to greet us today!" I say, still caught in between my roles as Daniel and Danny and in an intense déjà vu moment.

"Whoa, Daniel!" Claire says. "You're tripping back in time again."

I slip on a spinning log while trying to dredge up another log from my memory-attic as ten-year-old Danny in 1940. Then I relax and steady myself.

"I think I need some rest," I say, rubbing my eyes.

CHAPTER 6

Seattle: May 4, 1992

*(1940 continues to juxtapose
with the present)*

C laire and I experience another bit of history as we walk on the path along The Cut starring up at the bridge. The sun's rays illuminate a large white canvas banner strung between the towers. It reads OPENING DAY.

Mention Opening Day to any local and you'll learn most of the history I have been telling. The entire city is a beehive of boating activity, boats stretch from Lake Huron to Lake Washington. The drawbridge is the centerpiece where many vessels parade past the crowds on the banks of The Cut.

Claire continues taking photos of the procession of crafts of all shapes and kinds, the drawbridge, and the spectators. I continue to relive seeing my mom clicking away with her Leica back in 1940. Hundreds of seagulls soar overhead, and pigeons perch on the bridge towers and railings, jostling for the best spots for watching the spectacle of sailboats.

Reminding myself that the year is 1992, not 1940 is a constant challenge.

Elbow-to-elbow with thousands of eager faces crowding onto the bridge and the paths, Claire and I hope to get a bird's-eye view of the parade of boats. Next came the crew races featuring the Washington Huskies and their biggest rivals, the California Golden Bears.

History lesson nearly complete. While back on that special day in 1940, my memory-attic takes a 90-degree turn to a Dali painting I saw on exhibit in Paris on my way to Africa.

I have a distant look on my face, and Claire asks, "Where are you now, Daniel?"

"Controlling which memory returns at any moment is a problem," I say. "Right now, I'm recalling a Salvador Dali painting."

"I bet I know which one," Claire says, "does it have melting clocks in it?"

"That's the one."

"Dali's title for that painting is *The Persistence of memory*. It was on exhibit here at the Henry Art Gallery in Seattle."

Dali was a surrealist. He was depicting a dream state where time takes on a different meaning.

"Juxtaposing of past and present," Claire says. "Dali's images are very relevant to your memory-attic and what we are reenacting."

I nod, feeling a touch better, and return to my role as Danny.

Mom, Jer, and I look up at three lads who paused for a moment, a photo op, before running towards us off the bridge. We wave back at my Uncle Paul and his two friends as they greet us.

"This exuberant chap is my friend, Charlee Sang, he's our #7 oar," Paul said. "Franklin is our oar in waiting."

"And the lovely photographer is sister Connie, and these ruffians are her sons, Jer and Danny."

"Nice to meet you, Connie, Jer, and Danny," Charlee said. "Paul is always bragging about you folks."

Franklin smiled and bowed without speaking.

"I was wondering when you would introduce the lads," Claire says.

I don't take in her comment as I'm engrossed in the events of 1940 that are filling my consciousness.

"When is your race?" I say to Uncle Paul, oblivious to Claire's remark.

"The freshmen shell that Charlee and I row on races at noon," Paul said. "Charlee and I need to head off to the Shellhouse to prepare for our race. Franklin will keep you company."

"Keep us company?" I said, "he hasn't said a word."

Paul just laughed.

Connie held up her basket of goodies and said, "What about the picnic?"

"You'd better save some of Grandma's pie and vittles for us," Paul said.

Then he explained that after the race we'd have our picnic, and a taste of grandma's cooking. It'll give us some time to get acquainted, and to catch up on what's happening back in Spokane. We needed to make ready for the Christmas family gathering. After the picnic, we'll tour the campus.

Charlee's and Paul's first rowing race is about to

start. It's a proud moment, shared with family and his pals. Friends whom he thought of as extended family. Franklin helps us move our picnic to a strategic viewing spot along the western path of The Cut to get a view of the start of the race.

Connie spreads an old navy blanket on the rain-dampened bank of The Cut. A slender, petite teenage Japanese American girl appears with a large dog and asks if she can help with the picnic blanket.

"Hi, Tinya!" Franklin said. "Glad you could make it. These are Paul's family, Connie, Jer, and Danny."

"I'm Tinya Yoshino," she said. "I hope it's okay for my dog and me to watch the races with you folks."

Her English is excellent, and she says that Paul has tutored her and Franklin. She tells us about her dog, but the race starts. At this moment, my recall ceases to operate.

"Were Charlee, Franklin, and Tinya at Big Black Rock when Uncle Paul first told his new scary story?" Claire asks, once more returning me to the present.

"Yes!" I say. "I'll try to remember more about Tinya, when we get to the farm."

"You keep saying you can't force the memories, so don't."

Without warning, two 8+ man shells glide past our picnic perch. One of the coxswain's shouts, "Pull, pull, pull," setting the cadence for his crew.

They are in the water beneath the bridge at the starting line for the race.

"That's them, in the purple and gold striped jerseys," Franklin said.

Counting forward to oar #6, I see Paul, and oar #7, Charlee. I point, careful not to wave. Franklin explains that they are in a three-mile race against the freshman crew from Cal-Berkeley, their fiercest rival, and it's their first race of the season. It was a speech for Franklin.

The Cal Bears' scull passes by our perch, closer to the far bank, wearing blue, yellow, and gold jerseys. The shells line up under the bridge, I hear a gunshot, and the two boats disappear down the cut to multiple sounds of "pull, pull, pull." Because they seem to me to be going backwards, I get disoriented as they head for open water.

We didn't get to see the finish line of the race as it was in Lake Washington, over two miles away from our picnic spot.

"I remember being disappointed," I say. "I think Charlee and Paul's crew won the freshman race, but I don't remember for sure."

"It's strange not to recall who won the race," Claire says. "Defeating and winning is such an enormous deal in so many sports. And the archrival Cal Bears at that. Why would you block that out?"

After the race, Paul and Charlee rejoined us for the picnic. Paul said a prayer of thanks for the meal and the health and wellbeing of family and friends. We dined on a sumptuous meal packed by Connie and prepared by grandma. Grandma Jonson always worries we won't get enough to eat. We wrap everything in cellophane to keep it fresh for today and the train ride to Spokane. An oven-roasted chicken smells of lemon juice and spices, including rosemary. Uncle Paul volunteered to carve. We all pitched in and loosened Mason jars of grandma's sweet dills and pickled peaches. For dessert, we ate some of the biggest and best oatmeal raisin and apricot cookies on earth.

"I'm full," Connie said, "can we save the pie for the train ride?"

After our picnic, our reenactment continues with a tour of the University campus. Crossing the Bridge, we soon stand in Red Square gazing at Suzzallo Library. Majestic archways and fantastic stain-glass windows have me straining and gawking. Plunging me back to 1940. A beautiful woman is on the steps of the library looking up at the magnificent Gothic structure, snapping pictures with a Leica camera.

A tear flows down my cheek, and Claire wraps her arms around my shaking form.

Snap crank click... snap crank click... snap crank click.

Providing the sound effects is Claire's Canon, but I swear it's the sound of Connie's old Leica. A moment from my past in 1940 and one in the present juxtapose once more.

A tiny girl with a black ponytail points at me and says, "Daddy, why is that man crying?"

Smiling at her as she clings to his pants leg, her large brown eyes peering out from behind him, I say. "To cry is not always bad, these are tears of joy."

Snap crank click goes the camera again.

"Great pic!" a voice says.

Turning around I search for the source, is it Connie or Claire?

"Danny, you sure are the image of your uncle when he was your age, you could pass for his double," Connie said.

"Another tow-headed, blue or grey-eyed Jonson," Paul said.

Connie pulls two tattered photos out of her camera bag. A recent one of Jer and I, and an older yellowed photo of Paul at our age. She carried these with her everywhere. A quick comparison verified that we looked alike, but I thought, so does Jer and most of the Jonson's.

Connie was nine years older than Paul, and they were voracious readers and storytellers. She was standing with Paul in the old photo. I noticed that her hair was blond. It turned to light brown at her temples to grey over the years and to white in my nightmares. The black-and-white photo doesn't capture this.

She works as a secretary at a nearby university. But her passions are history, literature, and photography. She is our family photographer and historian. She's Jer's and my only parent since our father just up and left a few days after I was born. Uncle Paul was the closest to a father figure Jer and I ever had.

Claire looks at me, remains silent, sensing it's a painful topic for me.

"I'll bet that you will find the photo in the attic and with luck more of her photographs from that day at The Cut."

Claire flips open her spiral notepad and writes, search the attic for Connie's photos.

May 4th in 1940 was when Uncle Paul first introduced his friends. Friendship, family, and sharing was the goal that day, along with celebration and rowing. The sharing aspect is coming back to me now.

After the race, during our picnic and campus tour, Uncle Paul told of how he met his two friends.

They exchanged memories of their lives before coming to America.

"I'm sure mom kept a journal about each of them," I say, as Claire jots more notes in her spiral pad.

"I'll get us started," Connie said. "Paul Jonson is his name; rowing is his game."

He's a first-generation Swedish American, graduated from Spokane High School in eastern Washington a year ahead of his peers because of skipping 6th grade. He's a student here at UW campus in Seattle and #6 oar on the freshman rowing team, all before his eighteenth birthday.

"He was only 18, I figured older."

"Me too, when I was ten, I'd have bet my Schwinn bicycle he was over twenty."

Connie is Paul's middle sister. She skipped two years of middle school, hoping to attend college, and become a teacher; but the Jonson's lacked the means to send all five children to college. The two brothers, Paul, and Alec, and the oldest of the three girls received the family funding. The smartest and most diligent second daughter, Connie, did not, nor did Esther the youngest.

"I get it," Claire says. "Paul was the only Jonson to commiserate with Connie as he too had worked his tail off to get through high school early."

"Did you know back then that your mom skipped two grades," Claire says, "or did you learn that later in life?"

"Excellent point. You're correct. I'll restrict my recall to what I knew and experienced between 1940 and 1945."

My thoughts return to Connie finishing her narration about Paul. She spoke of her brother's passions for rowing and Far Eastern cultures, Pacific Rim history, and Asian languages. He chose UW as it has all these study programs. That and their reputation in the sport of rowing.

"Thank you, sis!" Paul said. "My genuine passion is for adventure."

He told of his fascination with Columbus and Marco Polo and many other adventurers. They braved the terra incognita, sailing into the unknown ends of the earth to discover lands and people. Their remarkable and hazardous tales led to his love for adventure and telling scary stories.

"Most of all," Paul said, "I wanted to join the prestigious UW crew teams."

"Why rowing?"

His passion for sculling began in 1936. He was listening to the BBC radio broadcast from Lake Grenau near Berlin. The UW crew of 8 plus coxswain became famous. The Husky varsity 8 defeated the favored British, eliminating them from the competition even before the medals were in contention. Then they shocked the world and won the gold medal at the Berlin Olympics, rowing to victory over the Germans. The Seattle Post Intelligencer newspaper declared that the Huskies victory over the Nazis was Seattle's greatest sports achievement and memory of all time.

All nine crew members were from modest working family backgrounds. That sparked some doubt about the Germans' being the super-race. Later, Jesse Owens, an African American, sprinted and jumped his way to gold medals, devastating the Nazi's claims of racial superiority.

"I joined the Freshman crew team at UW, where I

met Charlee Sang, and we started rowing and training together on Lake Washington," Paul said.

Paul explained that their days often began and ended right where we stood on the Montlake Cut Bridge.

"This skinny kid loves this very spot," he said.

Franklin is hanging over the rail captivated by the rowers as they come and go from the nearby Shellhouse, home for the rowing teams and their sculls.

"And that's the rest of my story," Paul said. "Might I add, I'm proud of my Swedish heritage and my family, and proud to be an American."

"I caught the Paul Harvey quote," Claire says.

This memory of the Berlin Olympics jars me back to the present.

"I wonder how Dawselle fared at the Comrades?" I say, "Did she make the RSA Olympic team for Barcelona?"

"Let's call her and find out," Claire says.

She calls, and it overjoys us, Dawselle made the South African team. Roses to be sent.

At this point during our time at The Cut, Franklin was the sole name I knew for the skinny callow lad standing on the Bridge. After the race at the picnic, I learned of his heritage.

Franklin needed a gentle assist to get started telling his story.

"Meet my young friend Franklin," Uncle Paul said.

He is a handsome lad, quick to laugh, flashing his toothy smile. Shy by nature and always avoiding direct eye contact. Franklin left most of the telling of his life story to Paul and Charlee.

They got him to nod his head and grin when Charlee pitched in with a story about how Franklin had arrived in America.

"Someone wrapped him in an old blanket, placed him in a basket, and left him at the doorstep of the Japanese Language School and Children's Home in Tacoma."

"At age 13, I first saw a boy, thin as a rail, watching wide-eyed as several shells rowed past under the bridge," Paul said. "We communicated in broken English, a bit of Japanese, and sign language that we made up as we went along."

Uncle Paul informed us Franklin had a keen mind despite a neglected education. He grasped unfamiliar concepts. Paul agreed to tutor him in English in return for Japanese lessons. Franklin had no money except what he earned from a Seattle-Times newspaper delivery route and running errands for the Yoshino's.

A small group of Japanese American Nisei children, ages 6-13, boys and girls from the JLS, started joining them to learn English. Tinya was another of Pauls' students. At first, they came to learn how to count money; they needed the math skills to survive in the city when they ventured outside the Nihonmachi or Japanese community.

"Nihonmachi," Claire says, "did you know that term as Danny or did you pick it up later in life?"

"My bad."

Uncle Paul repeated that he often saw Franklin standing atop the bridge as Charlee and his skull passed underneath, headed for open lake water.

"I'm sure he dreams of oaring one of these seats

one day," Paul said.

Franklin smiles back, flashing his pearly white teeth. His face often shows his admiration and envy of the two freshman crew members.

Uncle Paul wrapped an arm around the shoulders of his shorter companion and smiled.

"Paul and Charlee tell much of franklin's story, but I recall his expressing concern for his friend Tinya's safety."

But that memory may be premature. It came later when Tinya visited the family farm for the holidays with her constant companion, a black and white Akita.

"It was as if his life began at the JLS in Tacoma," I say. "But he, Tinya, and her dog were inseparable."

"Do you know where he was born?"

"Not sure!" I say, pausing as a fragment comes to me. "I recall that Uncle Paul asked the same question."

"Franklin, can you verify this?" Paul said, "You once told Charlee and me you were born aboard a ship."

I have no memory of where I was born," Franklin said as he stared down at his feet. "The Yoshino's told me someone left me in a basket on the front steps of the JLS."

"Okay, Charlee, enough about Franklin and me," Uncle Paul said, "your turn."

Paul reminded Charlee that in an hour, they needed to head for the Shellhouse. Keep it brief, he told him. Unlike Franklin, Charlee isn't shy about sharing. But he wasn't sure what his birth date was, nor am I. My best guess is that he was the same age as Paul. He's a broad-shouldered lad of 5' 10".

His story gets interrupted when they Paul says they need to suit up the race; but it was what he told us after the race that I can't quite member. Maybe it will come to me.

On the steps in front of Suzzallo Library.

Charlee sweeps an arm in a circle. His sweep encompasses the campus from the Montlake Bridge to the buildings that lined the Lake Washington Canal and back to Husky Stadium.

"We know this plaza as Red Square, as you can see, it's at the crossroads to all parts of the campus."

Once more, it reminds me of a castle and grounds.

"Is it Charlee we hear from now?" Claire says.

"Correct!" I say, adding, "Well, almost, it's Danny remembering what Charlee said."

The conversation turned serious. After Connie and the lads discussed their backgrounds, Uncle Paul suggested that Jer and I take a tour of Suzzallo while the adults conversed. We felt left out.

Besides his affinity for telling scary stories, Uncle Paul loved history, and so did Charlee Sang. Together they introduced Jer and I to Suzzallo Library and the great adventurers, Marco Polo and Christopher Columbus. They also instilled in me a lifelong wander lust and a love of adventure and the sea.

As we entered the south apse of the impressive Gothic structure, a hand-painted world globe hung overhead. I looked up at a neck-straining angle. We are in a vast wood-paneled reading room, stacks of books so high I got dizzy gazing up. I stared at the leaded-glass windows and the arched ceilings that rose to a height of 60 feet.

A slender young assistant librarian asked if she could be of help.

"What are the words on the gold ring around globe?"

Charlee looked the librarian in the eye and said, "Please let me answer that question."

These hand-painted world globes are hanging at this south apse and another at the north apse. The names of famous explorers are etched on the ring, Leif Ericson, Marco Polo, Columbus, and others.

Before Charlee could continue the litany of famed explorers, I broke in saying, "I know about Christopher Columbus; we studied him in school last month."

"I remember asking another librarian where to find Marco Polo's Travels," Charlee said. "Marco Polo is the only name on the globe I recognized."

We were laughing but our gaiety ends when Charlee said, "My family died fighting at Marco Polo Bridge during the Japanese conquest of Manchuria."

"The visit to Suzzallo was instrumental in my development of what mom called my wanderer's spirit of adventure."

"Connie warned me years ago about your vagabond ways," Claire says.

What I remember most about the conversation at Suzzallo was that the adults excluded Jer and me. Gossip and rumors ran rampant in the news about what was going on in the Japanese Language Schools up and down the Pacific coast. The JLS in Tacoma was a frequent target of gossip. Some accused them of training and housing Japanese sympathizers. I recall seeing newspaper headlines tacked to telephone poles all over Seattle and Tacoma, 'Yellow Peril,' and 'Japs Go Home.'

The laughter ceased, but not the taunts of passing students. These taunts were distressing to all of us, but more so to Franklin and Tinya, who lived at the children's home run by Mr. and Mrs. Yoshino. They resided there with over thirty orphans. I'm recalling that both Franklin and Tinya's surname was Yoshino.

Claire says, "I'll do some research on the JLS's."

Charlee continued his story. He escaped the Japs' clutches and fought for the Kuomintang against the Japanese Occupation Forces. They fought several skirmishes before arriving at Marco Polo Bridge. Outnumbered and outgunned, the Japanese defeated them.

Charlee paused, looked at Connie, and said, "Is it permissible to tell your boys about my parents' deaths and my escape from the Japs, it's a rather bloody tale?"

Connie looked at Charlee, and said, "No more talk of Japs, and please save the bloody parts for later. Tell us how you got to America."

Orphaned at 13, Charlee wandered south to the port city of Hong Kong, where he signed on as a cabin boy on a tramp steamer headed for Hawaii. They continued to Seattle, where the ship docked. He spoke only a few English words when he enrolled at a school in Tacoma. Later he improved his English under Paul's tutelage.

"I got bullied every day by the biggest boys at high school, they called me a Chink," Charlee said. "Some called me a slope head, others a Jap, sorry Connie."

"It became tiresome, correcting these bullies when they taunted me," Charlee said, explaining that it only made it worse when he responded to their taunts.

"The verbal and physical beatings continued, and they fueled my dreams of getting back at them when I was bigger."

Charlee is a Freshman at the University of Washington this Fall. He's full grown and the worst of the bullies have flunked out of high school.

"At university, I expected the hazing to lessen," Charlee said, "Today, it seems more painful because the taunts come from educated classmates."

Charlee spoke of overhearing a group of students at Red Square. They were jesting about how people suspect Japanese Americans from our language school of spying on the Naval bases from Tacoma to Bremerton.

"I'm sure they thought I was a Jap," Charlee said.

Connie flinched at the disparaging word, and Charlee again said, "Sorry, Connie."

"He's too modest to tell you," Uncle Paul said, "he graduated from High School in two years."

"My days start here at this magnificent library," Charlee said. "Reading the newspapers."

He was eager to learn about what was happening in the land of my ancestors. He wanted to know more about the Marco Polo Bridge Incident, the Rape of Nanking, and the Japanese conquest of Manchukuo.

His remark jars a log loose from my memory-attic. I tell Claire that I recall when Jer and I were inside the library before the discussion got intense. Uncle Paul picked out two newspapers from a rack that included the New York Times, the Washington Post, several London newspapers, including The Telegraph.

The first was a recent LA Times with the headline, "ALL JAPS SOON TO BE REMOVED FROM CALIFORNIA!"

The second was an editorial in the Post entitled, "WE ARE ALL AMERICANS."

"And that's my story," Charlee said with a grin, "Let's stretch our legs and pick up some Coca-Colas at the cart across the square. My treat!"

We borrow Paul's pocket-knife and pop off the caps of our nickel Coca-Colas from their green glass bottles, and gulp down the sweet cold liquid. Charlee takes a big swig of his Coca-Cola and burps, without apologizing, smiling.

"Let's you and I do the same," Claire says, "My treat!"

As we return to Red Square, Coca-Cola's in hand, I ask her how much they cost.

"A Coke costs fifty cents."

I recall another detail.

"Let's sit here on the steps for a moment longer and finish these sodas," Charlee said.

We are joking and reliving history lessons and finishing our Coca-Colas.

A rowdy group of students strolls across Red Square, hurling insults at us.

"Jap lovers!" "Yellow peril!" "Chinks!" "Dirty Japs!" "The

bastards are selling us out to the Emperor!"

Franklin's face turned ashen.

"Ignore them." Charlee said, "White people can't tell one Asian from another."

"Charlee's use of that single phrase has significance," I say to Claire.

"I see what you mean," Claire says, "Charlee's point about bullies in High School and his comment that all Asians look alike to whites, seems to be the focus of what they discussed at Red Square."

Distracted and angry, the three lads and Connie could not shake the insults hurled at them. But it was Charlee who taught us an important lesson.

Not to retaliate when bullies display ignorance. Soon the students tired of not getting a reaction. Regardless, their ugly words rang in their minds, starting an intense discussion. That's when Uncle Paul and Charlee ushered Jer and me inside the library.

CHAPTER 7

Continuing to search deep in my memory-attic for details of Opening Day, Charlee's remark about all Asians appearing the same echoes in my head. I'm sure Claire is correct. We need to find out how that saying pertains to Uncle Paul's new scary story. The connection evades me for the moment, but it intrigues me at the same time.

"I recall Uncle Paul mentioning a letter he received from Charlee Sang early in the war, but I can't place it."

Fragments such as this are perplexing, and it shows in the furrowed brows on my face.

"You're suggesting that something about that letter may come down the sluice later," Claire says. "Perhaps he was alerting you not to dig into these taunts until the war is over?"

"A warning?" I say, "but why?"

Uncle Paul, Charlee, and Franklin spoke with mom at length that day at the Montlake Cut and on the steps of Suzzallo Library on Red Square. When Jer and I returned from reading the newspapers, the lads were asking Connie for her opinion on what to do if our nation gets drawn into the war in Europe.

Connie discussed how Japanese and Chinese immigrants came to America. For the same reasons as the Swedes. Escape from starvation, seeking a better life, hoping to find work, putting an end to oppression. They brought with them farming techniques and the knowledge to build the irrigation systems of California's central valley.

Focusing on my ramblings, how does Claire manage to remain patient with my outbursts and my log jams? She amazes me.

"It seems clear to me they were planning and scheming something that day," Claire says.

Connie speaks of their fears and worries about the safety of their friends at the JLS in Tacoma. Of particular concern are two Japanese teens, Franklin and Tinya Yoshino. They also discussed concerns about the Japanese and their spreading military occupation of Manchuria and Korea in the 1930s.

"But what were they scheming?" I say with frustration in my voice. "I can't recall much other than that they sent Jer and me into the Library to read the newspapers, so the adults could make serious conversation."

"Berating yourself won't help," Claire says, "You've already recalled considerable and in fabulous detail."

When the fellows and Connie finish sharing narratives. I asked Uncle Paul the question I wanted an answer to all day, "Any new scary stories to tell us?"

"I have one brewing in my head," Uncle Paul said, "but you must be patient until I conjure up an ending to my story."

"What's it about?"

"A Chinese sentry, a terrifying fellow and his bear."

"He has a pet bear?"

"That's all I'm giving away today."

Reeling in these fragments is a start on my memories of that story. I glance at Claire, giving the moment a bit of emphasis and to reset us in the present.

"Right here on this very spot where we had our picnic is where Uncle Paul first mentioned that he had a new scary story that he was saving for Christmas eve at the annual family gathering," I say.

The fragment fits in between so many details of that day that I'm surprised I recall it.

"Can you recall more details about Uncle Paul's scary story," Claire says.

"It needs to be told on location," I say. "Big Black Rock is a landmark on the Jonson farm in Spokane, and it was Uncle Paul's favorite storytelling venue."

Claire writes Big Black Rock in her notepad and underlines it twice.

My focus and my memories shift to events from another time and place. I'm far away on the beaches of Durban, running with a sizeable Rhodesian ridgeback and Dawselle and some of my graduate students from WITS.

My mood darkens. Claire sees my frustration and tries to comfort me.

"Let's play tourists," she suggests, "how about a trek around the UW campus, so I can take some photos of this beautiful place?"

Once more, I'm reliving the day at The Cut listening to the snap crank click sounds and watching Connie taking pictures with her Leica.

"Mom stopped taking photos after Uncle Paul died," I say to Claire.

"Connie lost her brother," Claire says. "She repressed the loss."

"That camera was another link between a mother and her youngest son," Claire says. "As I suggested before, the attic is a must on our reenactment list."

I try to pull my thoughts together. What was the critical topic of conversation that day?

Another detail from the time at Red Square comes down the sluice.

The taunts changed the tenor of our talks that day, from crew racing and a fabulous picnic to history and personal biographies, to getting acquainted, to a more intense tone as I noted.

When Jer and I returned from the library, the lads and Connie were seated in a circle on the front steps.

Connie said, "Our neighbors in Spokane are calling people nasty names."

She always tried not to use the actual epithets.

When she saw Jer and I returning from Suzzallo Library, she paused as she gathered her thoughts. Everyone was on the edge of their seats, eager to discuss more of what was of concern to them.

"It's dreadful that some groups of immigrant Americans should mistrust and demean others," Connie said. "We have one thing in common, we are all loyal Americans."

"You also mentioned that your mom flinched at the use of the word 'Jap'," Claire says.

'Jap' and 'Yellow Peril' were derogatory terms used

by locals. But rumors and taunts started long before the war. Some locals thought Chinese, Japanese, and other Asian immigrants loyal to their homelands. To them, it meant they were disloyal to America. But these people had taken the oath of American citizenship.

"That's it!" I say, "loyalty and the safety for all Americans regardless of heritage; that was the theme of their conversation."

"You mean the theme for their strategic planning session," Claire says.

"Thanks for getting me back on track."

"The tenor of Charlee Sang's telling us about how white people can't tell one Asian from another never changed that day," I say. "None of them could get the taunts out of their minds, and they sensed danger."

Tacoma HS bullies', ugly news headlines, and taunts.

"The students at Red Square never took the time to talk to us," Connie said.

"Jer and I were in the library for much of the adult's discussion," I say. "But I remember that Connie started a journal about the heritages of our extended family members."

"Once more the attic beckons," Claire says, making a notation in her notepad.

"Before we head for the attic and mom's photos," I say, "Charlee said Asians look alike. I remember wondering at the time if Charlee and Franklin could pass as brothers."

In the photos Connie showed us at The Cut, Paul and I are hard to tell apart. I discounted her comment because Paul, Jer, and I are kin. I recall how different Charlee and Franklin were in one regard. Charlee always looked me straight in the eye when he spoke to me. Franklin looked away as if he were seeing someone behind me.

"That's what Danny thought," Claire says. "He focused on 'all Asians looking alike' as a remark about Charlee and Franklin, not about the broader topic of Asian cultures."

"Okay, we now know what they were discussing," Claire says, "the safety of Asians and their Japanese friends at the JLS."

Claire shares that her research shows that 1940 was a time of increasing animosity, ugly rumors, and rising racial hatred in America. Nazis to the east and Japs to the west.
The climax came in December 1941, with the Japanese attacks on Pearl Harbor. We can only speculate about what they were scheming the year before that catastrophic event.

"I agree," I say while holding up my hands and shrugging, "a plan was in the making, but to what end?"

Connie mentioned a plan that day at Suzzallo, and they all seemed distraught and intense about the personal safety of all Asians, not just Japanese.

"It seems they had a secret purpose.".

"You don't suppose that Uncle Paul's secret reason for his scary story and their secret are the same?" Claire says.

The reenactment of childhood memories from the 1940s juxtaposes with the present. The memories are descending more rapidly and increasing my confusion.

"I crave something," Claire says, "care to join me for fish-n-chips?"

She's trying to keep my disparate thoughts organized and mission-focused and lift my spirits.

"Stay with me, Claire, or I just might lose track of where we are going."

CHAPTER 8

Opening Day

Festivities continue after dark in private homes, at bars and restaurants in the Montlake District. Claire and I can hear the revelry as we depart the campus; but our first reenactment is complete.

What have we learned? A plan was probably in the making based in part on all Asians look alike proposition and how offending racial taunts are. But to what end? Uncle Paul is working on a new scary story. Charlee Sang is an orphan from Manchukuo and an American citizen. Franklin Yoshino is also an orphan, but he was born at sea. He and Tinya, a foundling, lived at the JLS in Tacoma where Paul taught them English.

Watching the setting sun as it emblazons the copper roofs atop the twin towers is as beautiful today as it was fifty years ago. Walking across the Montlake Bridge, we hope to ride the trolley south to Seattle's Waterfront District. Once there, we'll catch the ferryboat to Bremerton to spend the night before our next reenactment. The clackety clack and clanging of the 24th Avenue Trolley comes up behind us. Together we run, grabbing the trolley's hand bars and swing aboard, laughing.

Walking along the waterfront, we are engulfed in the full spectrum of odors of the fish markets. It's not pleasant. But the smell of seafood frying guides us to dinner at Ivar's Acres of Clams. What a place. I remembered it in March of 1945. It was an amusement house and aquarium, and a restaurant. They cover the walls with fishnets and autographed photos, including one of Harry Lillis 'Bing' Crosby, Jr. A mounted sailfish fills the wall behind the cash register, with a picture of the crew that caught the record-setting fish in 1939. A glass cabinet is full of fishing trophies.

Before our next reenactment, my last visit with Uncle Paul, we will ride the ferryboat. Meanwhile, my anxiety is peaking. Besides, Claire and I crave some fish-n-chips.

Now there are two restaurants on Pier 54, Ivar's Acres of Clams, and Ivar's Fish Bar. Claire and I decide on The Acres. We grab a booth that has a view of the harbor full of fishing vessels and hungry, aggressive seagulls. I place two orders for fish and chips and an order to go for Uncle Paul.

In the 1940s, this Seattle landmark was known as Ivar's Salmon Shack. Ivar was a Seattle icon, a Scandinavian immigrant, and a notorious promoter and entrepreneur in the same vein as circus magnate P. T. Barnum. Mom said he was a folksinger and entertainer, and he was Swedish or Norwegian, she wasn't sure which. Folks here called him the "King of the Seattle Waterfront". He opened a clam and seafood restaurant on a Pier close to Colman Dock, and the ferryboat terminal. His promotions included clam eating contests.

To spread rumors is bad, a value instilled in me at an early age. But some rumors are stories that bear repeating. I attribute these values to Connie and Paul.

A rumor persists to this day that Ivar made up a story about a child falling into the water and getting dragged under by a giant octopus. To attract customers, he held an octopus-wrestling event. They roped off the area, and it became an instant tourist attraction. Rather macabre, I thought, but I was only 13 and I kept a safe distance from the ropes along the edge of an inlet covered in dark black oily scum. Jer leaned over the barrier, hoping to cath a glimpse of the creature's tentacles or its big ugly eye.

Mom pulled him back and said, "Gerald Wallace, don't you be tempting fate."

Mom insisted that we buy a takeout bag of fish-n-chips for Uncle Paul. We scarfed down our bags of delicious fish and chips chased with vinegar and walked along the waterfront to the ferry terminal.

We caught the 12:15 ferry from Seattle to Bremerton to visit CPO Paul Jonson at the Naval Hospital.

Claire and I arrive at the Seattle-Bainbridge ferryboat terminal almost an hour before the next ferryboat departs. The Kalakala stopped running decades ago, so we pay for round-trip fares to Bremerton on a different ferryboat, the Kalama.

The change of boats takes us off script in our

reenactment.

"The devil is in the details," Claire says.

Her paraphrasing of an old German proverb about the details of a plan is a warning that hidden problems can disrupt any plan.

I'm both eager and hesitant as we wait to board.

"It's all right to be nervous, Daniel," Claire says, grasping my hand.

Connie, Jer, and I sat on a bench at Seattle's waterfront, waiting to board the MV Kalakala. Folks at the terminal are bustling about trying to stay warm on a chilly spring day, drinking hot Ovaltine and chattering about who won and lost yesterday's race.

While we wait, the ferry patrons argue about a boat race. I sense that I'm on the verge of remembering a piece to the history I couldn't recall earlier.

Eavesdropping on the dockside gossip, we overhear chatter about an impromptu race between rival ferryboats the previous day. An ongoing rivalry existed between two ship Captains of the Black Ball operating company. Motor Vessel Kalakala is a shiny silver ferry that operates in the Puget Sound. She was notable for her streamlined superstructure and art deco styling. The Kalakala was the flagship of the Black Ball Ferry Line. Patrons said she rumbled and shook because of misaligned engines. When challenged to a race her Captain feared that if he declined, she would appear weaker than her rival. The Willapa was a steel-electric class motor vessel. It doubled its passenger capacity to 1,500 when she transferred from San Francisco to Seattle waters.

The Willapa and The Kalakala left the dock in Seattle at the sound of a landing whistle from a third ferry. The race was on. The Captain of the Kalakala urged his chief engineer for more power.

"My money was on the Kalakala!" one man said.

One passenger from the day before argued that the ships were side by side, when they neared Rich Passage.

"I was on the Kalakala yesterday," says a weather-beaten old man. "We had the inside track at the narrow passage, and I heard the Captain ask his First Mate to check the tide."

"She's high," the First Mate hollered.

He reckoned the Captain didn't want to risk the ship grounding on Orchard Rocks. The Kalakala gave way, allowing room for the Willapa to pass inside.

"The Willapa may have won the race," another passenger said, "but her Captain put both ships at risk of hitting the Rocks."

The victorious captain sounded his boat whistle with a long loud blast and two short ones, what they call a warp and two woofs, as he reached the landing at the end of the race.

Several onlookers nodded, but aboard the Kalama Claire and I overheard more of the arguments over who won the race all the way to Bremerton.

"We could ask some old-timers hanging around the docks today who won that race," I say to Claire.

"And start an argument," Claire says with a grin, "I

think not."

"I'm still curious about the name Kalakala."

"Connie told me it's the Chinook word for bird."

To my eyes the ferryboat is a giant silver whale, not a bird.

"I once overheard a Swedish patron at Ivar's call her Kackerlacka, which means cockroach," Connie said.

"Thanks for telling me about the Kalakala race with her rival ferryboat, The Willapa," Claire says. "Now, will you please tell me who won the freshman skull race on The Cut?"

"You know, I've been trying to recall," I say, "that log seems jammed up."

The big motors churn up the water aboard the Kalama ferry to Bremerton, and my anxiety returns as I start to recall another day in the Spring of 1945.

To anticipate is to be frustrated. My sense of anticipation rises, and I'm not sure I want to go through with this reenactment of the events of the day we spent with Paul at the Naval Hospital. Learning to forge ahead with dark and sad memories. Claire has tried to prepare me for this but to no avail.

Claire and I are about to reenact a painful and somber event in Bremerton. My level of anxiety is unbearable. The icy breeze has nothing to do with why I'm shaking. She wraps a plaid wool blanket around me as we take seats on the benches aboard the ferry for the thirty-minute ride. She opens a thermos of hot beverage and pours two cups. I haven't drunk Ovaltine in fifty years.

"Where did you find this beverage, I thought Ovaltine went out of business many years ago?"

"They serve it in the galley," she says with a laugh.

She is brilliant at this reenactment therapy. The skill is in the details.

I dose off in Claire's arms, the Ovaltine effect, and my dreams take me to a fateful morning.

My brother and I slept in the bedroom over the front porch. Jer could sleep through anything. I enjoyed our perch as it oversaw most of the morning activities. A soft clinking of glass bottles being carried up the steps to the front porch door wakens me. The creaking of the lid to the woodbox as it opens, then the cover closes with a thud. More clinks as the person leaves the front porch and crunches across the gravel driveway to the neighbors. The crate was there for deliveries of all kinds. The first delivery at 6 am this morning was Mr. Carey, the milkman.

I got dressed and slid down the banister into the kitchen. Grandma had already taken the milk in and was mixing pancake batter.

"Rooster, don't you be sliding down that banister," she said. "Before you get to your chores, I need more buttermilk for these pancakes I'm making. Can you catch Mr. Carey?"

I got lucky, reaching Mr. Carey before he started up his truck.

"Morning, Mr. Carey," I said. "Grandma needs a bottle of buttermilk."

Grandma rewarded me with a cup of hot Ovaltine and a platter of buttermilk pancakes, apricot preserves, and apple juice. She slipped three oatmeal and raisin cookies in my lunch tin. It doesn't get better than this; I told her. On the walk to school, I shared the cookies with Essie.

I'm the early bird who retrieves the Spokesman-

Review newspaper out of the bushes so the adults in the family could read it over breakfast and coffee. We listened to the radio almost every day for updates on the war. The entire family sits around the kitchen table after the morning meal to listen to Paul Harvey and the news.

After the news, I take in a load of firewood for the potbelly stove. As I hang up my parka and Navy pea cap on the back porch, a treasured gift from my Uncle Paul, I hear voices out on the front porch.

It's another of the delivery services prevalent in the 1940s. There's a chill in air as our lanky, gray-bearded postman. He strides up the path wearing a fur-lined rain cap with earflaps. Mr. Stevenson walks with a limp past the ancient oak tree, saluting the two yellow ribbons. As he climbs the steps, he pulls out a bundle of mail from a leather bag slung over his shoulder.

He tips his hat when Connie opens the screen door, and hands her the mail saying, "Morning Missus Johnson, got an official-looking letter for you. You must sign for it. Hope it's not unpleasant news."

Mom signed and hesitated before opening the envelope. She sat on the front porch swing in the cold, rocking and crying while clutching the letter in her fist. Then she drops it, and it flutters into a puddle of rain-water at her feet. I reach to recover it. It reads, Official Document Department of the United States Navy.

I recall the day when the Speke's learned the fate of their oldest son in a Western Union Telegram.

"Is it terrible news, mom?" I said, almost afraid to ask.

"Yes and no," mom said, "your Uncle Paul is ill, and he's being shipped home to Bremerton Naval Hospital in two weeks."

Grandma was standing behind me. Without saying a word, she shuffles back into the kitchen.

CPO Paul Jonson came home in April 1945 from Subic Bay in the Philippines. He had enlisted two weeks after the day of FDR's radio broadcast about the attacks on Pearl Harbor and declaring war against Japan. He served for three and a half years in the Navy. Mom and grandma had received postcards and letters from him since then. I had last seen him at the Christmas 1941 family gathering.

I didn't know how ill Uncle Paul was; my joy was about this survival and that we would visit him soon. Jer bet me a licorice stick that he had some scary stories to tell about the war in the Pacific. I couldn't wait to find out about his recent stories.

Mom made some phone calls, and within a week, she secured a part time secretarial job in Seattle at the Helen Bush School to be nearer to Uncle Paul. Bremerton being only a ferryboat ride from Seattle.

"Should have reckoned that that was a sign that Uncle Paul's illness was serious."

I collect myself. Claire takes my hand, and we enter the Naval Hospital.

"Feels as if I'm entering a place where sailors go to die," I say to Claire. "I once visited Varanasi, where thousands of Hindus go to die at Hotel Death. They believe that dying there releases them from the cycle of life and death."

We all prayed for Uncle Paul to get well, but I could see and detect death all around the hospital from the moment we entered the swinging double doors.

A nurse wheeled a pale-skinned, watery-eyed

man towards us. He tried to stand but slumped back. He's wearing a blue dressing robe and white pajama pants and his slippers are several sizes too large. They keep slipping off his bone-white feet. Jer and I take turns putting them back on. He looks to be much older than my Uncle. He appears shrunken and weak, but his voice is steady and familiar.

It's my Uncle Paul; he is 22 (I learned that later). He asks the nurse to push him back to his hospital bed. She complies, and we follow. He motions to stop by a grey footlocker at the end of his bed, and she helps him open the lid. A black leather case falls out on the floor.

Mom retrieves it and snaps it open.

"A Purple Heart medal, were you wounded?" Jer said.

"That makes Uncle Paul a hero, right mom?"

"Being a hero is about doing the right thing."

Uncle Paul retrieved something else besides the Purple Heart medal from the footlocker at the foot of his bed at Bremerton Naval Hospital.

Still traversing about this hotel for the dying, I struggle hard for a few minutes trying to recall what that something was. A visage of my Great Aunt Selma hovers over me as I search amongst piles of bodies and bones instead of the usual logs.

I pop in and out of reality, seeking stable ground.

Connie hands me the fish-n-chips.

I hand Uncle Paul the bag from Ivar's and tell him the tale of the ferry boat race.

"I see you haven't lost your knack for telling tales," Uncle Paul said.

He ate the fish-n-chips and said, "Thanks Danny, just what I've been longing for since I got home. Navy

chow is good aboard ship, but the green Jell-O and pow-
dered eggs here at the hospital are tasteless."

The nurse puts a straw in his glass and helps him
take a sip of water. Drool rolls down his chin. The nurse
wipes his face with a towel.

"Have you boys been to the motion pictures this
week?" Uncle Paul said.

"We saw a western double feature a week ago at
the Clemmer," Jer said. "Gary Cooper was mistaken for
an outlaw in 'Along Came Jones', and Tex Ritter fought
in a range war in 'Marked for Murder'."

"Fabulous action movies," Uncle Paul said. "Did
you see the newsreel? It showed my unit disembarking
here on Bainbridge Island."

"No," Jer said, "but there was a Popeye The Sailor
cartoon called 'Shape Ahoy'."

I head for a box of popcorn during newsreels.

"They showed us the newsreel here at the hospital," Uncle Paul said. "If you look, you might see me in
a group in wheelchairs coming down the ship's ramp."

Then he told us about another kind of hero, a war
correspondent. I don't recall his name.

"They did a marvelous piece about him in that
newsreel. You ought to see it," Uncle Paul said.

"Last Christmas we saw 'Going My Way' you need
to see that film, it stars Bing Crosby as Father O'Malley,
he's terrific," I said.

I never saw that newsreel; but I recall the feature
film 'Going My Way' and the sequel, 'The Bells of St.
Mary's', which premiered around Christmas of 1945.

Jer and I enjoyed the double feature movies with a
cartoon and a newsreel. All for two bits, a quarter, at our
favorite movie house in Spokane, the Clemmer Theater.

I also recall sneaking in by climbing up the rear fire-stairs. The theater owners put a chain and lock on the fire exit to prevent non-paying intruders, and the fire inspector darn near closed them down for doing that. Der Bingle, Bing Crosby's nickname, was also on the radio and remained in my head for days, crooning 'White Christmas' in his mellow tones while I hummed and whistled along.

CPO Jonson got exhausted, and the nurse suggested we wrap up our visit.

CHAPTER 9

I t's getting cold and another log gets jammed. Claire is seeking to calm me, but trauma has me in its grip, and I'm working far too hard to remember.

"Are you trying not to remember something?"

I relax enough to recall a detail about the second item from Paul's footlocker.

As we depart the Bremerton Naval Hospital, Connie helps Paul replace the Purple Heart medal in its case. Reaching into the footlocker, he pulls out an envelope and hands it to her.

"The last letter I got from Charlee Sang," he said. "It came through the military APO system, so I don't know where they stationed him."

Mom was about to open the envelope, but Uncle Paul closed his hand around hers before she got the letter out.

"Read it later, the letter will help you locate Charlee and Franklin and Tinya now that this horrid war is almost over," he said. "I have lost touch with all of them."

"Do you recall the weekend at the Montlake Cut Bridge when we celebrated Charlee and I making the

Huskies freshman crew team?"

"What a wonderful time," Connie said.

She mentioned taking several photographs of Paul, Charlee, and Franklin standing arm in arm on the bridge and putting them in an album.

Claire beams.

Uncle Paul's words resonate with both of us. Claire is thinking attic and we're both thinking clues Charlee's letter.

"They excluded you and Jer from the serious adult part of their discussions at Red Square after the skull races," Claire says.

I didn't need reminding, but Claire is trying to put things in context for me. I'm floating somewhere between past and present.

The pause calms me more and serves as the impetus that jars another log loose, and my recall continues.

Struggling to remain awake, Paul's eyes droop, then he recovers with a start.

"With this war ending," Uncle Paul said, his voice weakening. "We got the news while aboard ship about Executive Order 9066 in February 1942. Franklin and Tinya are Japanese and subject to internment. I couldn't write Charlee back as our mail is being checked and mention of the Japanese Language School and the name Yoshino would get censored. We need to change the plan."

"He said, the plan," Claire says, "I knew they were scheming something; we are on the right track."

"Now what I need from each of you are your promises to track them all down, Charlee Sang, Franklin Yoshino, and Tinya," Uncle Paul said. "They are all family, and we need to know what happened to them and to reunite our family when this horrid war ends."

I remember being fixated less on this vital promise and more on whatever new scary stories Uncle Paul had, they too were never told. It was the last time I would see my favorite storytelling Uncle alive. Most of our extended family, no longer worked or lived in Spokane or Seattle when CPO Paul Jonson died at the Naval Hospital in Bremerton two months later.

"Typical of the stoicism in the Swedish members of my family, we never spoke of his illness nor of his passing," I say to Claire.

"Could it be that with your extended family members gone you had little choice but to deal alone with your grief?" Claire says. "Repressing your childhood memories of them was your only relief."

I take several minutes to get a grip on my emotions.

"Then, with the second promise of reuniting your lost family, you became traumatized, you faced an overwhelming task."

Reenactment of the last visit with Uncle Paul is freeing up some memories about the many times I retold scary stories to children in the neighborhood. But his demise brought an end to my services as his storytelling apprentice. The central activity of my life ceased. I assumed I was no longer needed and that coupled with his departure blotted out the second promise and my recollections of the missing family.

Let me restate Uncle Paul's last words: "You must

promise to find and reunite our extended family members after this war ends."

"I'm sensing that he feared their plan might have failed during his absence," Claire says. "Is this something we need to investigate?"

Until this moment of recall stirred by Charlee's last letter, I have repressed Franklin and Tinya being sent to one of the Japanese American internment camps.

Trauma and repression can lead to dysfunctional behavior. Claire explains how, in my case, that isn't true. Yes, I shirked family responsibility and wandered abroad, but I pursued a successful career. I appreciate the uplift.

Revealing the cause of my childhood memory repression is only a start, my trauma runs deep. I failed my favorite Uncle at the most important promise he ever presented to me. Paul, Charlee, Franklin, and Tinya were all so intertwined in my childhood, it's a package memory. It's as if they all died at once. It was too much for me, so I blocked it out.

"There, at last!" I say to Claire.

Now, fifty years later, the memory of my favorite Uncle's death is vivid. It returns with a strong twinge of regret. No, more than regret... more than a sense of failure and guilt over not fulfilling the second promise.

I've spent fifty years burying my failure to keep that second promise to find and reunite family. Now it's resurfacing and joins my sadness over the departures of my extended family members.

"It's the two promises together that have me intrigued," Claire says.

"What do you mean, the two promises together?"

"I'm guessing there is much more to Uncle Paul's last story than scaring off trespassers from the family farm."

"Back to square one?"

"Not quite," she says. "We need to uncover what happened between promising to retell the scary story and pledging to find and reunite relatives after the war."

She explains that regardless of whether I told Uncle Paul I kept the original pledge, what we need to know is whether there is a link between the promises.

"My deep feelings of guilt are about my failure to reunite the family, or are they?" I say as I wrestle to understand.

"Here's what I'm hypothesizing," Claire says. "We need to know the reason for Uncle Paul making you promise to tell and spread his story while he was away."

"By uncovering his secret reason, we can jump-start our efforts to keep the second promise, to find lost members and reunite the family."

"I believe you have it," Claire says, "It's a start."

I will need to dig deep into my memory-attic to find clues and an answer to what Uncle Paul's secret reason was. But the reenactment at The Cut provided some clues. First, the story itself, which I'm recalling in fragments. The story somehow holds the secret to why Uncle Paul had me spreading the scary tale all over the neighborhood. But it has been fifty years, and self-doubt and failing memories are obstacles I may not overcome, not without help.

"I may need a touch more help with this memory-attic thing than first expected."

"Did Connie take any photographs of Tinya and the lads?" Claire says. "I could send those photos to various government agencies and county records offices and newspapers to help me investigate each of the lost family members."

"Perhaps you will find her photos at the farm."

"The attic!" I exclaim with a sense of urgency in my voice. "If Connie's Leica and her photo albums and family records are in the attic, we must retrieve them before the auction."

Her laughter fills the air.

Our visit with Chief Petty Officer Paul Jonson at Bremerton Naval Hospital in the Fall of 1945 was short, a sad memory, not a joyful homecoming as Grandma and mom had prayed for. Jer and I continued to include Uncle Paul in our evening prayers.

During my global wandering, I mentioned earlier about visiting Hotel Death in India. That visit intermingles with a nightmare of a ghostly figure falling through space and plunging to his death.

After I discuss the nightmare with Claire, she says, "Bremerton Naval Hospital was CPO Jonson's Hotel Death. You still seek answers to something linked to your uncle's death. The question could be, what is your Hotel Death?"

"I blotted out of my memories of his emaciated, wheelchair-bound form. I didn't want those as my last image of him."

One more thing comes to me as we take the ferryboat back to Seattle's Pier 50. They scheduled CPO Paul Jonson for interment at the U. S. Navy Memorial Cemetery on Bainbridge Island. But grandma and mom

contacted the Department of the Navy with the help
of a lawyer. That was when I met Connie's friend Sara
Swenson. They persuaded the Navy that CPO Jonson's
remains get delivered to the family graveyard. With my
storytelling services no longer required, I went into a
funk.

Returning to when Jer said he didn't have a memorial service planned for mom. He also said there was
no need for me to return home. I felt a deep sense of
worthlessness. I had no role in laying my mother to rest.

A surge of fear came over me before I agreed to
meet and bury mom's ashes at the family cemetery.
Upon reflection, it comes to me I didn't want to return
to the cemetery and perhaps risk revisiting my memories of Uncle Paul's death.

My feeling of being worthless and having no role
in the ultimate act of laying her to rest is the same as
when Paul's body got delivered to the cemetery at the
farm.

Could this be why I have stayed away from the
farm and repressed my childhood memories?

I recollect crying over Paul's grave. I tell Claire I
had never seen a dead person in an open casket before
that day. When I got up the courage to look at the grey,
lifeless face of Uncle Paul, I felt ill. My great aunt Selma
stood beside me and leaned over and kissed his forehead. Then she insisted I do the same. Pretending to
make a kiss but not making contact, I ran outside behind the barn and lost it.

"What a dreadful experience for a boy," Claire
says, "no wonder it traumatized you."
Claire wraps her arms around me as I shake all over.

"Soon after the war, your mom found work in St.

Louis. She moved you to find employment but also to give you a chance to experience fresh memories," Claire says. "She saw what occurred and sensed a powerful need for a change of venue."

The difference being she came back to the farm years later, I never did.

Now, fifty years later, my memory-attic overflowing with international adventures. Uncle Paul and his secret lie buried in the maze along with my childhood and my lost family members.

"The rest of his story will come out of hiding, it's not forgotten," Claire says, "only repressed."

Claire explains repression. The psychological attempt to direct one's desires and impulses toward pleasurable instincts by excluding them from one's consciousness and holding or subduing them in the unconscious.

I'm reminded that she is a clinical psychologist.

Repression is a defense mechanism. But some memories don't just disappear; they continue to influence our behavior.

"How about an example?"

For example, a person who has repressed memories of abuse suffered as a child may later have difficulty forming relationships. Freud's psychoanalytic theory, notes distressing memories, thoughts, or feelings as often involving sexual or aggressive urges or painful childhood memories, it pushes these unwanted mental contents into the unconscious mind.

"Lots of stuff to add to the reenactments list," Claire says. "We need to discover things that led to and take us past the trauma blocking event. We may turn up some answers at Big Black Rock and the family farm."

"What a day!" Claire says, "Let's take a break. We'll find out what the secret is all about."

It's 2:15 am when Claire and I catch the ferry and return from Bremerton. We are both looking forward to an evening alone at her house. I need to stay rooted in the present to recharge my batteries and get a grip on the repression that has consumed me for fifty years.

An earlier topic resurfaces.

"Have you met Mr. and Mrs. Slater?" I ask as I read the name on the mailbox of the old Halverson's residence on the way up Hillside Drive to Claire's home.

"It's not the Slater's, it's Ansel Slater," Calire says. "He's a horticulturist. He moved in two weeks after the Halverson's left for Oregon."

"You'll meet him soon," she says, "he pops in from time to time, he's helping me plan a Japanese rock garden for my yard, below the rear porch."

My jealousy flares up. But I choke off my inclination to say no, I don't want to meet Ansel; I want to get rid of him.

I realize Claire and I have been having an ongoing argument since I made the crack about the spite houses having a magnificent view, and she shot back that her place has its own glorious view. I'm just now sensing she wants her home to be mine and hers. Jealousy is so petty and so counterproductive, but I'm not above it.

"What kind of name is Ansel?" I say as the candles flicker out on the flower-patterned kitchen tile counter. I put the remaining boxes of another order of Chinese take-home in the fridge. A pile of dinner dishes remains stacked in the sink.

"Remember Uncle Paul's directions for Connie," I say, "he wrote to start at King Street Train Station."

"I remember," Claire says as she pulls the comforter close.

"We all left together by train for Spokane after the picnic at The Cut," I say, adding, "Our reenactment of the train ride starts early tomorrow morning."

"That's nice!"

She's snoring as I spoon around her and fall asleep under the goose down comforter.

CHAPTER 10

5 am PST

A series of shrill child-like screams shatters the quiet calm. Claire is in front of the bedroom window, silhouetted in the silvery moonlight. I take a mental snapshot, feeling confident the image will last me for as long as my memory-attic operates.

"A baby squirrel is clinging to a limb up in the cypress," she says, "I think it's lost its mother."

Wiping a space in the frost on the glass with her palm, she uses her finger to draw a circular frame around the tiny creature.

"She must have fallen out of the drey during the storm."

"There was a storm outside last night?" I say, "I didn't notice."

Ignoring my attempt at humor, she stands by me and watches as the tiny bundle of fur continues an incessant flicking of its curly tail and screams for help.

"Should we rescue her?" I say, backing up a pace to continue admiring her silhouette.

"You know, kits are born blind. Let's give her mom

a chance to find her."

The nightmare of mom's last call resurfaces. There is an umbilical bond between a mother and off-spring.

Soon I'm too engrossed with the silhouette changing into a warm body that wraps around me as Claire smiles and says, "Mmm, that was a wonderful stormy evening."

"We have time for a morning run before we head for King Street Station," I say, feigning disinterest for a few seconds.

"Can our run wait for another 30 minutes?" Claire says, pulling me back under the comforter.

Returning to Claire's house after our run through the arboretum, dawn is breaking, and stillness prevails, dare I say ghostly quiet. Her burglar alarm system lets her know if anyone has broken in during her absence by playing the big band music of Glenn Miller's Orchestra. She loves 1930s and 1940s music, her favorites being Glenn Miller and Count Basie. I make a mental note to box up the old records mom used to play as a gift for her. I'm guessing they're in the attic at the farm.

The music comes on if someone enters the incorrect security code or if a window or door is ajar. Entering by the rear door, I notice it's unlocked, but all is quiet. Claire doesn't seem the least bit concerned.

I remark on the missing music when Claire holds up her finger to her lips to shush me and points out the window.

Mother squirrel has returned to the nest, flicking

her tail back and forth, she has found her kit.

"I love happy endings, don't you?"

"I forgot to reset the alarms after the power went off last night."

While I put her matching luggage and my leather duffel in the boot of her Peugeot, Claire prepares French press and croissants with mango jam for breakfast.

"Who won the race?" she asks.

"You know, I'm not sure," I say. "Are you referring to the Montlake Cut and Paul's freshman rowing team; do you mean that race?"

"Yes, wise guy!" Claire says. "I find it strange that you don't recall if the UW Huskies won the freshman race against their biggest rivals, the Cal Bears."

"You said that Franklin stayed with Connie and you at the picnic site along The Cut, so you could at least see the start of the race, if not the finish as it was out of sight on Lake Washington. So, who won the race?"

To ask is okay, but why now?

As we slide the garage door open to get into her Peugeot for the drive to King Street train station, Claire shrugs.

"We can always look it up in the Seattle-Times archives," she says. "I have a hypothesis, if you'll listen to it?"

"Naw! Not knowing is okay by me."

I picked a lousy time to upset her with my flippant remark, as she is turning the key in the ignition and starting the engine of the Peugeot. Claire hits reverse and backs out of the garage into the rain. She suffers from a condition known as road rage.

Five minutes of absolute silence prevails.

With pursed lips and fire in her voice, she says, "Whether you want to listen, here's my hypothesis. You mentioned that Franklin was shy. But you also said he was exuberant when Paul and Charlee returned after the freshman crew race."

She pauses, shifts the Peugeot into first gear and, tires spinning, speeds up down the street.

"That was your choice of words, exuberant," she says as she shifts into second gear. "I think that's a sign they won the competition."

She waits me out. I grin. She shifts into third gear.

"OK, I get it," I say, "Franklin, the shy one, wouldn't have been that giddy unless they won."

Downshifting into second gear, she skids around a corner on the slippery wet pavement.
I have upset her. I should have remembered that when Claire is driving, she gets intense. After a brief cooling down period, I almost choke, getting out my apology for being so glib.

She stares straight ahead all the way to King Street Station, utter silence prevails. I turn my attention to the forthcoming train ride and the Jonson family farm, the next reenactment. Her list now includes Big Black Rock, the cabins, the Falu red farmhouse, the attic, the barn, and Oldman Speke's country store with a note to sort it out later.

We spin out, coming to a stop on the slippery surface of the rain-soaked parking lot next to King Street station. Claire is still simmering. She parks in the long-term section as close as she can to the entrance. She turns off the engine, we disembark, get her luggage out of the boot, and she locks the Peugeot. As if by magic, her road rage subsides.

I remember rows of canvas topped Model T's and Model A Sedan, all in black, lined up in a 1940s funeral procession. Glancing up as the rain comes down, I glimpse the time on the six-story clock tower hovering above the station. That landmark hasn't changed.

"We're early," I say, "may I buy you an espresso and tell you one of the first stories Uncle Paul ever told us? It's about an avalanche. Want to hear it?"

"Will it take long to tell?" she says, still a touch snippy. "Our train leaves in ten minutes."

"Okay, I'll tell it to you during the train ride," I say. "It may jog my memory."

We pick up our tickets at the AMTRAK counter at King Street Station from a dude with slicked-back black hair, wearing a green plastic visor. Handing us our tickets, he says, "Track 5 and the # 34 double berth in the third sleeping car."

"We are in Seattle, don't overdramatize this gloomy departure," Claire says, recovered from her rage. "We get a lot of this dreary rain; it dulls the mind."

"So far the reenactment list idea is paying off," she says, "Let's enjoy the train ride, and I'm anxiously awaiting the avalanche story. I'm also looking forward to seeing Ms. Sara and Jer."

"Are you sure we're in first class?" Claire says with a look of disdain as we arrived at Track #5, climbed aboard, and located berth #34.

"These bunks are the best accommodations on this train," I say. "I'll flip you for the upper bunk."

The conductor punched our tickets as I threw my leather duffle on the upper bunk of the berth. Claire's matched luggage is in the baggage compartment, but she carries her overnight bag. Most of Claire's and my travel is by airplane, and I prefer to keep my luggage close. Once I air-freighted a trunk from Johannesburg to Seattle. The airline tracked it to its last known location on the Ivory Coast and said that it's being rerouted.

Claire kicks off her shoes and settles into the lower bunk and dozes off. I remove my hiking boots and prop my feet on a pillow. I'm looking forward to being drummed to sleep to the rhythm of the clickety-clack, of steel wheels on iron rails. A steady rain falls as the train pulls out of King Street Station. By the time we are a few miles from the station, the repetitive clickety-clack becomes a constant hum, and I drift off.

My dreams take me back to December 1940, and the ride to Spokane on the day after the races on the Montlake Cut. The first snow of the year was falling, more sleet than flakes. Uncle Paul, Charlee, Franklin, Tinya, mom, Jer, and I return to the farm for the annual family gathering for the Christmas holidays.

Uncle Paul spent his meager savings from his tutoring on train tickets on the Cascadian Line for his three friends.

December 1940 was a time of discovery and excitement. Franklin, Tinya, and Charlee are travelling with us to our traditional gathering for the holidays. During the train ride Uncle Paul and Connie frequently refer to Franklin, Tinya, and Charlee as family, something I only now realize.

As we prepared to board the Cascadian Line of the Great Northern Railway at King Street Station, Uncle Paul began our journey by asking us if we wanted to hear a true scary story. The tale is about a train wreck and an avalanche that destroyed a town on this route to Spokane many years ago.

Uncle Paul's enticement of a scary story has Jer and me on the edge of our seats. We flip the seatback in front of us 180 degrees, Paul and Connie and I sit opposite Charlee, Franklin, Tinya, and Jer, then we settle in our seats. No first-class bunks, we couldn't afford them. The engineer pulls the chain on the steam whistle, and we hear a long shrill note. It repeats a second and third time, and the remaining passengers clamber on board. The train jerks several times, and we are underway.

"Tickets, tickets! " The porter said as he passed by snapping and punching holes in the passengers' tickets. Soon he made a return pass and said, "Anyone care for a nickel Coca-Cola?"

The porter returns with a tray of cold green glass bottles. He wipes the moisture off each bottle with a towel and pops them open with a bottle opener attached to his key chain and a ring of keys, passing them to each of us with an enormous smile.

Powerful engines strain as the train crawls up the steep grade towards the next town. The Cascadian is a milk run, stopping at every speck of a town between Seattle and Spokane, making it a 9-hour journey; faster trains were too expensive and booked.

The train soon jerks, squeals, and slows at an insignificant town, and I peek out the window where I see the name Tye on the depot house. We screech to a stop to take on a single passenger and her entourage comprising a white miniature poodle and several pieces of leather luggage.

Uncle Paul settles into the seat between Charlee and Franklin, and opposite Connie, Tinya, Jer, and I, says, "Are you ready for that story I mentioned before we left King Street Station?"

"If you don't tell it soon," Charlee Sang said, flashing his white teeth in a broad grin, "I will tell your sister who I saw you with at the dance last night, after the races."

"I wondered where you lads had disappeared to after the picnic," Connie said, "Tell me more."

"I don't take well to blackmail, my friend," Paul said, feigning anger at Charlee and feinting a left jab before starting his story.

"They call this town we are passing through Tye; before an immense avalanche, it used to be Wellington's town. Back in 1910, Wellington was a mere whistle-stop high on the Cascade mountain range on the west side of the Cascade Tunnel, that's the grade we are now climbing so."

"What's a whistle-stop?" I say.

"I know that one," Jer said, "When the station master blows the whistle, he notifies an oncoming train that there is a passenger to pick up."

"Thank you, Gerald," Uncle Paul said with a nod, Jer smiled, and he returned to the avalanche story.

A horrific blizzard fell for over a week in February 1910, burying Wellington's tiny town under ten feet of snow on the worst day of the storm.

"Ten feet of snow," Jer said, "that's as tall as the front porch on the farmhouse."

"I suspect that is an accurate estimate," Uncle Paul said as he wiped his forehead with a red and black bandana before adding, "Shall I continue the story, or are there more remarks from the peanut gallery?"

Satisfied that he had our full attention, he folded

his black and red bandana and returned it to his back pants pocket. It reminds me of one of his storytelling lessons. No story can be told until you capture the audience's full attention.

By the last day of February, the cold and snow stopped, and warmer, rainy days took over. On March 1, a thunderstorm produced a lightning bolt strike that caused a large slab of ice and snow to split free from Windy Mountain. In recent years, forest fires had cleared the slopes of the trees that might have slowed the avalanche before it smashed into the town and the railroad station and the two trains that were approaching. Ten feet of snow, a length of eight football fields and half again as wide bulldozed smack into the town.

No one could leave the depot during that snowstorm. Wellington Station had snowplows; but they were inadequate to the task. A call for help went out to surrounding towns. No one could plow through the vast snowdrifts, and the snow kept accumulating as more avalanches blocked the tracks in and out of the area.

Uncle Paul paused once more for effect, then continued.

The danger begins when a passenger train bound for Spokane from Seattle and the mail train destined for Seattle are crawling along the hill near the town of Tye, on a collision course.

Almost all the passengers are asleep. Only the crew members aboard the two trains are awake. The two engineers had both stopped at Wellington to avoid a collision.

Paul's audience gasps in relief.

No one aboard either train had time to react as a

thunderous clash of ice and snow mixed with pine trees smashed into the engines and passenger and freight cars. Both trains toppled down the hillside for over 100 feet and came crashing to rest half-submerged in the Tye River. 100 people suffocated in the snow and ice.

Heroes were born that day among the passengers and crew. Strangers risked their lives to pull twenty-three passengers to safety out of the icy water of the river, the deep snow, and the tangled wreckage. No one claimed credit for the rescues, that's the way of genuine heroes, not until a local newspaper reported that it was a gruesome sight.

"21 weeks later, in the summer, they recover the last of the bodies when the snow and ice melt," Uncle Paul said, letting us absorb the enormity of the tragedy.

The Great Northern Railway built concrete snow sheds to deflect any future avalanches along these tracks, and several years later, they dug the Cascade Tunnel. Wellington brought on intense feelings of disaster among the townspeople and visitors. They rename the town, Tye. He pointed out the train window at the sign on the stationhouse roof.

Sometime later, Wellington depot was closed, and the town became a veritable ghost town before it burned to the ground. They then changed the town name to Tye. The Iron Goat Trail passes near the old site.

"What's the Iron Goat Trail?" Jer and I said in unison.

"We'll trek it together someday when it's not snowing, and I'll tell you that tale."

We never did.

The sheets of snow and sleet continued falling,

and we saw little for the rest of the train ride. Nine hours after leaving Seattle, we reach Spokane. Jer and I pressing our faces against the frosted windows and making ice crystals by blowing on the glass while staring wide-eyed, looking for signs of an avalanche. We had survived the dreaded avalanches and learned of the ghosts and heroes of Wellington.

May 7, 1992, the train whistle screeches, and the sleeper car shudders and jerks several times before coming to a halt. Unlike in 1940, today, we disembark at the Spokane Intermodal Center, the new train depot in Spokane. They tore down most of the station I knew as a child. Only the two-story red brick Amtrak station house remains.

Claire is with me, but I'm alone with my memories.

I swear I'm on the lookout for avalanches following my dream infested train ride from Seattle. The image doesn't go away until Claire and I step off the train in Spokane, blinking in the bright early morning summer sunlight, I had forgotten it was summer, no snow in sight.

I am uncertain whether I told Claire the Avalanche Story or only recreated it in my dreams.

Uncle Paul's avalanche tale lingers in my thoughts and soon loosens something else from my log jam of memories.

Claire only has four suitcases with her, but that's enough for me to leave her at Spokane Intermodal Station while I walk to the rental car office in the southeast corner of the parking lot, happy to stretch the stiffness out of my legs.

"*I'm dreaming of a White Christmas, just like the one...*"

The music comes from a speaker on the corner of the station house roof over the rental car office.

"Damn, that's der Bingle," I exclaim as I enter.

"I love that song, too," the girl at the rental car counter says, "I can never get enough of it, even when it's not Christmas."

"I just recalled an earlier visit," I say, "it was right after an avalanche blocked the train tracks over in Tye."

"You know that it's nearing the end of Spring?" the counter girl says with a giggle. "I was just checking out the new stereo, and I put the first record on the turntable I recognized."

She's a wisp of a girl, about five foot nothing with eyes that sparkle, and she's a bundle of historical information about her hometown, Spokane.

"Did you know that Bing Crosby came from near here?" she says. "My grandma saw him perform at the Old Clemmer Theater."

I pulled my driver's license and a credit card from my wallet and handed them to her.

"Nice to meet you, Dr. Jonson, I'm Ginger," she says as she checks some paperwork and asks me if I want insurance.

I say no. The credit card covers liability. Ginger hands me the keys to a polished and vacuumed late model black and silver Cadillac Seville that smells of cedar.

"A Cadillac is the only vehicle available this morning," she says, "the dentists convention has everything rented. I charged you at the mid-size rate."

My dreaming or reliving of the Wellington avalanche story has loosened another piece of the puzzle
from my memory-attic. The Bing Crosby songs from
Ivar's and now at the Spokane Intermodal Center. I
again recall Uncle Paul's remarks about newsreels and
movies at our last visit with him in Bremerton. Am I
being drawn by der Bingle's music or led by his ghost, as
Claire had joked? But brought to where and why?

The Clemmer Theater became the State Theatre
and, it's being renamed the Bing Crosby. It's a quick walk
from the Old Davenport Hotel. The Old Davenport Hotel
is in downtown Spokane, a mile or so south of the Spokane River on the corner of Sprague and Post Streets.
The hotel is where Uncle Paul first showed me a large
oil painting in the grand lobby. Christopher Columbus's
three sailing ships. Columbus's name is on the globe
in the apse at Suzzallo Library, and now this painting.
What does it mean?

As I thank Ginger for the history lesson, she jots
down the phone numbers for Hunt Realtors and the
AAAAA security service on the back of the car rental
form. Der Bingle continues singing "*White Christmas*".

In the Cadillac I take a few minutes to familiarize
myself with the radio, the a/c, and other gadgets. I half
expect more of Crosby's singing when I push a station
button on the radio.

Which of the ghosts is leading me by the nose,
Bing, or Columbus?

Back at the train station, I pick up Claire and her
luggage so we can head to the farm.

"Did I tell you the avalanche story and about der
Bingle's ghost and the Old Davenport Hotel?" I say.

" Yes, dear," Claire smiles and says, "And the re-enactment list grows ever longer."

Ghosts or no ghosts, I feel compelled to follow Columbus and der Bingle to the Clemmer Theater and the Old Davenport Hotel after we attend to business at the farm and inter mom's ashes.

CHAPTER 11

To see something familiar, that's my first aim as Claire and I drive east in the Caddy from Spokane. An enormous sign for the Inland Paper Mill appears. It was once the source of over a thousand jobs, several Jonson's and Nordling's once worked there, but it's boarded up. We cross the Spokane River on the old Argonne Bridge and head south through Millwood, which is a ghost town. The rain stops, but the wiper blades don't.

I'm driving on paved streets and passing rows of recent housing developments, a shopping mall, and a business park. These images are not congruent with my memories of dirt and gravel roads and rock-strewn fields and apple orchards. After crossing the Spokane River comes Grant Park. I slow down, expecting to see the three-story red brick schoolhouse where I was champion marble shooter. They bulldozed the school playground of my childhood. A new sprawling single-story Grant Elementary School and the asphalt parking lot has replaced it.

Five minutes further on East 9th Street, I spot a green framed billboard advertising Speke's Country

Store [Open daily at 7 am]. At last, something familiar.

I know I'm close to home when we drive past Speke's. I glance at the clock on the dashboard; it reads 6:35 am, meaning the store won't open for another 25 minutes.

We'll return and pick up some supplies and say hello after we check out the farmhouse.

"To recognize a little of the neighborhood would be nice," I say as I fumble with the wiper controls.

"How long has it been since your last visit?" Claire says.

"Two years, but rarely after my childhood."

The farm served as the hub for our extended family. Christmas holidays signalled a time for the family to gather. Relatives came from all over the states and even abroad. Gatherings began in December when Charles Frederick Jonson and Matilda Nordling Jonson broke ground and built a barn in the valley. My anxiety intensifies as we get closer to the origin of these memories.

A few miles southeast of downtown Spokane, I spot the rocky terrain that marks the edge of the glacial age and the southern boundary of the land. Big Black Rock casts a protective shadow over the homestead in daylight. My increased heartbeat foretells that I'm close to home.

Five blocks further south on the new blacktop, I catch sight out of the driver's side window of a red farmhouse. I realize for the first time that it has been 50 years since the family last gathered here for the Christmas holidays. It also hits me. I haven't visited mom and the farm more than for a few brief visits in the thirty years I've spent living abroad.

My anxiety resurfaces as the Cadillac's tires

crunch across the gravel in the driveway, and I park alongside the farmhouse. I'm on familiar ground. Jer and I helped Uncle Paul lay the sand and rocks.

When I open the car door, I'm greeted by a soft breeze that hints of rain. It's a pleasant 65 degrees Fahrenheit, and my lingering thoughts of trains, scary avalanches, and winter snowstorms subside.

I'm wearing jeans, a purple tee shirt with UW Huskies stenciled on the front, and my favorite leather flight jacket. It doesn't repel rain. I drape the coat on the driver's seat and run around opening the passenger door for Claire. Before we can dash for shelter of the porch, a squall rolls in.

"I'll get some rain gear from the house," I say, "wait in the car."

If I'm lucky, Grandpa Jonson's rain slicker is hanging on the rear porch. I grope along the sill over the rear-porch door, disrupting a colony of cockroaches and a black widow spider, until I find the hidden door-key. Some memories remain useful as I slip the key in the lock and enter.

Draping the rain slicker over our shoulders, Claire and I enter the kitchen. I notice that the air inside is free of the musty odor of a place that no one has lived in for years. A sudden chill comes over me.

Memories dance all around me as Claire and I do a quick exploration of the house. I'm at home in familiar surroundings. I feel the eerie presence of ghosts.

In Grandma's kitchen, I turn the faucet handles and the pipes croak with a dry cough. I flip on the light switches to no avail. Missing fuses means there is no point in flipping the circuit breakers. It gets down as low as 45 to 50 degrees after the sun sets this time of year.

With the heat and water turned off, we'll need some heat if we want to stay overnight.

I gather up an armful of logs from wood box and take it into the living room. The fireplace is gas, explaining the sizeable white cylinder I had glimpsed while coming down the driveway. That's a change since my last visit. Grandma's kitchen still has her wrought-iron potbelly stove. I check the stove pipe for wrens' nests, crumple up some newspaper and insert kindling and two.

Claire rummages through some drawers and cupboards in the pantry. She finds a box of wooden safety matches and a dozen candles in a tin container. Using one candle, she drips some wax onto the lid; then, she seats the candle in the soft wax. It solidifies for a minute before handing it to me to start the fire in the potbelly stove. She places the candle on the breakfast table to light up the room.

"What a lovely, crocheted tablecloth," Claire exclaims.

One of grandmas crocheted white tablecloths covers the kitchen table and a lovely bouquet of fresh flowers sets in the middle. It's just the same as what grandma picked every summer and spring day.

I swear to Claire that I detect oatmeal and raisin, or is it oatmeal and cranberry cookies baking in the oven?

As the potbelly stove warms the kitchen, I set up a second candle lamp and head for the attic. I pull the rope, and the trap door opens. Down comes the ladder. I expect a blast of dust. It has been closed for months. It's a dangerous climb up the rickety wooden rungs to see what's stored up there that I might want to keep from being sold at auction. The plan is to transport whatever Jer, and I keep. We'll rent storage space at Speke's Country Store. I begin with a stack of two dozen cardboard boxes lined along the west wall.

In the flickering candlelight in the dusty attic, I read the label on a top box, 'Sundry linens'. The box is open. I'm guessing it was the source of the crocheted tablecloth on the dining table. Someone has been here before Claire and I arrived.

I carry the linens and a second box down the shaky ladder to the kitchen table. There is an old-fashioned ringer washing machine, but no water means no clean sheets for Claire and me tonight. Not acceptable.

I lift the ladder and close the attic.

Soon I discover that they disconnected the service to the wall-mounted telephone.

Claire suggests that we make a quick trek around the property before driving to the country store to make phone calls and pick up supplies. We only get as far as the garage when a gentle rain starts up.

Five months have elapsed since mom died. I'm expecting the farmhouse and out-buildings to look neglected. We walk around in the drizzle and inspect the grounds around the traditional Swedish farmhouse. Two stories, an attic, and a food cellar, a fresh coat of paint covers the farmhouse. It raises my curiosity because it comes to me that not just anyone knows how to apply this special Falu red paint.

We run into more evidence of people being on the grounds. An enormous sign is on the front lawn between the house and the venerable oak tree. It announces to passersby that the estate is up for AUCTION. That old oak is at least a hundred. I recall the two yellow ribbons tied around it during the war years to announce to all that we had family serving in the war. That ugly sign does not belong next to the sacred oak. I almost take it down before reminding myself that mom had given the responsibility for selling the family farm to her lawyer; but I still find the big sign offensive.

Sara Swenson, mom's attorney, or the Hunt Realtors firm are the party responsible for the auction sign. Perhaps they hired a caretaker to manicure the place.

The grounds surrounding the house are mown. The smell of cut grass mingles with the odor of rotting apples from the nearby apple orchard. Garden beds tended by my grandma and mom for decades are weeded.

The peonies and tulips, nurtured by the sun and the spring rains, are the same flowers as in the kitchen vase. They are colorful accessories alongside the painted Falu red siding of the house.

"Damn!" I say, thinking, who wouldn't want to buy this place.

"Damn what?" Claire says.

She startles me as I think its grandma's ghost admonishing me.

"Damn we have ghosts, and I remember why I loved this place as a child."

Claire laughs and smothers me with a hug.

Fresh cut grass encrusts the lawnmower. I find a chainsaw in the toolshed. Hard to make use of a chainsaw without gas, and the 4-wheeler is useless for doing a tour of the orchards and forest.

I check around the three-car garage and see a paint-stained tarpaulin covering a vehicle.

I pull the tarp off a dusty old sedan, and say with joy, "It's

Black Beauty."

"Black Beauty?"

"It's mom's 1939 La Salle."

I blow the dust off a box of spark plugs and plug wires. They look to be in good shape.

The drizzle is slowing to a stop, so we gamble on walking to Speke's Country Store. We need a plan if we are to remain overnight. First, we need to walk up the road to Speke's to use the pay phone to call Ma Bell to restore the phone service. Calls to PG&E and the Spokane Water Department follow to obtain service. I lock the back door and replace the key on the sill. We walk the five blocks to Speke's Country Store.

That's when I decide to get the La Salle in running order at the first opportunity. Then we can return the Caddy.

I ask Claire to add some items to the list of household and grocery supplies. A 5-gallon can of gas, motor oil, some light bulbs, two flashlights and batteries, and a propane cylinder.

"We can't carry all that back to the farm," Claire says.

A red wagon hangs from the far wall in the garage. I get it down, oil the wheels and say, "The perfect vehicle for carrying supplies."

A youthful woman in her twenties with long shiny black hair and a Pepsodent smile greets us as I hold open the front door to Speke's for Claire.

"Nice to see you, Professor Daniel, may I help you and your friend?" the youthful woman says. "You don't remember me, do you?"

"I'm Angie Speke," she says. "Mr. Speke is my great uncle, I'll tell him you're back at the farm when he returns tomorrow, he'll want to know."

"I remember an Angie," I say.

"She's about so tall and 4 years old," I say, gesturing a height below my belt.

Then I give her a hug.

"Meet Claire."

"We need some supplies, and can I use the payphone to make some calls," I say. "We're in town for the auction."

Angie exchanges a twenty for two rolls of quarters from the cash register for the payphone. I open the yellow pages and call PG&E to restore the electricity at the farm. The service department clerk says they will repair it in 3 days. The PG&E clerk promises they'll send a man between 1 and 4 pm, and I need not be at the house if the fuse box is outside. I tell her it's on the back porch, I'll leave the door unlocked. My next call gets the phone service restored, a third restores the water.

The fresh coat of Falu red paint, tidied up flower beds, mowed lawn, grandma's crocheted tablecloth taken from the attic. These mysteries dance around in my head. I make a call to the one person who might have some answers.

Sara Swenson's message machine says, "Back soon, leave a message."

I'm getting more and more annoyed by these message machines. They are a fad I can live without.

I spend a quarter to call the reservation desk to book a room at the Davenport Towers Hotel in downtown Spokane. Rooms are booked solid. I still have a second roll, so I call the Red Lion by the Park on the north side of the river. The reservations clerk tells me there's a dentist convention in town, no vacancy until the day after tomorrow. I'd forgotten what Ginger told me at the car rental agency.

"There's a lot of stuff from our train ride that begs a place on the reenactment list," Claire says, once more expecting my next move. "The Davenport Hotel has some interesting ghosts, and the Clemmer Theater should be fun."

We placed the gas can and materials to get the La Salle operating in the red wagon. The propane cylinder is too heavy.

"Can you deliver the rest of the supplies in three days?" I say to Angie, "Tell your Uncle I'm looking forward to seeing him."

"Pleased to meet you, Ms. Claire," Mila says, nodding and waving as we trek back down 9th Street. Two smiling children pulling a red wagon.

CHAPTER 12

Tuning up the old La Salle and giving her a wash and wax is a joy. Remembering other childhood memories as I work. We bought an additional set of plugs and six quarts of motor oil from Speke's. I didn't want to risk using the ones I found in the garage. I tear off a piece of chocolate licorice to chew. Slip into a a pair of Paul's grease-stained bib-coveralls and relive his teaching me how to drain the oil and wash and polish the LaSalle. A voice in my head says, make sure you have the right tools. A rusted plug wrench is hanging from a peg on the garage wall. I grab a rag and some 3-in-1.

Memories crowd their way into my cluttered memory-attic, and I recall some details of Uncle Paul's scary story while I tend to the La Salle. My plan is to re-tell as much as I recall of his tale to Claire this evening atop Big Black Rock.

The battery is dead, meaning I can't start her up and check out my work and we won't be able to play the radio. Slipping out of Paul's oil-stained coveralls, I hang them on a hook next to the big, galvanized wash-basin. I wash up with a bar of Ivory soap and scrub the grease from under my fingernails. My knuckles need

some band-aids, which I find in a tin in the kitchen pantry along with some iodine.

Extracting the rundown battery wasn't easy, I put
it in the red wagon. Asphalt paving makes this a simple
trip, with no potholes filled with rain. Jer and I used to
pull this same red wagon and take empty Coke bottles to
Speke's to get refunds and buy licorice sticks.

The sun sets before I return from Speke's with a
used battery. I had to remove it from a pickup truck
with a blown water pump. It takes several tries and
chokes before the La Salle spits a few times, coughs, and
roars to life. I check the headlamps, which are dim and
toot the horn. It gives off the sound of a goose honking.
Headlights and taillights go on my growing list of items
to buy at the Cadillac dealer in Spokane.

It takes two hours to clean and gap the spark
plugs, adjust the ignition points, and repair the plug
wires. These are all things Paul taught me. A rebuilt
ignition system and extra plug wires will have to wait.
I give the La Salle a wax job, finish with a hand buffing,
no electricity for the power drill. She has a shine that befits the childhood nickname we gave her, Black Beauty.
With a stiff copper wire brush, I clean the wide whitewalls. The tires still have some tread but, they'll need
replacement soon. A gauge from the toolbox works well
enough to check the tire pressure. Can I purchase a set of
these old wide whitewalls in town?

Pushing the heavy car out of the garage takes an
effort. Black Beauty crunches down the gravel driveway
to the front of the house where Claire is standing by
the venerable oak tree. A flood of childhood memories
about the postman, yellow ribbons, and so much more
comes cascading down the sluice. I told Uncle Paul's

story many times, but there are still fragments hidden deep in my memory-attic. What Claire calls details of my repressed memories.

"She's beautiful!" Claire says. "Let's give her a test ride, take a spin into town."

"First, I need to get her rolling down 9th Street to jump start her and charge the battery."

We push her to the corner. To Spruce Avenue which heads downhill. I jump in and hit the ignition switch, pop the clutch and the engine chugs to life as Claire cheers.

"Better yet," I say, "I'll drive Black Beauty into town, and you follow in the rental Caddy."

The plan is to return it to the airport to drop off the Caddy. Then we'll have dinner at the Red Lion Bar & Grill and spend the night before visiting the Davenport and the Clemmer Theater. Claire grabs her overnight case, and matching suitcases and gets in the rental Caddy to drive to Spokane Intermodal. The windshield wipers of the Caddy are still flapping full force from yesterday's rainstorm.

Claire powers down the window and says, "Listen to these wipers, can you fix them?"

The worn rubber blades screech across the dry glass. Fingernails on a blackboard. I fumble around with several switches and knobs on the Caddy's dash before finding the lever that should turn the wipers off. No luck, so I reach under the dash and disconnect the wire so Claire can drive into town in peace. Crossing her fingers, she mumbles something of a prayer that it won't rain.

I follow her in the LaSalle and park behind the Caddy at the Spokane Intermodal. The rental car clerk isn't the same girl as when I picked up the Caddy. I tell her that Ginger made a note about the broken wipers when we picked it up. She sees a notation on her copy of my rental agreement. I expect to get a bill in the mail.

By the time we arrive at the Red Lion Hotel, the Bar & Grill is closed. The desk clerk says room service is available. We order steak sandwiches, fries, and chocolate shakes. Within an hour, we snuggle into the king-size hotel bed and are sound asleep.

We book a two-night stay at the Red Lion Hotel in Spokane. I make a call on the hotel room phone to Sara Swenson's law offices. All I get is another annoying, "Back soon, leave a message at the tone."

Finishing making calls, my curiosity gets the best of me. I wonder if we might visit the Davenport Hotel and see the Christopher Columbus painting.

"Now there's a disparate fragment from your childhood visit to Suzzallo Library," Claire says. "Sounds fun."

"You know that the Davenport has been closed for years?" the Bell Telephone operator says.

Ginger, the rental car girl at the train station, had mentioned that it was closed in 1985. I ran down to the Red Lion Hotel parking lot and fumbled through the papers in the glove box I had transferred from the Caddy to the LaSalle. I recover the AAAAA Security phone number Ginger wrote on my rental form. Then I return to our hotel room and call.

A pleasant female voice says, "AAAAA Security, how may I help you?"

Claire is laughing as I resist the urge to ask, 'was that 4 or 5 A's?'

"Yes, I hope so," I say. "I'm Professor Jonson, my

colleague and I are in town for today and tomorrow, and we're doing some background research on the Davenport; is it possible for us to tour the hotel?"

I told her I wanted to look around and satisfy a historian's memories and curiosities about the art collection and the fabulous Spanish architecture.

"Hold please," the AAAAA clerk says, "I'll check with Security."

"Professor Jonson, I've scheduled a security guard to meet you and your party at the west side entrance at 8 am tomorrow."

I thank her.

After a five-mile run along the Spokane River, Claire and I order double espressos and croissants in the Red Lion coffee shop. I sip while reading the local news, a habit from years of international travel. While we walk from the Red Lion Hotel to the Davenport, my brain tries to connect the dots. Dozens of memories tie to that last visit with Uncle Paul.

At 8 am, we arrive at the old Davenport. A frail, diminutive man with a snow-white goatee greets us at the entrance on Spruce Street. It remains a majestic Spanish renaissance-style structure, even in its current state, with an eight-foot-high fence and scaffoldings surrounding it and a sign saying, "Closed for Renovations".

The security guard is wearing a starched, pressed blue uniform, and a captain's cap. My guess is that he's in his late 80s and most likely of Japanese ancestry. He has a massive ring of keys attached to his belt, and he's swinging a two-foot-long flashlight on a leather thong.

He sees me staring at the flashlight and says, "The power is off in most of the hotel."

"Dr. Claire Parsons, and Professor Daniel Jonson," I say, bowing slightly. "We hope to see the Columbus painting and other artifacts."

"Welcome, Doctor Professors," he says, returning my bow, "My name is Samuel Yoshino."

The Yoshino surname has me excited, and Claire jabs me.

Rattling the keys attached to his belt, Mr. Yoshino stretches the keyring out on a retractable line, and selects a large brass key. He inserts it in the bolt lock at the top and repeats the process for the lock at the bottom of the service door.

The entrance opens onto an immense room. Mr. Yoshino switches on his flashlight. He sweeps the hotel lobby with a broad illuminating beam. As we walk through the lobby, I swear der Bingle is crooning, "*I'm dreaming of a White Christmas.*"

I pause and cock my head, seeking the source of the sound.

"Is that Bing?" Claire says.

Mr. Yoshino cocks his head while cupping his right hand behind his ear.

"I hear it too," he says. "Der Bingle haunts this place. He is still singing, even for a tiny audience of three."

I feel as if der Bingle has led me here to this place. Claire's smiling with delight.

Whatever that means.

Mr. Yoshino says," Shall we check out the Columbus painting?"

Claire and I marvel at the Renaissance Spanish architecture. When we reach the center of gigantic lobby, the glass panels in the ceiling give the place the look of a large atrium. The vast cathedral room is alive in beams of sunlight but has no plants. They cover most of the furnishings in tarps, and the area has a dusty mausoleum smell. Mr. Yoshino shuts off the flashlight. An elegant carved marble mantle tops an impressive stone fireplace.

"The first fire in the lobby fireplace was lit in 1914," Mr. Yoshino says.

He tells us the story of the hotel proprietor, Mr. Davenport. He decreed that as a symbol of hospitality; the fireplace is to burn year-round.

"At some point, they converted the fireplace to gas," Mr. Yoshino says. "It's not safe to keep it lit with only the occasional watchman looking in on it."

He flips the flashlight on and shines the beam on a huge oil-painting over the chimney.

"Is this the painting you wish to see?" Mr. Yoshino says. "It portrays the three famous ships sailed by Christopher Columbus in his discoveries of the unknown world, the Niña, the Pinta, and the Santa Maria."

Flat-footed and transfixed, I take in every detail. I'm flashing back to the Suzzallo Library and the south apse with the hanging sphere with the great explorers' names, including Columbus.

Why does it feel as if we are sailing, and I'm being led to the Hotel on a ghostly ship?

Last night at the Red Lion Hotel I dreamed of sailing the seas with Columbus. It was a dream I had in my youth, returning after a 50-year hiatus. In the dream Paul is Columbus and he is telling us of the movies and newsreels and the spheres hanging in the apses of Suzzallo Library.

Mr. Yoshino continues our tour, explaining the

traditional Spanish architecture. Ornaments such as griffins and eagles and dolphins, all with mythological relevance, are everywhere.

"That accounts for the decorating style of the hotel lobby," Claire says, "may I take photos?"

"I'm very sorry," Mr. Yoshino says, "management allows no pictures."

These are the same artifacts that I remember from when Uncle Paul brought Connie, Jer, and I here, but everything seems dull, musty, and not as colorful as I recollect.

"Louis L. M. Davenport sold the hotel in 1945, died in his suite on the top floor in 1951. His wife Verus died in the late 1960s," Mr. Yoshino says, adding, "I suspect haunting."

The Davenport's only son died some years ago. A demolition crew determined that they could set the entire city block size building with explosives and drop it in 20 seconds.

Local protestors, supported by several historians from nearby Gonzaga University, picketed in front of the hotel for two weeks. Their posters claimed the people of Spokane would suffer the nightmare of asbestos poisoning. Fear of asbestos poisoning saved the hotel from demolition. Salvage was too expensive, so she has remained closed for many years.

"We heard der Bingle crooning when we first entered," Claire says.

Mr. Yoshino explains that visitors often comment on der Bingle's singing, and they claim to see glimpses of flowing, white-sheeted figures dancing in the ballroom. A ghost legend he enjoys most is about each successive owner taking more than they gave to the property.

"It's told by old-timers living in these parts that Mr. and Mrs. Davenport chase the ghosts of these greedy and neglectful landlords."

"When did you arrive here?" Claire says.

He explains that after being freed from an internment camp in Idaho, there was no work. Wandering the streets of Spokane one evening, a beautiful deep voice crooned a Christmas song. He followed the singing to an open alleyway door behind the Davenport Hotel. Samuel sat on a street curb, listening until the music stopped, scattered applause coming from inside. A handsome man came out of the rear entrance into the alley. He too was on a cigarette break. He tapped two Lucky Strikes out of a green pack, offered me one, I accepted and lit his.

"Name's Harry Lillis Junior," he said. "How was my version of White Christmas?"

"I told him it was beautiful."

"Next time, come on in out of the cold, you'll be my guest."

"I was positive he told me his name was Harry Lillis," Mr. Yoshino says. "Six months later, I was walking past the Clemmer Theater and saw a poster with his photo on it, Bing Crosby to appear here Christmas eve."

"Shall we visit the Clemmer next?"

Claire nods.

"In March of the next year, I was still unemployed when they closed the Clemmer Theater for renovations," Mr. Yoshino says.

They nailed a notice to the front door that read, "Night-watchman needed, enquire within or call SPO-1778".

"I got the job, and a year later came over to the Hotel, been here ever since," Mr. Yoshino says with a smile.

He recalls that they had a basement full of film canisters. All the Crosby movies and hundreds of other films. The room is an archive of 1930-1950 movies, cartoons, Movietone, and RKO newsreels.

This sparked my memory of Bremerton when Uncle Paul asked if we had seen the newsreel about returning from the war. I remember his discussion of movies and Bing's films.

"Any chance those film canisters are still in the Clemmer Theater basement?" I say.

"I've got a key for the rear entrance here on my ring," Mr. Yoshino says, "Let's have a look. Anything you want to see?"

Jer and I once snuck in by this same side door that leads to a fire escape. Uncle Paul often spent his meager savings on Jer and me to go to the motion pictures in the early 1940s.

Bing Crosby's voice was crooning *White Christmas* when Jer and I arrived with Connie and Paul fifty years ago to view a double feature at the Clemmer. That music became an integral part of our Christmas gatherings. That album must be in the attic. But, at this moment, the newsreels capture our attention.

"Perhaps we'll find a copy of the newsreel Uncle Paul mentioned," Claire says.

"Something to do with his ship and crew returning in wheelchairs from the Philippines," I say. "That occurred in March or April 1945."

All these details rattled around in my head as we strolled down Spruce Street, me not recognizing much of anything in a town I once knew well.

"The Clemmer is now the State Theater," Mr. Yoshino says.

Ginger had told me that.

Fifteen minutes later, Mr. Yoshino shows Claire and me a room full of canisters marked Newsreels and dated by month and year. We carry the two bulky canisters dated March 1945 and April 1945 to the viewing room. Mr. Yoshino sets up the projector and we watch in fascination, narrowing it down to a newsreel that shows a Pacific Fleet hospital ship disembarking hundreds of wounded. Several sailors in wheelchairs are being rolled down the ship's ramp to dockside.

I choke up a bit, thinking one of them might be CPO Paul Jonson; but the grainy quality of the film makes an individual face nothing more than a smudge. Then the film switches to a headline, "*Japs being repelled in bloody fighting in Okinawa*." There were several scenes of mounds of bodies lying on the rocks below the cliffs at a place the narrator called Naha.

My list of ghostly tour guides expands. Why have Uncle Paul, Columbus, and der Bingle's ghosts led us all this way, for what?

It came to me that at our last visit to Bremerton, Uncle Paul had a reason for mentioning the newsreel about the hospital ship's return. He wanted us to see that the Japanese were losing the war in the Pacific at a horrific price to both sides. He also showed us a news clip about one of Uncle Paul's heroes, a war correspondent named Ernie Pyle. The article reported that a sniper had shot and killed Pyle, and they buried him on one of the Ryukyu Islands. Pyle's earlier editorials included a prophetic remark that a burial far from home is not for him.

That comment was eerie, and it has me returning to when Grandma and Connie got the official communication from the Navy about Uncle Paul's remains being buried in Bremerton.

Connie might have seen the newsreel, and she and grandma had been carrying out Paul's wishes when they lobbied with the Navy to return his casket to the farm. Maybe the ghosts of Columbus and der Bingle led me to find this newsreel. Uncle Paul also wanted a burial at home. It's all a bit too late, confusing, but somehow it makes sense.

"I hope you enjoyed the tour," Mr. Yoshino says.

"When I visited my Uncle Paul at the University of Washington in Seattle in the early 1940s, I met a friend of his, a teenager named Franklin Yoshino," I say. "I recall him saying that he lived with a family that ran a Japanese Language School and Children's Home in Tacoma."

"Is there any chance that you are that Yoshino?"

The old man smiles, and says, "Yoshino is a common Japanese surname."

He explains that over one hundred children who lost their parents were orphans who lived with his wife Mikki and him. They ran a Japanese Language School in Tacoma and provided the children with a home. Many of the children took the Yoshino surname when they registered for public school.

"There was a Franklin among the orphans," Mr. Yoshino says. "He had a young lady friend, a beautiful girl."

Mr. Yoshino describes her as a foundling. Remembering them both because they were with the other orphans when the authorities came to the JLS and Children's Home in the winter days of March 1942.

"They separated my Mikki and me at Camp Harmony Relocation Center in 1942," Mr. Yoshino says. "I went to one camp, she and the children to another."

His eyes are filling with tears as his voice turns into a murmur.

"In 1943, I received word via the prisoner grapevine that my Mikki had died at Mindoka Camp," Mr. Yoshino says, pausing and gathering the strength to continue.

"My sadness never ended," Mr. Yoshino says. "When released from the camps at the war's end, I felt alone in the world."

He explains how he came to the Davenport Hotel after being released from Kooskia Internment Camp in Idaho in the summer of 1945.

His composure returns, and he reveals he was on a government watch list for running the Japanese Language School in Tacoma. He bounced around for a year before being sent to Kooskia Camp in a remote part of the Bitterroot Mountains in Northern Idaho. It was a camp for suspected spies, and once there, he gets assigned to a work gang to build roads and bridges.

"I have never returned to Tacoma."

He doesn't recall adopting Franklin or Tinya, and he tells us he has heard nothing of them since 1942. He remembers that Tinya was not her real first name; it was a nickname given to her by Franklin. He also suggests that we contact one of the organizations that keeps records of the internments and victims of EO 9066.

I reach into my backpack and take out one of my

business cards, handing it to Mr. Yoshino in the traditional Japanese two-handed gesture with a slight bow.

"Domo Arigato Gozaimasu, Yoshino-san!" I say.

I ask Mr. Yoshino if he can do us a favor and recommend us to the real estate company who owns the Old Davenport Hotel and the State Theatre. Might we borrow these film canisters for a few weeks, so my colleague and I may study them?

"I'll do my best," he says. "In the meantime, please take the canisters."

Our tour of the Clemmer Theater and the Old Davenport Hotel ends.

"If you can show me photos of Franklin and his friend Tinya, I might remember more about them."

"If we find photos, may we contact with you here at the hotel?" Claire says.

"Please do."

This meeting with Samuel Yoshino and the surname and first name information is a fantastic bit of luck. I see Claire underline the word ghost next to der Bingle and Columbus in her notepad.

"Serendipity!" I say to Claire.

"Samuel is delightful," she says with a smile, "he's lived through a lot."

Our encounter with Mr. Samuel Yoshino at the Old Davenport Hotel is a fortuitous bonus inspired by the train ride. I'm thinking it increased the number of events on Claire's List of places to visit and activities to reenact from my childhood. An increase when the list should be dwindling. Instead of shrinking, the list grows with each reenactment and brings more memories and more questions, but too few answers. It's a never-ending list and I'm the pet hamster chasing each event, going around on a wheel until overcome by sheer exhaustion.

We drive Black Beauty back to the farm after a visit to the Spokane Cadillac dealer. Claire turns on the car radio and finds some traveling music on a country music station. We have extra plug wires, ignition system, sparkplugs, black-wall tires, and a new battery installed. Assorted parts and white-wall tires for the La Salle are on order. More karma than one has a right to expect.

Speke's Country Store

KOBX 91.1 FM Public radio is broadcasting the morning weather forecast after Johnny Cash sings *"Riders in the Sky."* The weatherman predicts Intermittent showers all day.

In the early 1940s, some of our neighbors in Spokane called them Japs and Slopes and Chinks and other horrible names. Jer and I often heard the same taunts from the day at the races on the Montlake Cut at Speke's Country Store. The radio was full of claims that we must place these people on 'watch lists' or imprison them before they betray America. People identical to Samuel Yoshino, what a travesty.

I turn Black Beauty into the parking lot of Speke's Country Store, and Claire and I dash in as the rain comes down in sheets.

We're greeted by Angie and a small child clutching her floor-length apron.

"I have your order ready, shall I deliver it or put it in the car?"

While I pump the gas into the La Salle, I ask Angie if she has some roses that I can purchase for placing at Connie's grave.

"I'm so sad about Connie," Angie says, "We love her so much. We sold a large gentleman the last of the roses only 30 minutes earlier; but I have some lilies, they're fresh this morning?"

She shuffles off to the storeroom, brings me the lilies wrapped in butcher's paper, and holds them out for me to smell.

"I think Asiatic lilies best if they have no scent," Angie says.

"Lilies will be fine."

Claire is standing, staring at the exhibit on the wall. I'm reminded of how long I have been away. But Speke's Country Store and the 'wall of honor' are still here. Some memories are forever.

Meanwhile, next on, Claire's List is the Jonson's farm and interring mom's ashes. We've already determined that ghosts haunt the farmhouse, but this time we'll be spending the night, likely with some family spirits.

Five blocks down from Speke's on E. 9th Street, the following memories are forming. Why now and not three days ago when we first showed up?

They paved over the potholes that were so challenging to both bicycle and wagon alike and a storm shower is darkening the morning sky.

❖ ❖ ❖

Mom and Uncle Paul told Jer and me many stories. None more captivating than the family history of the Jonson and Nordling families emigrating from Gothenburg, Sweden in 1905 to escape famine and start life anew in a land of wonder and promise.

The four of us spent evenings huddled on the floor in front of the stone fireplace, while the adventures of relatives past came to life. Uncle Paul's telling of these stories sparked my earliest interest in history and adventure even before seeing the globes at Suzzallo Library. His scary stories and our mutual sense of adventure bonded us.

One family of Nordling's pushed on to the north, to the western tip of Lake Superior.
The beautiful lakes of northern Minnesota lured one family of Nordlings, or perhaps it was the fatigue of months of travel by sea and rail.

The Jonson's accompanied them; but when they reached St. Paul, Grandpa learned that the Northern Pacific Railroad would transport them for free all the way to Washington state.
Passing through the panhandle of Northern Idaho, another family of Jonsons set up a homestead by Lake Coeur d'Alene. Spokane was the last stop. Grandpa carried a Northern Pacific Railroad flyer that promoted inexpensive farmland plots along the Spokane River Valley. Suitable for settlement and development. That was his map to a fresh beginning for his family.

My earliest childhood memories began here at Big Black Rock and the Jonson farm, as they did for Jer and most of the Jonson's who are first and second-generation Americans. The farm served as the hub for Christmas gatherings.

Why didn't we start our reenactments here? Claire thought the place might overwhelm me, so she wanted me to ease into my return, so we began with Opening Day.

Connie is the middle daughter of three, and Uncle Paul, the youngest of two brothers. Alec was born in Sweden. The other Jonson children were all born at the farm. Esther died at an early age. Doc Hansen delivered Connie and me in the same room, thirty years apart.

It's a gloomy overcast morning as a storm rolls in. A single light flickers and darts about in the bedroom upstairs over the front porch as the LaSalle crunches to a stop in the driveway next to the farmhouse.

"At least the PG&E folks got the power on," Claire says.

"I'm not so sure," I say, "that could be a flashlight."

"That dancing light's coming from Jer's and my room," I say.

Someone's looking for something. Could it be the ghostly dude who broke into the attic or the house painter?

The light flickers again and goes off. I circle the house to get in by the back porch, hoping that our arrival hasn't scared the intruder off, intent on catching the culprit. I enter as I always have, via grandma's kitchen, but the key is missing from its secret location over the door.

Glancing over my shoulder, I see a Landcruiser that looks like it returned from a safari in the dust and mud of the Masai Mara. It's parked in the shadows behind the garage, so I didn't notice it at first. I write wash me on the hood with my finger.

The rear screen door bursts open.

"That's a classic vehicle, scratch it, and you buy it!"

The silhouette of a stout gentleman stands filling the door well. As I approach, he flips on the porch light. His girth and a shock of unruly white hair give him the appearance of Big Daddy, the family patriarch in the 1958 movie, "Cat on a hot tin roof". He's brandishing a flashlight in his left hand while struggling to slip his right arm into a sleeve hole of grandpa's old rain slicker. My U.S. Navy pea cap on his head. The one Uncle Paul gave me.

He points at the cap and says, "Look here what I found."

"Hey, that's my cap!"

"Good to see you, big brother, how are Amanda and the grandchildren?"

"You too little brother," he says, hugging me and including a big wet kiss. "Everyone's well, and Lilly sends you one of her special kisses."

Lilly is Jer's four-year-old granddaughter. You guessed it, she has flaxen hair and blue eyes, Swedish on her father's side, and the last time we talked was by long-distance from Joburg.

"She is always pulling on the poodle's ears, giggling in delight and going on about her African uncle."

"Go figure!" Claire says as she runs across the porch and gives Jer an enormous hug.

Why I'm of interest to Lilly remains a puzzle. Maybe it's the musk scent of my aftershave lotion. I've only spent a few days with her, could be a favorite Uncle thing. Could be my beard. Perhaps my storytelling.

"I saw the upstairs lights flickering on and off a few minutes ago," I say. "I was certain I was about to catch the culprit who broke into the attic."

"Sorry, Sherlock," Jer says, "didn't mean to spoil your detecting."

"That bouncing light was me and my flashlight," he says. "PG&E must have turned the power back on yesterday, but I was inspecting the bulbs upstairs, so I reckoned we'd need some bulbs and fuses."

"The house is too clean to have vacant the past six months since mom passed."

"Was it Sara's doing?" Jer says, "You know, fixing up the place before the auction."

I nod my agreement, willing to attribute the mysterious house and barn painting and general grounds cleanup and the tablecloth to our family lawyer. But not yet ready to dismiss my ghosts' hypothesis.

"We both know that the real secret behind Falu red paint. You can restore it over and over by using a brush to bring back the luster and make it look the same as a fresh paint job," Jer says.

"That's right," I say. "So, the painter has to be someone who knows about the county of Falun, its famous red paint and all, most likely a Swede."

"That's why I thought it was a family ghost."

"Back at you brother!" Jer quips. "Maybe the ghost is a Jonson. They all know about the refreshing of Falu red paint. Uncle Paul is my candidate."

"Meanwhile, ghosts won't take care of the business at hand," Jer says as he picks up mom's urn.

Somehow Jer's and my decision to inter mom's ashes here in the family cemetery, just doesn't seem right.

"Are you sure we should inter mom's ashes here?"

"It's only a pot of ashes," Jer says in his pragmatic

way.

"What if the new owners don't want our family graveyard," I say, adding, "besides, it may violate some city or county ordinance."

"I get it, " Jer says, "you think we must move all the graves and urns after the sale."

We agree to ask Sara when we meet with her about the auction, she'll know if we can leave the graveyard intact. Meanwhile, we head for the cemetery.

CHAPTER 13

Handing the basket of lilies to Claire, I pick up the roses. Jer cradles the container with mom's ashes in both hands and follows us to the cemetery.

Fifty paces from the back porch, between Uncle Paul's cabin and Big Black Rock, is a square plot with a wrought iron fence marking the cemetery boundary.

Standing with my head swirling with fragments from my memory-attic, Claire steadies me as I struggle to stay with the task at hand.

The urn is solid silver with a single line of flowers etched in a ring around the center. They're lilies. How's that for kismet!

"Splendid choice of urn big brother."

"I had Connie's stone etched by a carver in Yuma and brought it up with me in the Landcruiser," Jer says, pointing to the marker which leans against the fence.

"It's beautiful," Claire says.

Jer smiles and places the silver urn with Connie's ashes next to the remains and gravestone of her brother Paul. Claire arranges the lilies on a circular flat stone that marks the vortex of the burial ground. I place six white roses at each grave, pausing at last at Paul Jonson's marker. The encryption reads: Home is the sailor, home from the sea. We place Connie Jonson's marker next to Uncle Paul's.

The encryption reads: *I hope you have found peace.*

A distant bugler plays taps as a misty rain falls and blends with my tears; some tears reach the soil that has nourished three generations of Jonson's and Nordling's. I stand at attention, right hand over my heart.

With Jer at my side, I feel closer to mom, to Uncle Paul, and to family past and present than I have for years.

I begin to tremble. Claire enfolds me in her arms.

As I kneel beside Paul's and Connie's gravestones I say, "I kept my promise. I spread *The Chinaman's Story* to every child within ten miles, all over the neighborhood while you were away at war."

It was an immense relief to me to speak these words to Paul. I almost didn't notice that I had spoken the title of Paul's story.

"You're reliving Uncle Paul's coming home from the Pacific, Daniel," Jer says. "I sense him too."

It takes a moment for me to realize that my Great Aunt Selma's spirit is standing next to me. She leans over the casket and kisses Uncle Paul while saying a prayer.

Then she insists that I kiss him. I peer into the casket, avoiding looking into my uncle's face. Paul is dressed in a black Navy uniform and with his hair pasted down, he looks old, and his pallor is pasty. His eyelids flutter, and he stares at me. His blue-grey eyes are the only thing about him I remember. A small drool of liquid is coming out of his lips. He seems to want to say something.

I turn to Aunt Selma and say, "He's not dead."

Jer says as he encases me in a bear hug and says, "Aunt Selma told you to kiss Uncle Paul's corpse, and you ran like hell. I found you curled up and shaking up on Big Black Rock ten minutes later."

Jer places the Navy cap Uncle Paul had given me on my head. The shaking stops.

"As good Swedes, stoic and all," Claire says, "I'll wager the two of you never mentioned that event again."

It's the traumatic incident that blocked so much of my childhood.

Childhood memories come cascading down, revealing details associated with Uncle Paul's scary tale of the Chinaman. We pause at the base of Big Black Rock, his storytelling venue, where I apprenticed. I repeat what I said to Uncle Paul in 1945.

"I promise you we will find Franklin, Tinya, and Charlee and reunite the family."

This homestead is a treasure trove of mysteries, and there are several ghost candidates with brushes for restoring the Falu red paint, laying out tablecloths, and chopping firewood.

"That confirms it," I say, "we have ghosts. I'm ruling out grandma, but my guess is, Connie?"

"My guess is still Uncle Paul," Jer says with a grin, "not Aunt Selma."

"Sara Swenson isn't a ghost, but she's my best judgment," Claire says. "Could it be the ghosts are welcoming Connie, Jer, and you home?"

We gather in the kitchen for coffee. It's a fine time to render a summary of our reenactments to Jer.

Claire and I review our visits to Opening Day at the Montlake Cut Bridge, Bremerton, and the Old Davenport Hotel and the Clemmer Theater where we met Samuel Yoshino.

"I remember when we snuck into the Clemmer via the fire stairs to see a double feature," Jer says. "Darn near got the theatre closed when the owner put a padlock on the backdoor which was a fire-exit, and the Spokane fire department inspector heard about that."

Intrigued, he says, "That was a terrific weekend we had at the Cut with Uncle Paul and his pals. How can I help with the investigation?"

"You already are helping big brother."

"Sometimes it's good to come home," Jer says with a warm smile. "Mom always said you were a born wanderer. That's what this whole memory-attic thing you're wrestling with is all about and could explain the family ghosts."

I chuckle at his ghost remark, but his comment about family sinks in, causing a painful spike in my feelings of guilt.

The guilt and failure remain, but it comes to me that at least I'm not alone. I sense that Jer has similar guilt, but at least he returned home to visit mom and take care of her, so I don't ask. I realize that I have not delivered what I promised, because I wandered off doing my Columbus and Marco Polo act. He and mom are right about my being a wanderer.

As I finish my executive summary, I ask Jer a question that has dominated my thoughts since Claire and I started our reenactments.

"How much of *The Chinaman's Story* do you remember?"

"That was one of Uncle Paul's best scary stories," Jer says.

"Do you remember why he asked me to spread that tale amongst the children in the neighborhood?"

"To scare off trespassers," Jer says. "I think he worried about family safety and pilfering while he was away fighting the war in the Pacific. Why do you ask?"

He told us that story the year before the attacks on Hawaii. He couldn't have known the war was coming.

"When he made me promise to spread the story, I thought he meant while he was away at university."

"Interesting point," Jer says. "That throws a unique light on why he had you spread that story all over the place."

I explain that Claire and I are working on the hypothesis he had a secret reason for that story, not only to scare off intruders. We speculate that the Chinese sentry story is crucial to a second promise to reunite the family. It's essential to find out what happened during and after the war years to Charlee, Franklin, and Tinya.

"No wonder you were so upset when we placed mom's ashes next to Paul's," Jer says. "I knew that Aunt Selma freaked you out. But you need to remember that mom and I also promised Paul to reunite the family when the war was over. We were all at his deathbed in Bremerton."

The source of my intense feelings of failure wasn't what blocked so many of my childhood memories. It was a single traumatic event. But Jer's telling me he and mom shared in that promise. I took it as a personal pledge and that exaggerated my sense of failure and loss when we buried Uncle Paul.

Claire reminds me we still have the mystery of the key reason behind Uncle Paul's story of the Chinaman to solve. If we can uncover this secret, we may find out what happened to our lost family members.

As night falls and a crescent moon appears, it disappears and reappears in the wispy cirrus clouds, Big Black Rock beckons. It's time for me to tell Claire and Jer the rest of *The Chinaman's Story*.

CHAPTER 14

Big Black Rock

*(1992 & 1940 juxtapose
once more)*

I t's getting dark, and there's a sliver of a crescent moon, it's the perfect time for me to unveil the story which is finally free to flood my memory-attic with details.

"Let's climb up and build a fire," I say. "I'll tell you *The Chinaman's Story* just as it was told to me."

We each gather an armload of firewood from the shed. As we start our ascent, I recall a favorite line Uncle Paul often quoted. It's from a 19th-century poet and world traveler whose poems inspired him.

"Above Coblentz, almost every mountain (rock) has a ruin and a legend. One feels everywhere the spirit of the past, and its stirring recollections come back upon the mind with irresistible

force." (Bayard Taylor, 19th c.)

To look things up helps when my memory fails. I looked this quote up and used it in a lecture last year.

Big Black Rock is the place where Uncle Paul first told his scary story of the Chinaman. To reenact his first telling, I'll replicate details of how he set the scene for his story. Building anticipation in those who are present is a storytelling technique I learned from observing Uncle Paul telling his stories. He taught me to look for this in the eager faces of the children.

December 7, 1940, my 10th birthday, we are at the start of our annual gathering for the Christmas holidays at the Jonson's farm. Our extended family has doubled in size in recent years and is about to adopt and expand by three. We expect over thirty adults and children to arrive on the Great Northern by rail and the Greyhound buses, and in a variety of Hudson's, Ford's, and Packard's. The automobiles will join mom's La Salle with its wide whitewall tires as it sits in the garage next to the farmhouse. My favorite morning chore is to polish her, she's mom's first car. The kids in the neighborhood all called her Black Beauty.

Relatives came to the farm in Spokane from Bremerton, Tacoma, and Seattle to the west and Missoula and Coeur d'Alene to the east. A dozen children were in attendance on Big Black Rock when Uncle Paul first told his story. Some I remember, some I have forgotten. The Chinaman's Story just isn't the same without the youngsters, but I expect to see their faces in the flickering firelight suggesting their spirits are present. I'm optimistic and expecting more details will occur to me as I tell the story.

We called the Jonson farm 'The Hub' because it

lies midway between Seattle and Missoula. The estate comprises a hundred acres of apple orchard, Falu red house, and barn, punctuated by a huge rock. We are all drawn here at Christmas to partake of Grandma Jonson's delicious meals and pies and to to listen to Uncle Paul's scary stories.

On Christmas eve 1940, we welcomed three special members into our extended family. Charlee Sang, Franklin Yoshino, and Tinya Yoshino. They are orphans who each have fascinating stories to tell about their heritage, which I've recalled to Claire during our visit to The Cut. Uncle Paul befriended these three orphans over the past year while at the University of Washington in Seattle, and soon we will adopt them. It's their first attendance at an annual Christmas gathering.

Christmas 1940 and

May 1992 are juxtaposing

A crescent moon and a partnership of stars are visible in the chilly predawn skies. Grandma has been up baking for hours before I slide down the banister to start my daily chores.

It was a brisk Christmas morning. My fingers and ears feel as if they might break off. I blow some warmth into my hands and slip them into leather work gloves lined with rabbit fur. Then I head for the woodshed to cut and carry an armload of firewood for the potbelly stove in Grandma's kitchen. I'm completing my chores, stacking wood when my older brother Jer, often confused as my tow-headed blond, blue-grey eyed twin, comes out of the barn with a basket of eggs. We trek back to the farmhouse.

Diverting our attention is a tantalizing aroma. Grandma's fresh out of the oven pies are cooling on the kitchen windowsill. Six strawberry-rhubarb pies are ten feet above the snow-covered ground, sending their delicious message.

Jer glances at me, and I glance back, signifying that we are in synch. I drop my load of firewood back on the woodpile. He places the basket of eggs atop the wood. We each grab a sturdy wooden apple crate from the stack leaning against the outer wall of the barn. Stacked one on top of the other, the boxes serve as a ladder that enables me to reach the kitchen windowsill.

One of the six pies cooling on the kitchen windowsill goes missing.

Scrambling as fast as we can, we get to the creek behind the cabin Uncle Paul is building near Big Black Rock, out of sight from Grandma's kitchen windows.

Jer scoops a handful of pie into his mouth, yelping as the hot strawberries and rhubarb burn his tongue. He pauses, but only long enough to blow on the second handful. We polish off our looted pie, belching and gloating in what we have done. With the evidence of guilt on our lips and chins, still licking our sticky fingers, our tee shirts stained with blobs of strawberry. Grandma's strawberry-rhubarb pie is worth whatever happens next.

Uncle Paul's lanky frame, carpenter's tool-belt on his hips, is upon us without our noticing. He's carrying the two apple crates we left stacked under the kitchen windowsill and the basket of eggs.

"Found these eggs in the woodshed and the crates under Grandma's kitchen window," Uncle Paul says, "better let me dispose of that pie tin."

"Be sure to clean yourselves up in the creek and rinse out those stains from your shirts. Then take a load of firewood and this basket of eggs to the kitchen."

"I have to drive into town and pick up some building supplies. I won't return until just before dark. Gather the children and meet me atop Big Black Rock at dusk. I have a new scary story to tell you all, a story you must never forget."

Every family has a story and needs a storyteller. During my childhood, it was my favorite uncle, Paul.

Before he begins, he leans close to me and says, "Pay attention as at story's end tonight, I will request a promise from you as my apprentice storyteller."

The punishment for nicking one of Grandma's strawberry-rhubarb pies would have been harsh. In our family, we pass the edicts of Grandpa Jonson down to every child. There is a willow branch hanging on the wall behind the outhouse in the barn that Grandpa used to enforce them. If you do not intend to keep a promise, don't make it. If you steal one of Grandma's pies?

"Uncle Paul saved you two from several hours of peeling potatoes and onions under the watchful eye of Grandma Jonson," Claire says.

"That's what we thought," Jer says. "He earned our undying trust that morning, and thanks to Uncle Paul's keeping our secret, Jer and I were sure we had pulled off the perfect caper."

"Meaning you must keep any promise you made to him," Claire says.

"You and your brother were real rascals," Claire says. "But for heaven's sake, please get on with telling us Uncle Paul's story."

Anticipation builds as Jer and I run around the farm spreading the message that Uncle Paul is at Big Black Rock about to tell one of his stories. No one tells scary stories better than my Uncle Paul.

As darkness descends, children and guests are on the path climbing up The Rock, including our newest family members, Charlee, Tinya, and Franklin. Connie and the youngest children join us at the crows-nest on Big Black Rock, where Uncle Paul has a campfire going to ward off the chilling cold. The fire also provides a guiding light for the climb. He has set the scene for his telling of his new scary story.

A crescent moon slips in and out of a blanket of clouds. A faint line of pale blue light on the western horizon fades from atop the rock. We can see glimpses of moonlight reflecting off the tin roofs of the farm buildings and the two cabins. Uncle paul's cabin is between The Rock and the farmhouse. We tucked the other cabin amidst the pines and cedars that populate the forest below the apple orchards. A breeze carries an odor of compost, rotting apples and vegetables from behind the barn.

Uncle Paul glides out of the shadows behind the fire. He coughs into a red and black checkered bandanna.

He points at the crescent moon as it makes another appearance between the passing clouds, as if on his command. There is a shimmering haze surrounding the arced sliver of the moon, giving it an eerie look. He motions with his arms for all the children to gather in a around him by the fire.

He folds the checkered bandana and stuffs it in his left hip pocket. An attention focusing device, as is the crescent moon and his soft tone.

I will unknowingly copy these movements throughout my career as a university lecturer.

Eager faces dance in the firelight, awaiting the new scary tale and huddling close to the fire to ward off the chill as darkness descends.

Before he can start, Cousin Stella says, "It sure is scary up here on this big rock."

"Do you want to hear the legend of Big Black Rock?" Uncle Paul says, pointing up into the night sky and adding.

Mom, Jer, and I have heard him tell the history of The Rock's origins many times; for the benefit of new-comers, he continues.

"When the moon appears, you might glimpse smoke coming from the cabin in the woods."

Everyone looks upward, the clouds separate, and we get an unobstructed view of the horseshoe moon. I'm not sure if we saw the faint trail of smoke; but, if you asked any of us, we'd swear we did.

"I see it," the children said, one after the other.

The Spokane tribe has a legendary tale of how, many hundreds of years ago, earth suffered through an ice age, and massive glaciers formed. Later, tempera-tures rise, the glacier melts, and a mighty river stretches across the land. The rushing water pushes the rocks for miles until this gigantic rock came to rest here in the Spokane River valley.

"What's a glazer, Uncle Paul?" Cousin Stella asks.

She's a precocious flaxen haired, blue-eyed 6-year-old Nordling.

In case I forget to mention it, all the Nordling and Jonson children, my brother and I included, are towheads with blue or gray eyes; it's our Swedish genes.

"A g-l-a-c-i-e-r," Uncle Paul said, pronouncing the word one letter at a time.

A glacier is a massive avalanche of snow and ice that sweeps down a mountain, snapping off trees and dragging them, changing the landscape forever.

"What of the Chinaman?" Stella asked.

"Is it Charlee Sang?".

The children looked at Charlee, who was blushing.

"No, not Charlee," Uncle Paul said, turning to Charlee to explain.

"It's said that the Chinaman traveled from far away on the opposite side of the Pacific Ocean to escape war and devastation in a place called Manchukuo," Charlee said.

"Where is Man-mooch-ko?" Timmy Nordling said, struggling to pronounce the strange word.

"M-A-N-C-H-U-K-U-O lies thousands of miles across the Pacific Ocean from here," Charlee Sang said in a whisper while nodding and apologizing for his interruption.

Charlee told us the name Manchukuo conjures up hate among survivors of the Japanese occupation of the 1930s. The Japanese invaded our homeland in Manchuria. They renamed it with a Japanese word, Manchukuo, which means Manchu or puppet state of the Japanese Empire.

"No apology needed," Uncle Paul said. "The Japanese controlled the Chinese and forced many of them to export what they grow on their own lands. Japan did not have enough land to meet the demands for rice and other food crops. You know about farms and how we need them to grow our own strawberries, rhubarb, potatoes, and apples. Grandma uses them to make her wonderful dishes for the holiday meals."

I flinched at the mention of Grandma's dishes, thinking of the strawberry-rhubarb pie escapade. I didn't dare glance at Jer; but Uncle Paul winked at me.

This kicked off a game he played with the children.

"What is your most favorite of grandma's meals?"

In unison, the children said, "Gram's stew."

Except for Timmy, who said, "Straw-barby pie."

Uncle Paul said, "Me too, Timmy, but I meant mealtime favorite, not dessert."

Timmy blushed and said, "Gram's so-stew."

"And what goes into Grandma's stew?"

"Sweet potatoes," Jer said.

"Idaho potatoes," Stella said.

"Crab-by apples," Timmy said with a giggle.

Each of the other six children listed names and favorite ingredients, crabby apples and others are not in grandma's stew.

The Nordling twins, Herbie, and Helen, both loved Grandma's brown sugar yams. Clifton Jonson, a second cousin, was 6, he preferred turkey legs as did Millicent, a shy girl who nodded when Clifton said turkey legs. The two eldest children other than Jer and I were Sandy and Clara, Uncle Al's kids from Coeur d'Alene. They licked their lips and said cranberry sauce.

Franklin and Tinya remain silent as they have yet to experience Grandma's gastronomic delights.

Uncle Paul paused, then began telling "*The Chinaman's Story*."

A man lives with his wife in a cabin he built in the woods below this vey rock. They have a small greenhouse to grow vegetables in the winter to feed them. They are from China. He is a small but powerful man with ugly crooked yellow teeth and a black ponytail that hangs down his back. She is slender and beautiful. Their companion is a fast and vicious Asian bear. Folks call it a moon bear.

Timmy stammers, "A b-b-bear!"

"Why's it called a moon bear?" The Nordling twins asked in unison.

"Bears in our woods are solid brown, this one has a white bib in the shape of a crescent moon," Uncle Paul said. "Like the bibs grandma makes you wear when eating her vegetable and meat stew."

The Chinaman rescued the bear from a zoo in Tacoma after she mauled the caretaker's dog. He brought her to his home and trained the bear to protect his cabin from intruders, including children. She eats vegetables and greens, but she loves meat.

Uncle Paul lowers his voice and looks at each of the sets of eyes across the fire.

"Never let the moon bear see or hear you, or she will chase you down," he said. "If there is moonlight as there is tonight, she'll detect you, even in the shadows."

He hesitates as the youngsters look around in the growing darkness behind them, searching for a pair of glowing eyes peering at them from behind the fire.

"The moon bear is fast, faster than a bicycle," Uncle Paul said.

"Is it faster than an American Flyer," one of the boys said.

"Faster than the blink of an eye."

"So, stay far away from the cabin, when you see smoke rising from it over the trees. That smoke means the Chinaman is cooking up a feast for his dinner, and the moon bear is on guard and awaiting her evening supper."

Uncle Paul gestures for the children to move closer. He points up just as the clouds separate enough to allow a view of the moon. Remembering the wisp of smoke, they saw when they arrived. Everyone's head turns upward in unison. With the magical moonlight streaming down, Uncle Paul's voice turns softer in tone, drawing in his audience.

"What do you think is the moon bear's favorite meal?"

Timmy stuttered, "St-at-stew."

"That's right, Timmy, and if the Chinaman grows his own potatoes and vegetables, what is he missing for his stew?" Paul said, lowering his voice.

"M-m-meat."

Uncle Paul jumped up and said, "Meat, that's right, meat, and he prefers the flesh of little boys and girls."

A trail of small footprints spreads across the fallen snow from the rock's base to the safety of grandma's kitchen.

Uncle Paul and I were the last to leave Big Black Rock that winter night. The clouds grew denser, and snow fell, blocking the sliver of crescent moonlight and stars. When we put out the last of the embers of the fire, it plunged us into total darkness.

Before we start the climb down, he spoke to me in earnest.

"I have a promise to ask of you, Danny, one you must swear to keep."

He held my arm and sat me back down.

"I'll be needing you to promise to spread *The Chinaman's Story* to all the children in the neighborhood," he said. "You must continue to be my apprentice storyteller while I'm away."

I put out the fire and spread the ashes. Was it Uncle Paul who taught me fire safety or was it, Smokey the Bear? We climb down and return to Grandma's kitchen.

"I've always wondered why Uncle Paul chose you to be his apprentice storyteller," Jer says. "Now, I know why, I reckon I've always known."

"Wow! That was some story," Claire exclaims as we warm up over the potbelly stove.

"Now, I know where you got your flair for the dramatic."

"It may take me a few minutes to digest what all this means," she says. "I'll make us some French press."

While we sip our coffee she says, "The story explains why keeping a promise to your Uncle Paul was so important to you. It also reveals that your family has some strong traditional values, including keeping important secrets and promises."

"So, you kept your promise," she says.

"Sort of," I say. "I aimed my storytelling as a warning to keep trespassers off our farm."

"But I never learned why Uncle Paul wanted to keep them off our property. He had his secret reason. But he kept Jer's and my secret. That was reason enough for me to keep my promise to spread the tale no matter how long he was away and no matter what the secret reason."

"That's my recollection, too," Jer says.

"A year later," I say, "after the attack on Pearl Harbor, it came to me; how did Uncle Paul know a year ahead that war was coming to the Pacific?"

"When Uncle Paul said away," I say. "I was thinking he meant to Seattle to study at the university and to continue rowing."

"The full impact of the Japanese attacks on Pearl Harbor and the war in the Pacific had yet to become clear to you," Claire says.

"My focus was on my apprentice duties and keeping my promise. I spread the story everywhere children gathered. When the war in the Pacific dragged on, I continued in my role of apprentice storyteller in Uncle Paul's absence for three more years."

"I'm inclined to agree that there is a secret reason behind *The Chinaman's Story*," Claire says. "Something more than keeping strangers off the farm while he's away."

Uncle Paul's storytelling was renowned in our family, and I was proud that he took me on as his apprentice. This made it a joyful and easy task to keep my promise. I cheerfully spread the scary tale of the Chinese sentry and his frightening moon bear among the children in our neighborhood.

I told the tale in the school playground while shooting marbles and on weekends at the country store when picking up a wagonload of groceries for Grandma. Soon it became local folklore at Speke's, where people gathered around the fireplace to get warm and hear news and gossip.

Children spoke in whispers of the scary Chinaman and his moon bear.

"There's a Chinaman and his wife living in the cabin at the rear of the Jonson farm."

"He's got a colossal bear guarding the place."

"The bear eats children."

I embellished and added more to the story to make the legend grow. All this according to instructions Uncle Paul had given me.

"There's the matter of Bremerton where Uncle Paul posed a second promise, to find and reunite the extended family after the war," Claire says. "Failure to keep that promise explains one source of Daniel's guilt."

"That's not precisely accurate," Jer says. "Daniel and I discussed that promise earlier. Uncle Paul made all three of us, Connie, Daniel, and me, pledge to find and reunite lost family members after the war."

CHAPTER 15

Spokane River Valley,
Jonson's Farm

"I'm glad I postponed my flight another day," Claire says. "Being with you and Jer when you interred Connie's ashes gave me a genuine sense of family."

Lingering in my brain is my sense of failure. Even after interring mom's ashes and learning about the traumatic event that has blocked my recollection of my childhood and retelling The Chinaman's Story.

The next reenactment may provide some relief. I'm not convinced that the daunting task of fulfilling our second promise isn't my personal failing. My memory-attic remains a cluttered log jam. The irony of rummaging through a real attic doesn't escape me.

"Scavenger hunts are such fun. It's good Jer will be here with you to share the adventure."

Claire and I hop in Black Beauty; she's humming along nicely with her new tune up. We're up early to drive to Spokane Intermodal for her 6 am PST flight to

Seattle. She is giving a televised seminar tomorrow on 'The lost civilizations of the Americas'. On our drive across the old Argonne bridge over the Spokane River, a layer of dingy white fog slows us to 20 mph. It's a gloomy day, and the mist clings to us, turning the thirty-minute drive to the airport into an hour.

"We'll be on time."

"Attics are treasure troves of memories," she says. "May I remind you that Mr. Tanaka, at The Japanese American Repository (JAR), needs photos of Franklin and Tinya."

"You're referring to Jer's and my scavenger hunt?"

"Smart aleck!" she says. "Those items are important. The photos might jar loose some more logs."

"My brother and I once found a favorite toy train stored for an eternity in a trunk in a dusty old attic," Claire says.

The metaphor about the toy train in the seaman's trunk in the attic clicks for me. Maybe CPO Paul Jonson's Navy footlocker is up that rickety ladder. But it also occurs to me that this is the first time she has mentioned having a brother.

"Could Connie have kept Charlee Sang's last letter?"

Clever boy."

Her point is to get me enthused. She's succeeding.

"I'd love to stick around and track down the ghosts with you," she says."Don't forget the parcel Sara has been keeping, for Jer and you to open together."

But I have forgotten.

"I'll miss you, big guy," she says, "but at least you and Jer will have some bonding time before the auction to scavenge and to share memories."

"Miss you too," I say, "Send me a videotape of your seminar."

Watching Claire's flight depart on time, and I stay at the terminal until the aircraft lifts off, banks, and disappears into the low-hanging clouds headed for the Pacific. I glide along in the Old LaSalle, and as I near the farm, Claire's earlier words come back to me.

"Someone is guiding us on this investigation."

I wasn't always sure what she meant until now. She implies a ghost, and Connie remains my ghost of choice.

A shower erupts as I pull into the driveway, so I put Black Beauty in the garage and dart inside. I don't have time to feel sorry for myself at Claire's departure. A copy of her revised reenactment list is on the kitchen table, and I swear it has grown since The Cut. The next reenactment is starting the attic scavenger hunt with Jer and finding those photos for JAR and Samuel.

Roasting coffee and buttermilk biscuits warming in the oven greet me as I burst into grandma's kitchen soaking wet. An eerie sensation comes over me, more than mere déjà vu.

"Dig in!" Jer says. "I stopped by Speke's Country Store this morning while you drove Claire to the airport. Picked up some fresh biscuits."

"There's a mason jar of apricot jam in the fridge."

Taped to the fridge is a Barnstormers Feed & Grain four-year (1989 -1992) calendar. There are several notations on it for each day from January 1989 to December 1991. They are in mom's handwriting. Every note begins with the same word, remember to call Sara. Remember to go to Speke's for groceries. Remember to call Daniel on his birthday.

That last entry chokes me up.

I pencil Sara Swenson in for today at noon, but it's 1992. It's an expired calendar. August 9 has a note about the Barcelona Olympics in Claire's writing. She made the same mistake I had.

To call Dawselle in South Africa, I need to connect to the long-distance operator. She says the lines are busy and to try again later.

My impression is that I've only been away from the family farm for a brief time.

I tell Jer about that haunting nightmare I had before he called me in Africa to say to me mom had passed. It surprises him at how it parallels what happened to her.

It has been such a brief time between mom's death and the nightmare in Africa. Then on to Opening Day at the Montlake Cut Bridge, to Bremerton, to the train ride, to burying mom's ashes at the hub of our childhood. All before uncovering the source of my trauma.

"While Paul was at university his first year, I delivered what I first promised," I say to Jer. "Now we need to get back to work on Uncle Paul's secret behind why he created *The Chinaman's Story*."

"What secret is that?"

I tell him Claire's version of what troubles me. When Claire and I reenacted the visit with Uncle Paul at the Bremerton Naval Hospital, we uncovered a memory I've repressed ever since. I've been hiding from my failure to keep my second promise to him. I was so horrified by Uncle Paul's death that I repressed my memories of Charlee Sang, Franklin, and Tinya. My entire childhood got lost, or at least suppressed in the depths of my memory-attic.

My goal was the pursuit of adventure abroad, living far away from the places and events of my childhood. I was seeking to escape anything that would remind me of my memories of death, guilt, and failure. It became the motivation for my pursuing a life and career abroad.

"I get it, " Jer says, "Mom's death started you reliving the death of Uncle Paul. As I told you earlier, you forget that I too suffered that loss, mom, and I also made that promise."

He goes silent for a moment.

"I'm only now starting to forgive you for abandoning your family and wandering off."

My brother's forgiveness is a refreshing drink of water for a drowning man.

CHAPTER 16

The Scavenger Hunt Begins

The attic trapdoor opens easily. I pull down on the rope to lower the folding ladder. The hinges don't squeak, someone has oiled them since I first climbed into the attic.

"The ghost has returned."

"Ghosts again?" he says, looking at me and raising his arms in surrender. "It wasn't me."

It must be the same ghost who rummaged around in the attic and got the crocheted tablecloth. Mom's lawyer Sara Swenson may have hired someone to tidy up the place.

"I saw the auction sign out front," Jer says.

We have a lunch meeting with Sara tomorrow to complete plans for the sale. Might she resolve our ghost dilemma?

"I prefer the more logical explanation of family ghosts," he says with a wily chuckle.

We continue playing our childhood game of 'which family ghost'.

A scavenger hunt wouldn't be much fun alone.

Jer is the first to climb up the shaky ladder into the dusty attic, one rung at a time. We expect having to brush aside cobwebs as we go deeper into the attic, but whoever has preceded us has swept away some of them. He crawls back into the attic, into a dark corner. He uses a flashlight, panning back and forth into the corners.

"Could use some lights back here, dark as a cave," he mutters as he crawls full face into a giant cobweb, "Damn spiders!"

"Remember whose house you are in and watch the profanity," I say with a poor imitation of grandma's voice.

I hand him a box of new light bulbs. He inserts a new bulb in a fixture in the center of the attic and pulls on the chain.

"Voila, we have light."

If we are to keep our second promise, we also must discover more about what happened to Charlee, and Franklin and Tinya. The nightmare that led to my recall of my last visit with Uncle Paul triggered this investigation; then came the presidential apology to Japanese Americans interned 50 years ago; and third and fourth our visits to the Montlake and Bremerton in early 1992.

It comes to me more than once that without Claire's help, I might never solve this cold case. The fortuitous meeting with Samuel Yoshino was huge. Now Jer is at my side, adding a touch of fun to our scavenger hunt. His presence lessens my personal stress and depression. It's as if we are recapturing our mischievous partnership, strawberry-rhubarb pie episode, and all. I can't shake the thought of our ghostly guide.

Our reenactments have helped me restore details

that will help in our investigation. This reenactment involves searching in a real attic, scavenging for memorabilia and stuff to put in storage, so it won't get sold off at the auction. We are searching for clues to solving the secret behind Uncle Paul's story. Jer and I are now scavenging in the real attic of our family farmhouse, looking for treasures and photo albums to verify memories of our childhood and heritage.

Jer is the perfect partner for the scavenger hunt since he can verify memories tied to actual objects, we find in the farmhouse attic. He was there, or should I say here with me, 50 years ago. We were inseparable during those years.

Making a game of our attic search helps a lot. It encourages outbursts of memory with each photo and treasure we discover. I'm learning that the details of my childhood are far from lost. I haven't eliminated my guilt feelings; but having Claire and now Jer on my team has sparked my optimism. Together, our investigation into the disappearances of Franklin and Tinya will succeed. The secret to how that ties into the mystery behind Uncle Paul's secret reason for concocting the tale of the Chinaman and to fulfilling our second promise remains hidden, but it doesn't seem so unsolvable.

It's all about family, runs through my head. Thanks in part to Jer's remarks to me when we placed Connie's ashes in the family cemetery and his forgiveness for my wandering ways.

Dusting off several more boxes on the top of a stack along the wall near the trapdoor. We get frustrated by the lack of sufficient light, cobwebs, and dust as we climb up and down the rickety ladder. Minimizing the cursing becomes a necessity.

With each item we find, there comes a lengthy exchange.

"I found the old RCA Victrola," Jer hollers out from the depths of the attic. "Lend me a hand with it. We can crank it up and play some 40s swing music to set the mood."

We muscle the large console down the ladder. It comes to life with a hum and some static.

"They don't build them this quality anymore."

One box labeled 'records and music' is open and only half full. Popular Music 1935-1945: Count Basie, Benny Goodman, Tommy Dorsey, Artie Shaw, Dizzy Gillespie, Bing Crosby, and Glenn Miller.

"Didn't Miller and his band die in a plane crash on their way to a USO concert in 1942?"

"That sounds right," Jer says. "Put the Miller album on the Victrola and crank it up full volume so I can hear in the back of the attic."

Soon the entire house shakes to the rhythms of... *'In a sentimental mood'*.

"In the mood, very appropriate," I say, remembering that this tune is one of Claire's favorites.

This will make a fabulous Christmas present. I don't always forget the important stuff.

Dawning in the depths of my memory attic is a kernel of a memory. Connie was at the center of what the lads were scheming and planning that day at the Montlake Cut and later at Red Square back in 1940. She has played more of a role in this mystery that we are trying to solve than I suspected. Connie knew how to keep a secret.

◆ ◆ ◆

The kitchen wall phone shatters our routine. Ma Bell is testing the restored service. It rings again.

"How's the scavenger hunt going?" Claire says. "Dare I ask, how are you and Jer getting along?"

"We're spending a lot of time reminiscing," I say. "How did your TV lecture go?"

"We had over a hundred guests in the UW Radio & TV studio," Claire says. "I'll send you a cassette and a news clip from the Seattle-Times. Got some nice reviews."

Claire tells me she started her investigation of Franklin and Tinya at the office of the Seattle-Times and the Japanese Internment Archives at UW in Suzzallo Library. She also called a colleague at the DOD in Washington DC to do some military service records checks on Charlee Sang.

"I've been talking with Samuel Yoshino," she says. "What a delightful man. Samuel was branded by the government as an enemy alien and put on a watch list and sent to an internment camp in Idaho. It doesn't sit right with me. I got so upset, I called Sara Swenson and told her we need to sue the government."

Samuel Yoshino told her about all the orphaned children he and his wife housed in several cases adopted at the JLS in Tacoma. She's digging into the history of the Japanese Language Schools.

"I'll keep you posted," she says.

One of our most promising leads to date is Camp Kooskia. The internment camp they moved Samuel Yoshino to in a remote corner of the Bitterroot Mountains of Northern Idaho.

Samuel mentioned that several camp survivors moved back to Tacoma after their release in 1945. Some of them must be JAR members. We might get lucky and find someone who remembers Franklin and Tinya from the Camp Harmony Relocation Center in Puyallup. The camp is now only an archaeological project, an empty field.

"I contacted Mr. Bobby Tanaka at JAR," she says.

Their archives mention Samuel and Mikki Yoshino and the JLS at Tacoma; but they have no records of a Franklin Yoshino or a Tinya Yoshino. Tanaka wants us to come up with photos. Black and white photos will be best, along with some profile information which he can post in the next issue of the JAR newsletter. They can circulate a request in their monthly newsletter for anyone with knowledge of Franklin or Tinya.

"The deadline for next month's issue is Monday," Claire says, "Guess what I need?"

"Would some of Connie's Leica snapshots be of help?"

She doesn't react to my humor. Instead, she sticks to business.

"A photograph of Charlee Sang would sure help me with my search in newspaper archives, county and DOD military service records. Can you find me a picture of CPO Paul Jonson in uniform?" Claire says, adding, "I'm confident, Jer, and you will find these amongst Connie's photos while conducting your scavenger hunt."

"Something is about to pop." She says as she rings off.

I love Claire's enthusiasm, her never give up attitude, and it buoys up my sagging spirits whenever she gets excited about a clue or placing a lead in a newsletter.

Several boxes contain more albums with photos and news clippings. I'm learning to appreciate more with each carton of memorabilia, Connie really was an excellent family historian.

A box labeled 'Paul Jonson' gets me excited. It means that the search is on for real. The top item is an album of news clippings and pictures from our visit to Montlake Cut Bridge to see Uncle Paul's and Charlee's first race. We hit the mother lode.

A second album contains more snapshots from that day at the bridge. There's a note written in mom's handwriting: Paul and Daniel look alike.

These are the same photos mom used to carry with her in her handbag and used to compare Paul at age 7 and me that day at The Cut.

Four black photo holder corners remained pasted to a blank page. A note below the space for the missing photo reads '3 lads on the Bridge'.

I glance at the faded square on the wallpaper.

"Jer, do you know what happened to the painting that once hung over the fireplace?"

"What painting is that?"

The 3 lads' photo is missing. I show the album to Jer, who comes down the ladder with another box. He turns the page, and the snapshot falls out.

"Which one is Charlee, and which one is Franklin?" Jer says with a chuckle as he recovers it. The lads could be brothers."

"Franklin is Japanese and Charlee is Chinese," I say. "Why can't we tell them apart?"

"Didn't Charlee tell us that all Asians look alike to

white people?" Jer says.

The photos pile up, but they have one thing in common, poor condition. It's difficult to distinguish who is whom. Faces are only partial profiles in shadows or turned away from the camera or in group photos, too small to identify.

I stack each of the photos we find by name. Franklin and Tinya are most critical, as they will help with the JAR newsletter. Within a few hours, the snapshots of Uncle Paul have a slight edge over the collection for Jer and I, Charlee, and Franklin combined. We have only a single picture of Tinya, a partial profile.

I mark each portrait photo as I take it from an album to make it easy to return. Not wanting to mess up mom's diligent organization. Pictures of Big Black Rock, the farmhouse, the Falu red barn, and the two cabins. Photos of past Christmas gatherings. Grandma, mom, and other family members, all organized in albums but decaying with age. I'm guessing they will need restoration to be of any value to JAR and Claire.

Jer and I stop and reminisce over every photo, and now we have the music distraction. It's a pleasant one. We take time to argue about who won the race, Jer doesn't recall. I'll mention that to Claire.

At this rate, it will take us weeks to get through the boxes and albums. We continue stacking photos. In a box labeled 'Christmas 1941', I stumble on a picture of a couple decorating a fir tree with strands of popcorn and cranberries. 1941 was when Franklin first brought Tinya and her dog to our family gathering? The black and white Akita sits, head cocked, looking up at them. She could pass for the RCA Victor dog emblem on the old Victrola.

A notation below the couple reads, 'Tinya's Akita, Moonbear, sticks to her like glue'.

"We have photographs of Franklin and Tinya that we can send to Claire," I say to Jer. "But they are of inferior quality."

Claire and I talk about the 3 lads' picture, and some other snapshots mom took of Charlee, Franklin, and Tinya. Jer and I couldn't make out which figure is Charlee. He and Franklin look so much alike. Most of the photo's mom took are yellowing with age. And, so far, we only have a profile photo of Tinya.

"We have several pictures of Paul. Do you prefer in uniform or not?"

"You mentioned that Charlee Sang made that remark about all Asians looking alike," Claire says. "Have you had any luck finding the last letter from Charlee Sang that Connie was to open later?"

"Could be it's in the attic with some other stuff," I say. "We found a box of fabulous swing era music."

"I can hear Count Basie playing *'One O'clock jump'* in the background," she says, "Also, that's the third time you've mentioned the poor quality of the photos. Why don't you call Father L and see if he can restore some pictures?"

Claire's idea is terrific. I almost hang up on her without saying goodbye.

Our mutual friend Father Elly Kibet (Father L, as he is best known to colleagues and students), should be at Seattle University. He's a Jesuit priest and a full professor of theology and linguistics.

Five minutes later, I haven't been able to get through by direct dialing. I ask the Bell operator to try his apartment phone.

Father L is what I deem to be a modern Renaissance scholar and thinker. More than a theologian and linguist; he is an expert in stained-glass art and restoration of photographs, and a former world-class ten K and marathon runner. A Kalenjin, born in Kisumu near Mount Elgon in East Africa. In part because of his linguistics and encryption skills, students spread a rumor that he worked as a spy for the government.

I recruit Father L to our investigative team. I hope to solicit his help with restoring Connie's photos, aged and yellowed by time and neglect.

"Father Kibet here, how may I be of service?" a deep bass voice says in a tone like a BBC announcer. "Father Kibet here, can you hear me chaps?"

"Father L, Daniel here," I say, "how are you?"

"Daniel old chap, are you in-country?"

"Yes, I'm in Spokane," I say. "I was just talking with Claire, and we have a problem with some old family snapshots that need restoring, and she reminded me you were at Seattle U."

"I called earlier, but a Father Nye at the Chapel of St. Ignatius said you were in Korea."

"Returned last week, I forgot to inform the university operator. I forgive you for not calling me sooner."

Father L is fond of telling folktales. He and Uncle Paul would have hit it off.

I told him *The Chinaman's Story*, scary moon bear and all. Then I briefed him on the research Claire, and I are pursuing to find out what happened to lost family back after the Pacific War.

"We need your help in restoring some WWII vintage photos that my mom took," I say. "Claire needs clear portraits of Franklin Yoshino and Tinya Yoshino for an ad she hopes to run in the JAR Newsletter next month. With luck, a subscriber will identify Franklin and Tinya and give us some clues about their disappearances."

"Remember the hyena and their eerie yellow eyes peering out of the dark from across the river at our campsite on the Masai Mara?"

"When I told The Chinaman's Story to Claire, I could have used some of that scary stuff."

I'm sure the American CIA used Elly as a translator and decryption expert after he gained US citizenship. A year or two after earning his PhD in linguistics and archaeology from Harvard, he entered the priesthood; I think he was thirty. He experienced an epiphany; beyond that, his decision to become a Jesuit priest is a mystery. I consider it his private business. Respecting his privacy explains our continuing friendship. Heck, it's no problem for a Swede to keep a secret. Father L has developed a reputation as a restorer of vintage photographs in East Africa and later in the USA. The Jesuits assigned him to the faculty of Seattle University after they ordained him. He crosses the Montlake Cut Bridge twice a week to teach a linguistics class at the Suzzallo Library on UW's Red Square. It's a regular part-time gig for him. That is where I reached him by phone today with my request for his help in restoring Connie's portraits.

"I'll courier you a batch of mom's photos," I say. "They are all black and white and in sad condition. There's one of the 3 lads and a single photo of Franklin, Tinya and her dog."

Claire will call him for updates once he gets my package.

My last request is to identify which of the lads is Chinese and which is Japanese in the three lads on the bridge snapshot.

"Great talking with you, Daniel," Father L says. "Mark your calendar for the 12th of next month, there's a 10k race in the Arboretum."

The following day a reply comes from Father L, while Jer and I are still scavenging.

"I'm planning on keeping the originals in case you need me to do something else with these photos," he says. "Meanwhile, I'll send my restorations and blowups to Claire."

He explains that he restored one portrait photo restoration for Paul, one for Charlee, Tinya, and Franklin.

"The detail is good if I say so myself," he says. "Claire can use them for her identity searches and her JAR Newsletter advertisement. Tinya is only a profile, so I hope that will suffice."

"As for the second part of your request, to identify who is whom in the 3 lads' photo," Father L says. "I think I've solved your dilemma about whether all Asians look alike."

"The lad in the middle of the three is Paul Jonson," he says, with a titter. "When you receive your copies of my restorations, you'll have the rest of your answer."

Claire leaves a message in the morning.

"Father L's restorations are fabulous," Claire says.

The next day I'm holding my copy of the restored and enhanced 3 lads on the bridge photo. I inspect it under a magnifying glass.

Father L is correct, the lad on Paul's left is Franklin. He is Japanese, not Chinese. In the blowup, I can see slight differences in the eyes and his lack of facial hair. He is two inches shorter than Uncle Paul and Charlee, both of whom I estimate to be 5' 10", and in need of a shave.

I plan to share the restored photos with Jer for further verification.

Claire sent Bobby Tanaka at JAR copies of Father L's restored photos of Franklin and Tinya along with bios on them. A week later Claire leaves me a message on my answering machine. I find these new-fangled machines offensive, but when I hear her sexy gravelly voice, I think I should ask her to make a recording for my message system.

"The Newsletter has born fruit," she says, "I got a call this morning from a Mrs. Toho Yamasaki in Yuma."

Mrs. Yamasaki responded to the ad and photos of Franklin and Tinya that ran in the latest Newsletter. I told her the details of our search for Franklin and Tinya Yoshino of the JLS in Tacoma.

"She has some photos of Opa and Franklin and some other orphans," Claire reports.

"Orphans!" Claire says, "I thought the orphans' clue was an excellent one, guess what?"

"What?"

"I'm getting ahead of myself," Claire says. "Listen to this recording of the phone call I received from Mrs. Yamasaki two hours ago."

"Is this Professor Parsons?" A woman's voice says. "My name is Toho Yamasaki. I know the girl in the photo reprinted in the Newsletter, but her name is not Tinya. It's Opa."

"That was enough for me," Claire says, turning off the recorder. "Toho is one orphan from the JLS and Children's Home in Tacoma and a survivor of the internment camp at Manzanar."

"She also says the Yoshino's adopted her. They registered the adoption in Pierce County, not King County," Claire says. "Isn't that a hoot! I've been searching in the wrong county records for a week for a Tinya, and her proper name is Opa."

"Go figure," I say.

"Don't you mock me."

"Here comes the best part," she says, "Toho's friend Opa used to call her boyfriend Franklin. They were on the buses with her and the other orphans from Tacoma to Puyallup, that's the Relocation Center known as Camp Harmony. Then they disappeared."

Toho told Claire she has some photographs from back then. She mentioned she might have one of Opa and Franklin, but she wasn't sure. Claire asked if she would courier them to her in Seattle. She seemed very reluctant to let the precious photos out of her sight. To overcome the reluctance to part with her precious memories, Claire suggests that she knows the man who did the restorations of the portrait photos for the JAR newsletter. He's a Jesuit priest named Father Kibet, and he can restore Mrs. Yamasaki's snapshots for her.

Claire contacted Father L and asked him if he would call Mrs. Yamasaki and do whatever he can to persuade her to send him the pictures for restoration.

"Isn't this fantastic," Claire says. "We can compare Toho's photos with Father L's restorations of Connie's. This will give me accurate pictures to compare with DOD military service and county records."

"In my excitement, I almost forgot about Samuel Yoshino," she says. "I'll send him copies and get his verification."

"Don't forget to tell him you have located his adopted daughter, Toho."

"Got lucky," Claire says. "Father L says to tell you he just returned from a friend's wedding overseas. He says it'll be his pleasure to call Ms. Yamasaki. Told me to remind you of next month's race."

"I hope that his most excellent command of Japanese and his station in life might persuade her," Claire says. "You know how charming Father L can be. What do we have to lose?"

Father L calls me back within a few hours. He promised Ms. Yamasaki that he will care for and respect her photos. He plans to send her copies of his restorations, suitable for framing and hanging on her living room wall in Yuma, all at no expense.

I entertained no doubt about Father L's joining the team, nor about his persuasive powers. I imagined him speaking with Ms. Yamasaki in his usual dulcet tones. He would mix English and Japanese while reminding her of his priestly role and his professional skill in restoring photos.

He told me later that Ms. Yamasaki is a converted

Catholic. How's that for serendipity at work?

"Are Ms. Yamasaki's photos restorable?" I say, "Or are they in worse condition than Connie's?"

"I've never met an un-restorable photo," Father L says.

The next day Claire calls me again.

"Father L and I examined Ms. Yamasaki's snapshots," Claire says. "They are a diary of her memories of her years of internment."

Most of her pictures are black and white and yellowed with age, but Father L selected four that he is restoring.

In the first photo, a young couple is hugging, in what appears to be a desperate embrace. The blowup of Franklin shows a boyish man's full face, and it compares well with the lad to the left of Uncle Paul. That puts one mystery to rest.

But the girl's face is fuzzy. Again, we are dealing with a partial profile.

Mrs. Yamasaki first said that she didn't think she no more photos of Opa nor of Franklin. But she persisted and found a third snapshot in a shoebox. It features a group of the Tacoma JLS orphans from a year before the relocations.

She included a note that reads: "That's me in the second row on the far right. Franklin and Opa are in front of me in the first row."

Toho explains that she was 15 years old, and the Yoshino's adopted her at the time of the group photo. Opa was 14, one of her orphan friends at the JLS and Children's Home in Tacoma.

One thing she remembers was that Opa had this beautiful Akita that followed her everywhere. Any time a stranger walked between Opa and the dog, it rose and repositioned itself between them without making a sound. Look, you can see the dog seated and looking up at Franklin and Opa. The Yoshino's found the pair half-starved on the ferryboat docks. She wasn't an orphan; she was a foundling.

Mrs. Yamasaki recalled the day when the authorities moved the children in March 1942. She wasn't sure to which camp the Yoshinos got sent. After the war, when released, she stayed in Yuma and joined the local chapter of JAR. Later she met Mr. Tanaka from the Seattle chapter, who told her about Mikki Yoshino's death. Samuel had vanished and is not on the JAR mailing list.

Why he's not listed puzzles me. It was Samuel who first put Claire on to JAR. But that's his business. Perhaps he's not interested in reliving a painful past.

Claire thanked Toho for her photos and said, "Samuel Yoshino lives in Spokane. And I can put you in touch with him. He'll delight in hearing from you."

Claire gave her Samuel's phone number at the 5A Security firm in Spokane, but she is uncertain Mrs. Yamasaki welcomes this news.

"While Father L does his magic," Claire says. "I'll wrap up my research on Japanese American Relocation and Internment during WWII. I'll read you a summary of my report and courier the rest in the morning."

◆ ◆ ◆

Summary of Relocation Centers and Camps

In February/March 1942, the authorities rounded up everyone from the JLS and Children's House in Tacoma. They separated adults and orphans at a relocation center. Most of the Japanese American families who lived in Tacoma were first sent to the Washington State Fairgrounds at Puyallup for relocation. The War Relocation Authority named it Camp Harmony.

I'm horrified at the double entendre of that name.

Stage two was to move the prisoners from these temporary holding areas to more permanent camps, also constructed on Native American reservations.

Toho named the ones she knew in eastern California (Camp Manzanar), southern Idaho (Camp Minidoka), and northern Idaho (Camp Kooskia).

The criteria for how the authorities applied internment was geography, meaning coastal cities on the Pacific.

The camps were prisons.

After we spoke about Ms. Yamasaki by phone, Claire contacted the Pierce County (Tacoma) Records Office and sent me her report by fax.

Angie Speke got the fax the next morning. I should get a fax machine for the farm.

Exciting news. The Yoshino's adopted seventeen orphans from the JLS and Home for Children in Tacoma in the decade before the war. Pierce County adoption records list a Toho Yoshino, adopted by Samuel and Mikki Yoshino of Tacoma, March 7, 1932. No luck finding a history of adoption for an Opa Yoshino. My search for Franklin Yoshino was unsuccessful.

I also checked USA citizenship records. These records were a dead-end as age 18 was a requirement, and the two teenagers didn't qualify in 1942 at the time of their disappearance. But the 18-year-old age requirement for citizenship triggered another lead in my mind. DOD records, Franklin turned 18 in the spring of 1943 and may have enlisted.

After Pierce County, I'm flying to DC in the morning to meet with the DOD Military Service Records Office to delve into the three lads' military service. I'll let you know what I find by midweek.

I called Claire at her DC hotel the next morning.

"Hi Claire, it's Daniel."

"Thought that might be you, Daniel," Claire says, sounding groggy. "When I got into DC, it was past late. I'm doing fine, but the jet lag has me exhausted. I suppose you want to know why I need photos of Paul and Franklin."

"OK, so your name is Claire Voyant," I say. "Asking Father L for blowups of Franklin and Charlee, OK. But why Paul, what's that about? And why Tinya?"

"Claire Voyant, clever," she says. "I'm only following a hunch that came to me after I left Seattle. I'll call you if it pans out. Meanwhile, I need to catch two hours of sleep before I take the Metro subway over to the DOD in the morning."

CHAPTER 17

Father L's fantastic restorations of Connie's and Mrs. Yamasaki's photos have provided us with valuable knowledge and accurate images of Tinya, now Opa, Franklin, Charlee, and Paul.

I show the original photo of the 3 lads on the bridge to Jer while we continue to scavenge.

"Let's take another crack at which lad is Franklin."

"Franklin is on the left of Uncle Paul," Jer says. "Wait, make that to his right."

"Compare that photo with this restoration from Father L."

"For sure, Franklin is on Uncle Paul's left," he says, reverting to his first choice.

"Father L reports that Franklin is on Paul's right."

"All Asians look alike," he says with a sheepish grin.

We can't have it both ways.

Instead of celebrating our progress this morning, Jer and I sit on the front porch swing at the farmhouse sipping mugs of Kenya AA. We stare at the ugly 3'x3' sign announcing the FARM AUCTION. The auction sign faces sideways, for the benefit of passersby on 9th Street.

"What an ugly sign."

"It sure is offensive."

We sit for a few minutes as stares turn to glares. We both think of this ground by the ancient oak as hallowed ground.

Back and forth on the porch swing. Jer opens another album labeled 'Deliveries'. He flips some pages, pausing at a picture of a white truck that has ICE written on the side. They park the vehicle next to the same old tree with 9th Street behind it and a pile of bicycles scattered on the front lawn.

He shows me the photo.

Dodging the potholes on our bikes on 9th Street was a favorite game before they paved it.

I envision those delivery vehicles as they trailed dust down the dirt road, ringing their bells and tooting their horns. They all parked right here by the oak tree. Now that I recall these vehicles, I'm thinking they were another reason we called this place 'The Hub'.

"We started each day at the farm, before the sun came up, right at this spot."

"You did," Jer says, "I slept late."

My memory-attic soon fills with visions of the truck bringing the blocks of ice grandma used to refrigerate perishables. Or was it for us kids to chip a chunk off to suck on during a sweltering summer morning while I finish my chores?

"When I close my eyes, I can almost see Vinnie," Jer says. He was funning me about sleeping in. He had duties and errands the same as me. "You remember him, the wiry little iceman who you always described as the icepick murderer from a Sherlock Holmes mystery."

"Vinnie always chipped off two chunks for us to suck on before he delivered a block of ice to Grandma's cold cellar beneath the rear porch," I say. "He scared the devil out of me."

"I think it was right after we listened to a BBC radio broadcast of Conan Doyle's story about the ice dagger experiment," Jer says.

Running out of nearby houses or riding bicycles, a dozen or more children raced from a mile or more to catch up with the ice wagon. Chasing it until it parked in front of the big Falu red farmhouse opposite the venerable oak tree with the two yellow ribbons tied around it. They abandoned their bikes on the lawn. The Jonson farm was the first stop on Vinnie's 9th Street route.

All winter I continued to stoke the rumor fires at Grant Elementary by telling The Chinaman's Story during lunch hour and playground breaks.

Jer finds a cigar box in the attic fastened with a Christmas ribbon. It delights Jer and me when we find two yellow ribbons in the cigar box. He lays the ribbons on the kitchen table and smooths them with his hands, ironing the wrinkles of time out of them. The history of the yellow ribbons does a rerun in our brains.

Fixating on what else is in the cigar box, my attention is on a collection of mibs and shooting marbles, steelies and glassies. We had marble shooting contests on the cement playground behind Grant Elementary

School.

I draw a chalk circle on the porch deck, ten feet in diameter, and challenge Jer to a game of marbles.

"You were good at marbles," Jer says, reaching into the box and holding up a large steel ball bearing. "Do you remember the day you won that prize steelie from Fat Teddy?"

All the marble shooters in our neighborhood called them steelies.

"I remember Fat Teddy, zits and all," I say. "He took all the marbles from the smaller kids, win or lose."

"My favorite shooter was this blood red glassie," I say, picking it from the cigar box. I hold it up to the light to see it sparkle. I place it between my thumb and forefinger. "I shot at his half-inch diameter steelie, knocking it out of the circle, making it and all his mibs mine."

"After that day, your collection of marbles was the best in the neighborhood."

Jer's accolade brought a smile to my face. I had never heard him praise anything I did as a boy, not my storytelling, and not my marble shooting skills.

"Fat Teddy was about to beat the stuffing out of me."

"Then you did what Uncle Paul taught us," Jer says, "you told a story to distract him."

While we share memories of the playgrounds, I list the other venues where I told and retold The China-man's Story to keep my sacred promise to Uncle Paul. The school marked the western edge of our lives. The eastern boundary is Speke's Country Store. Where we deliver grandma's canned jams, and I tell Uncle Paul's story to gatherings of children in the parking lot while sipping nickel Cokes and chewing on licorice sticks.

These were the boundaries of our early childhood before we visited Uncle Paul for the races at the Montlake Cut. That day expanded my world to include adventures with Marco Polo and sailing the seas with Columbus.

"Check these photos," Jer says.

The clutter gets worse in my memory-attic as more photos of deliveries trigger childhood memories. Connie has arranged three photos in a row. Vinnie's ice wagon, the ice cream truck, then a bookmobile van. They parade before me as I gaze at them in the album.

"The dog's name was Sandy," Jer says, looking at a photo of my childhood friend Essie and her dog. "Hang on for a minute. I found an album marked 'Children's Books'."

He shuffles back into the living room, pulls out a bulky album and brings it to the front porch, sitting next to me on the swing.

A photo falls out of a long-overdue book stamped, Spokane Mobile Library.

It's a picture of the neighborhood children gathered around a big tan and white converted school bus. They print Spokane Public Library in bold letters on the sides. It came to our neighborhood every Friday and parked on 9th Street next to the gigantic oak.

Sometimes on warm evenings, mom and other times, Uncle Paul read to us while rocking on the swing before heading inside to bed.

Jer and I were ahead of most of our peers at school in reading and writing. Connie insisted that her sons read at every opportunity, and she read to us from books borrowed from the traveling library. Aesop's Fables, Albert Payson Terhune's beautiful dog stories about *Lad* and *Bruce.*

The overdue book is Ann Sewell's "*Black Beauty*," which has an original publication date of 1877. We named the old LaSalle after the stallion in her tale. It's also the first story mom read to my brother and me by candlelight. I open to a bookmarked page.

Black Beauty in recalling his childhood as a young colt, says, *"I've not forgotten my mother's advice. I hope you will grow up gentle and good and never learn bad ways."*

"The story was so captivating that we begged mom to continue the reading the next day."

"There's a point for you, mom could be our friendly ghost."

"Whenever I eat ice cream, I think of a specific delivery," I say, "and I ask myself, what happened to Black Beauty?"

"The old La Salle or the horse?"

The next morning, the ice cream truck rolls to a stop by the old oak tree.

"Ding a ding a ding a ding!" I say, pretending to be Sparks, the ice cream man ringing his cowbell as he came down the road.

"I'll take two dips of chocolate on a sugar cone and a single dip strawberry," Jer says.
"Don't you boys be spoiling your appetite before lunch," Grandma says from the doorway.

We sat on the porch swing, and mom continued reading from "*Black Beauty*". As I turn the pages, I notice a stain on page 41 that smudges an image of the black stallion. It's a muted chocolate color.

Ice-cream was the delivery the children in the neighborhood got most excited over. They heard the bell ringing down 9th Street a block before it arrives and parked, drawing crowds of dozens of children and a few adults.

"I wonder what the overdue library book fines total for fifty years," I say, grinning.

"For me, the ice truck was my favorite delivery," Jer says.

"Why?"

"Uncertain why," Jer says, "perhaps it was Sparks and his brass cowbell."

The big cowbell sent out a message of arrival as it reached the farmhouse. It was like Morse code... clang, clang, clackety, clang... clang, clang, clackety, clang.

Grandma told us that Sparks used to have a horse and wagon. He didn't want to give up the old cowbell for a modern siren or horn when he bought the truck.

"Do you get a sense of whether all this reminiscing is helping or hindering our investigations?"

"It's time consuming, and we drift off target," Jer says. "But I'm enjoying the big bands' jazz. Could be the real value to all this."

Settled back into our routine, we go uninterrupted for a few hours. Then it's time to change music albums on the old Victrola's turntable. It doesn't have an automated record changer.

As a Count Basie album ends, Jer fiddles with the old Victrola and the radio crackles to life with a burst of static.

An announcer with a pronounced British accent says, "Broadcasting from London on the BBC broadcast network with the first of a series of rebroadcasts of Arthur Conan Doyle's famous mysteries. We begin with "*A Study in Scarlet*", featuring Nigel Diggs as detective Sherlock Holmes and Warren Davenport as Doctor Watson."

We listen to the entire rebroadcast.

"Was Conan Doyle's description of Sherlock Holmes brain-attic your source of inspiration," Jer says as the broadcast ends.

"For what?"

"Your ramblings about your memory-attic."

I laugh and admit that it was.

"Another ghost," I say. "And another point for Connie."

"Did you find, "*A Study in Scarlet*" in that last box of books I brought down?" Jer asks, "I love that mystery."

"Me too and no, I didn't," I say, as Jer heads back up the ladder into the attic. "We still have some unopened boxes, could be in one of them."

I put a Benny Goodman album on the Victrola, and the sounds of "*The Charleston Stroll*" fills the house. Jer climbs down with another box. He places it on the kitchen floor and motions for me to join him in an impromptu jitterbug.

Still laughing as the stroll ends, he starts back up the ladder.

Jer's enjoying this scavenger hunt. My new partnership with Jer is changing my frame of mind. I believe at this moment that I feel closer to my big brother than I have in years.

"Should we keep this old stain-glass lamp?" Jer hollers down from the attic, "It has a few cracks. I can replace the wiring."

The lamp was a favorite of grandma's; she kept it on the nightstand next to her featherdown bed.

"Hand the lamp down," I say, placing it in the growing pile of items marked for storage."

It's the lamp that fell to the floor in my nightmare

about mom's last call.

I'm reminded that one reason for our scavenger hunt is to preserve family treasures and memorabilia before the auction. The auction had almost slipped my mind, perhaps because of the ugly sign on the front lawn by the old oak. That reminded me, along with my growling stomach, that Sara Swenson should arrive soon.

CHAPTER 18

A long black hearse crunches to a stop in the gravel driveway and blares its horn twice. On second look it's an Oldsmobile Custom Cruiser Station Wagon.

A tall woman, coiffed and attired in a white and blue suit, beams, and waves. As she steps out of the car, she adjusts her umbrella sized sunhat. Knots the scarf under her chin to tie the hat down as a gust of wind attempts to blow it away. Sara Swenson, attorney at law, has been one of mom's dearest friends for over thirty years. We never mention her age in her presence. She shares Connies penchant for literature and stories.

"Daniel, help me with this package," she says while unlocking the trunk.

The lid of the Olds doesn't want to stay up in the breeze. I wrestle with a sizeable picture frame wrapped in butcher block paper.

Sara opens the rear door of the car and picks up an enormous casserole dish.

"Hi, Doll! It's been too long," Jer says as he walks up, and she hands him the platter.

"Please put this in the oven?" Sara says while retrieving her leather briefcase.

"Does 350 degrees for 30 minutes sound about right?" Jer says.

"Mind if I pay my respects to Connie before we dine and get down to the business of the auction?"

Removing her scarf and sunbonnet, Sara stands at attention in the cemetery between Jer and me with tears rolling down her cheeks, making a mess of her mascara. She looks down at Connie's new stone marker, beside Uncle Paul's.

I hand her my checkered handkerchief.

"Miss you, Connie Jonson," Sara says, using a corner of the handkerchief to dab away a tear. "I hope you're at peace."

"Amen to that!"

Back in the kitchen, I pop a question I kept bottled up ever since Claire and I first arrived at the farm. I noticed a sun faded patch over the fireplace in the living room where a portrait hung for years.

"Do either of you have any idea what happened to that painting?"

"You caught us!" Sara says, almost blushing, "That's what you just carried in from the car."

It might get sold at the auction or damaged if left in an unheated and damp old house. She kept it at her office.

"The 3 lads painting is a commission drawn by the New Orleans artist, Heidi Pitre."

"So good of you to preserve it for us," I quip, emphasizing the 'us' as I glare at Jer.

"I called dibs the first time I saw the painting," Jer says with a smirk, adding. "Sara is my witness."

"Dibs, my ass!" I say, continuing, "You took the

painting to keep me from getting it, so why bring it back now?"

"Please, boys!" Sara says, her tone and use of the word boys reminding me of mom and grandma. "Grandma Jonson and Connie would never tolerate such language. I'm sure we can work out some sharing arrangement."

"Perhaps a King Solomon sort of division," I say as I feign a slicing gesture with a packing crate knife.

"Lawyers!" Jer says, feigning exasperation. We all laugh as I remember he's a lawyer.

"I believe I will leave the custody issue in your hands," Sara says. "I'm only the delivery girl."

Then it hits me. We hadn't solved a thing. Who gets custody of the 3 lads painting?

The timer for the oven dings as the smell of the tuna casserole warming in the oven distracts all of us. It makes a fabulous addition to our soup and sandwich makings.

"That was delicious," Sara says, as she dips a corner of one of grandma's exquisite cloth napkins in her water glass and dabs at her lips. "Now let's get down to business."

Pulling a book with a tattered cover and a package from her leather briefcase, she lays them on the kitchen table.

"Connie instructed me to give you this book and a parcel," she says, "but only if the two of you returned home."

She directs the return home comment at me.

"She also enjoined me to say a few words on her behalf," Sara says. "Boys, I trust you are together back at the farm. I'm hoping you remember this novel by Conan

Doyle, "*A Study in Scarlet*"."

Sara opens the book to a bookmarked passage.

"This passage will revive some old memories," Sara says. "Connie instructed me to tell you boys to remember to think backwards. Read this story once more, and it will help you get organized."

The passage is about Dr. Watson listening to Sherlock Holmes describe how his 'brain-attic' works.

"We've been searching in the attic for this novel for two days," Jer says as he thumbs through the pages.

The binding is about to give way. He hands it to me, opened to a second bookmark.

"This bookmark, it's a photo, of Franklin, Tinya and her Akita, Moonbear, dated Christmas 1941."

"How did mom know we'd need help to get organized?"

Sara shrugs her shoulders.

A skim through "*A Study in Scarlet*", and I rediscover that Arthur Conan Doyle is right about what he called the 'brain-attic'.

My thoughts return to the analogy of a 'brain-attic'. I prefer the term 'memory-attic,' as the brain devotes time to creativity and organization of memories.

Conan Doyle's character, detective Sherlock Holmes, states, "*One should properly furnish their attic.*" Sherlock had a well-organized brain-attic. My memory-attic is cluttered.

Unlike Sherlock's brain-attic, the attic of the family farmhouse is a dusty, cluttered collection of furniture, carpets, trunks, and boxes. But the boxes are an exception. They are all organized and labeled: Music & Records; Kitchen utensils; Poppa's stuff; Books; Grandma's memorabilia; Paul Jonson; Christmases Past;

Property Deed & Legal Papers; Deliveries.

I'm not surprised at the level of organization of these boxes and the picture albums. Connie and Uncle Paul read the mysteries of Sherlock Holmes to us on many evenings before bed. Then there were the BBC broadcasts. Those novels had taught Jer and me to organize whatever we did.

Sherlock's thinking backwards has been one of my best tools for organizing the clutter in my memory-attic all my life. Adding this thinking tool our reenactment efforts and the progress Father L made in restoring photographs of Franklin and Tinya, and my optimism is rising.

"Think backwards?" I say with incredulity, realizing what Claire and mom have had me doing for weeks.

I'm reminded once more that Claire thinks we're being led by a ghost.

Finding the source of my trauma lifts the cover of repression from my childhood memories. This couples with the shared nature of the second promise, lessening my feelings of guilt and failure.

It's our commitment, not my sole obligation, to find out what happened to Charlee Sang, to Franklin and Tinya after Camp Harmony. Uncle Paul's secret reason for developing his story of the Chinaman is now a shared mission.

Looking at the package, Jer and I are excited and apprehensive.

"Before I go any further," Sara says, her tone becoming solemn as she hands us Connie's package. "I need to explain something about the state of mind your mom was in when she gave me the book and package for safekeeping."

"It's written, so I can read it to you without breaking down in tears," Sara says.

Connie told me many a story about how your family's values were your grandmother's and grandfather's domain, including kindness and respect for others, honoring promises, and keeping secrets.

"Speaking of keeping secrets," Sara says, "your mom also left you whatever's in this package. Family documents, birth certificates, diplomas."

Sara explains that Connie is an extraordinary planner. Three years ago, when Connie first started giving these items to her for safekeeping, Sara figured she was planning for her departure from this world. Connie tried to transcribe the notes in her steno pads written many years earlier. That was when she also told me it worried her that her memory was failing; but she swore me to secrecy.

"When you have signed for it," Sara says, "I'll give it to you, boys."

Jer and I are about to sign for the package. Connie's handwritten notes on the 4-year Barnstormers' Feed & Grain calendar are evidence of her dementia. She had been leaving messages to herself for months so she wouldn't forget even slight things. What to make for dinner and remember to call Daniel on his birthday. Each note starts with remember. Once more I choke up.

I turn my attention to Sara's other reason for her

visit. I sense that Jer is as reluctant as I am to discuss the forthcoming auction. It represents an end, not a beginning to both of us. Together with Sara, we set Thursday, August 16, as the official date for the auction. There is one piece of business burning at me that can't wait any longer.

"Sara?" I say, "Did you hire someone to clean up the grounds and refresh the house and barn with a fresh coat of Falu red paint?"

"I thought something looked different when I drove into the driveway," Sara says. "I was here three weeks ago, and the house looked rather drab."

She admits that she sent her assistant by to put up the auction sign out front and that she reported that the place looks unkept.

"All the flower beds and grounds out front and back by the cemetery are so trim and weeded," she says, "was that you boys' doing?"

OK, that answers my first and second questions.

"Our ghost theories are back in play," I say to Jer while making a mental note to tell Claire.

"What about grandma's crocheted tablecloth on the kitchen table, and the stack of fresh-cut wood in the shed?" Jer says.

"Not my doing," Sara says with a look of incredulity, "I've no idea what you boys are talking about."

"Someone's been here before us, and they refreshed the paint on the house and barn," I say. "Not a simple task as Falu red is a special paint, based on a secret recipe that comes from a district in Sweden."

"Oh, yeah!" Jer says. "I almost forgot. Someone oiled the hinges on the attic ladder and trapdoor."

Sara stares at us as if we are ghostbusters from

the 1984 movie or read too many Sherlock Holmes novels. She adjusts her hair, tying it in a ponytail before donning her huge sunhat and securing everything with a blue-black ribbon and a lethal-looking six-inch hatpin. As she closes her briefcase, she gives us a puzzled look.

"I've contacted everyone I can identify with an interest in the forthcoming auction."

She tells us that so far, one relative has responded, Ernest Nordling. He called from southern California.

"I could use some help from you boys if you think of anyone I've overlooked," she says as she hands us a copy of her list.

"I also received a rather strange request in the mail a few weeks back from a Mr. R. Sang," she says, "It's postmarked Boston but without a return address."

In the letter, Mr. Sang asked about the Jonson family and said he wanted to pay his respects and condolences for Connie Jonson's recent departure.

"Connie never mentioned an R. Sang to me," she says, "Do either of you boys know who this Sang person is?"

"We adopted a Charlee Sang," I say. "But he was an orphan, he's the only Sang I've known. Claire is checking on Charlee Sang's military service records. Maybe she'll come up with something."

"Charlee Sang was an oar on Uncle Paul's skull for the UW Huskies," Jer says. "He was Uncle Paul's best friend at UW and enlisted in the Navy with Paul at the start of the war in the Pacific. We've been looking for a letter he wrote Paul."

He has been paying attention.

Sara pauses as if digging deep in her memories.

"I met Charlee Sang at the family Christmas gathering before the war, he was a friend of your Uncle Paul's."

"Who is this R. Sang?" Sara says. "I have another appointment in town."

"Meanwhile, I'll leave it to you boys to solve your custody quarrel over the 3 lads painting and investigate the ghosts you mentioned,"

"Before I leave," she says, "you boys open this package so I can attest to the fact that you opened it together in my presence as per Connie's request. But don't show me the contents. Connie said they are to keep them secret. Then I have one last chore."

Jer and I sign, and we hear her footsteps crunching on the gravel as she heads for the front of the house. She uses a black marking pen to mark the auction sign August 16, 1992, noon.

CHAPTER 19

Watching the taillights blinking as gravel spits out behind the Oldsmobile. Sara Swenson makes her departure from the farm, pale blue scarf flowing out the drivers' side window. Claire would admire her dramatic entrance and exit.

We are both staring at the package we just signed for. I glance at Jer. He looks back with a perplexed expression on his face.

I open the large envelope with a box cutter. It contains two stenographer pads with script in mom's distinctive cursive.

"Connie's journals!" I declare, as I thumb through the first memo pad entitled Family Heritages which has a segment on Charlee Sang's Heritage.

Handwriting was a skill mom tried to teach her sons. Her cursive is meticulous, but the scribbling is unreadable.

"Can you make out the rest of this?"

"When we went to high school, mom always said Latin was a fit foundation for studying romance languages, but this isn't Latin," Jer says. "There are a few Swedish words, and the titles bear a resemblance to her beautiful cursive for a word here and there."

"The title is intriguing," he says, holding up the second journal to show me.

I nod my agreement while thinking Claire needs to know about 'The Plan'.

Ten minutes later, I'm on the phone with Claire at her hotel in DC. The Hotel operator puts me on hold for several minutes.

Meanwhile, Jer skims through the pages of *"A Study in Scarlet."* An envelope sticks to the pages. He slides a brittle, yellowing letter out. Its condition is so deteriorated it crumbles as he unfolds a corner.

"Daniel," he says, "I think we found Charlee Sang's last letter."

"Bremerton," I say, "The letter sort of fell out of Uncle Paul's trunk."

"Damn!" Jer says, "that was spooky."

"Careful, Grandma's listening."

"As best as I can remember," Jer says, "mom never opened Charlee's letter, Uncle Paul told her to open it later."

"Then Paul said the letter may help in finding Charlee, Franklin, and Tinya after the war. Promise me you'll locate them."

"And here we are 50 years later with Charlee Sang's last message," Jer says. "We must find out what he wrote."

"We," I say, "We."

"You're starting to get it, little brother," Jer says. "You forgot, or as Claire puts it, you repressed the fact we all made that promise, Connie, you, and me. Emphasis on us."

"Emphasis on we failed to keep our promise," I say.

"Now you're catching on," Jer says, adding, "Mom and I also felt guilty."

The District Holiday Hotel operator says, "I'm ringing your party now."

Claire picks up on the third ring.

"Daniel, it's 2 am EST here," Claire says, sleep in her voice and annoyed. "This best be important! I just got in from Seattle, and I'm bushed."

"Sorry, I forgot the time zone difference. But it's important. Do you recall Bremerton and our reenactment of our last visit with Uncle Paul?"

"Yes."

"Do you remember my talking about Charlee Sang's letter to Paul when we reenacted the Bremerton events?" I say. "And mom's package, the one Sara Swenson just delivered to Jer and me?"

"Yes, and yes!" Claire says, "You became obsessed with your failure to keep your second promise to your Uncle Paul. And I remember he said finding Charlee Sang's letter might help in that mission."

"Now, may I please get some sleep?"

"Soon." I say. "That very letter fell out of the pages of a Conan Doyle novel, part of what was in the package mom gave Sara Swenson for safekeeping."

"Enough with the melodrama," Claire says. "I'm awake now, tell me what's in the letter."

"That's the dilemma."

I explain how Charlee's last letter is falling apart, and there are two of Connie's journals in the package written in code.

"One at a time," Claire says. "Tell me about the letter's poor condition."

"The paper is all yellow and it crumbled when we took it from the envelope," I say. "If we unfold it, it will disintegrate more."

"OK!" Claire says. "Now tell me what you mean by Connie's journals being in code."

"It stumps Jer and me," I say. "We can't make sense of the scribbling except for the titles. The first journal is Family Heritages and the second The Plan."

"The Plan sounds intriguing," she says. "I've been saying all along Paul, Franklin, Tinya, and Connie were concocting a plan at Red Square."

Her proposition about The Plan is that Connie and the lads wanted to keep Tinya and Franklin safe from anti-Japanese threats and abuse. The news was full of menacing comments about all Japanese Americans in the years before the attacks on Pearl Harbor. The menacing tone reached a crescendo two years later with EO 9066 and the forced relocations of Japanese Americans living on the coast.

"As for your dilemma," Claire says, "why is it you never look to the few friends you have for answers?"

"I called you, didn't I?"

"And woke me up," she says. "Call Father L and send him Charlee's letter and let him open it."

Claire reminds me that Father L is an expert at restoring all kinds of things and he's also a linguistics professor.

"I'm betting he can decode the scribbling in the journals."

"Let me know what Father L finds," she says

laughing. "Now, I need to get some sleep, bye, love."

She rings off before I ask why she's looking into Paul's military service records.

CHAPTER 20

Angie calls from Speke's Country Store. She has a fax addressed to Professor Daniel Jonson. I tell her I'll come and pick it up. I'm impressed by Claire's ingenuity in locating the nearest fax machine.

Executive Summary of research by Professor Claire Parsons, Department of Archaeology, U. W. (May 7, 1992)
Subject: (1940-45) Historical context of Internment of Japanese Americans.
War raged on two continents. Families on the American home front faced a battle of an unconventional kind. Japanese Americans soon became the most persecuted Americans in our country's history.
Let me first summarize the historical background before 1941. This applies to our investigation into finding out what happened Charlee Sang and Franklin and Tinya.
I have tracked backwards from the points of their disappearances. Franklin and Tinya vanished from the relocation center at Camp Har-

mony in Puyallup. Charlee Sang's disappearance traces back to Bremerton, where he didn't
enlist in the Navy with Paul.

Daniel was correct in starting our investigations even further back in time, beginning at
the races at the Montlake Cut Bridge. I agree
with Daniel that the three lads on the bridge
were planning something with Connie. They
started two years before the attacks on Pearl
Harbor and the subsequent issuance of EO
9066.

Claire's report continues with a segment on
Japanese Language Schools:

Many Japanese migrated to Hawaii in pursuit of
a better life in the last half of the 19th century.
Later they continued to the mainland and settled along the Pacific coast. Parents worried
that their children would get Americanized
and lose their cultural heritage and language.

So they develop Japanese Language Schools,
separate from the American public-school system. JLS's were where students studied Japanese language, culture, and other subjects from
Japan's national curriculum. Some teachers are
locals, they recruited many from Japan. JLS's
would submit a request for teachers to the Japanese consulate who forwarded their applica-
tions to the Japanese Ministry of Education.
Those selected were experienced teachers. If
the JLS is a startup, so they send a couple from
Japan to manage the operation.

This last part of my research brings up two
events that I am continuing to investigate:

1st event: Two Nisei, Samuel and Mikki
Yoshino are the managers of the JLS and Children's Home in Tacoma, Samuel gets put on a
"watch list". We knew this. But there's more.

Japanese Language Schools (JLS's) were failing

to impart sufficient Japanese fluency, and the younger generations spoke English learned in local schools and neighborhoods. Most Nisei seemed more American than Japanese and may have been less fluent in Japanese than some supposed back then. These findings seem to show the success of Americanization efforts. It's apparent in hindsight that American fears of Japanese espionage were unfounded as were the lists of suspected spies.

EO 9066 issued in February 1942. News headlines and signs are posted everywhere in Pacific Coast cities from Seattle and Tacoma to San Diego. Telephone poles, storefront windows, billboards at train stations spread the message, "INSTRUCTIONS TO ALL JAPANESE PREPARE TO MOVE."

I can only imagine what that meant to Franklin Yoshino, who may have been a proud and loyal American in 1940-42. More to come on his citizenship status. He must have felt threatened, fearing that the Tacoma JLS run by the Yoshino's was in immediate danger of being closed and boarded up. Meaning the authorities transported residents and students, including the orphans at the Children's Home, to inland internment camps. Adding to the posters and taunts the lads and Connie heard at the races, are the rumors that Samuel Yoshino was on a list of suspected disloyal spies. Franklin and Tinya loved and respected the Yoshino's who were the adopting parents of many of the orphans.

Mrs. Toho Yamasaki verified that Franklin and Tinya disappeared from Camp Harmony just before the orphans got transported to Camp Manzanar in eastern California.

Samuel Yoshino verified they send Mikki to

Camp Minidoka, where she lived until her death. Kooskia Camp was in north-central Idaho, 30 miles NE of the town of Kooskia. Prisoners from Kooskia labored on local dam projects such as the Anderson Ranch Dam. I verified with Samuel Yoshino that he and all the prisoners at Kooskia were on government "watch lists" and considered subversives. He confirms that rumors circulated in the months before EO 9066 that he and others were on such a list. People suspected they were spies with loyalties to the Emperor and not to America.

While researching the lists, I had a disparate thought I am tracking.

2nd event: Uncle Paul taught English at the JLS in Tacoma.

More to come after I visit the DOD.

Another line of investigation is about orphans. I found some news headlines and articles in the archives at Suzzallo Library about the closing of Japanese Language Schools, including the JLS in Tacoma. My investigation didn't take off until I started examining what Toho Yamasaki told me. I call this the orphans angle.

Official internment records for Manzanar Camp on the Nevada/California border list 100 orphans from the JLS & Children's Home in Tacoma, including Toho Yoshino.

Pierce County records verified that Mikki and Samuel Yoshino adopted many of these orphans, including Toho, but not Franklin or Tinya.

Claire's Closing Notes:

Parts of my investigations have left me with more questions than answers, but I shall persist.

1) Franklin's American citizenship is in ques-

tion. Another DOD matter I'm looking into. Major Nutting is checking to see if Franklin could be exempt if he is an American by birth. Did the authorities miss this point? He turned 17 in the Spring of 1943, and that would have made him eligible for the draft.

Note: I prepare this executive Summary before seeing Father L's decryptions of Connie's journals and his restoration of Charlee Sang's last letter. I'm at a dead end as regards Charlee Sang, but we'll search the DOD records further.

Whatever the circumstances, Franklin would have stayed with Tinya.

End Report.

The kitchen phone rings as I finish reading Claire's report.

"Did you get my fax?" Claire says, "I sent it to Angie Speke. I did some further military service records research that may surprise you, Daniel."

"Jer is here with me," I say, "I'm putting us on speaker."

"Oh, Good!" Claire says, "I have Major Nutting here with me, we're calling from his office."

"Greetings!" Major Nutting says, adding, "We are not on a secure line."

"You may both want to sit down for my report on CPO Paul Jonson's military service," Claire says.

"You checked out my Uncle Paul?"

"Hear us out, then I'll get to CPO Jonson."

She describes how she and Samuel Yoshino discussed his watch list status. It came to her that Uncle Paul tutored at the same JLS that Samuel and his wife

Mikki operated in Tacoma. If Samuel Yoshino were on the enemy watch list, could it be that Paul was too? It was only a premonition, a hunch.

"I don't think they subjected Swedish Americans to the same level of national paranoia about spies in our midst. At least not at the level Japanese Americans were."

"Even if they were," Claire says, "it would have been as Nazi sympathizers, not Japanese sympathizers. I get it. But here's the shocker."

"I'm seated," Jer says.

"Paul Jonson was on another of the government's espionage suspects lists."

"The military calls them security clearance checks," Major Nutting says.

"What?" I say in an astonished tone.

Claire pauses again. To calm me down. I don't.

Claire and Major Nutting report that according to the DOD's official records, Paul Jonson's application to the Navy for officer training status has a hold put on it. They pursued an investigation into his interests in and relationship with the Japanese Language School in Tacoma. In short, he needed a security clearance to be an officer.

Claire quotes from an official letter in Paul Jonson's file: "The JLS is a known subversive institution whose directors are being scrutinized for their connections to Imperial Japan. They hire Shinto trained priests as language and indoctrination teachers for their school."

"Wait, a minute!" I say, still startled by this revelation. "Paul tutored several of the children at the JLS in English. His first two pupils were his friends Franklin and Tinya Yoshino, but he was no spy, no subversive; hell, Uncle Paul was a patriot, earned a Purple Heart, died serving his country."

"Don't kill the messengers!" Claire says. "The Major and I are only telling you what we found in the military service records."

"Paul Jonson took his rejection for OTS in stride and enlisted in the Navy as a Seaman," Major Nutting says.

My annoyance abates somewhat over Claire's checking out Uncle Paul's military service records without telling me first. But my anger remains that this falsehood is a permanent part of his service record.

"Major Nutting, can you check into having this expunged from his official records?"

"I'll try," Major Nutting says, "but it may take some time, bureaucratic red tape and all."

"I'm finishing up here in DC and catching a plane back to Seattle in the morning," Claire says.

"Tell me the flight number," I say, "Jer and I will be there to meet you."

"Pacific Air flight 987 arrives at 7 am PST," Claire says. "You can fill me in on the scavenger hunt while we drive to the meeting at Red Square. I left my Peugeot in the long-term parking lot at Boeing International."

"We'll be there beautiful," Jer says.

"You were right about Claire looking into CPO Paul Jonson without checking with you first," Jer says. "He was a hero, no way he would ever betray his country."

I forgot he was in the kitchen.

"There's something in the attic I need you to help me with," he says.

CHAPTER 21

"**L**end me a hand with this carpet."

Jer has wrapped a Persian rug around a large crate. We wedge it through the attic opening and slide it down the ladder. He removes the carpet, cutting the twine with a flourish. Dust fills the air as he shakes and smooths it on the floor, and we place the chest on the magic carpet.

"Voila!" he says with a Cheshire cat grin broadening across his face. "Feast your eyes on the treasure chest I found."

It's a footlocker stored deep in the attic all these years, unattended or forgotten, or so I think until I see the broken latch.

Stenciled on the front side of the gunmetal grey footlocker is CPO Paul Jonson, Property of US Navy. The Navy had sent it with his casket to the 9th Street address, and mom stowed it away.

If mom opened it, she wouldn't have broken the latch. Was it the same someone who rummaged in the attic before we arrived?

"Jer, did you snap this lock?"

"No, must have been our friendly ghost."

Think backwards runs through my head as Jer, and I set about discovering what is inside, we are Sifting through the reminders of CPO Paul Jonson's Navy life, a sacred task.

I lift the lid with Jer leaning over my shoulder. A leather case lies on top of the other items in the locker. It contains CPO Jonson's Purple Heart. As I take the medal out of the footlocker, it slips from my grip, falling to the tile floor. I'm chilled by a cool ghostly breeze that crosses Grandma's kitchen.

"Wow!" Jer says. "That sure was creepy."

"You felt it too," I say. "Same as when Uncle Paul dropped the medal at Bremerton Naval Hospital."

"He said something about heroes don't need recognition."

"Never knew the footlocker was in the attic, did you?" I say. "No one would have dared open it. It was the sacrosanct property of a departed loved one."

"No one except Connie," Jer says. "Besides, I remember Uncle Paul giving her that red and black shawl for Christmas the year the Japanese attacked Pearl Harbor."

Jer unwraps the scarf, revealing a machete. Mom must have placed it in Paul's footlocker. But why?

"Do you remember when some local children called the Spokane Police and reported that they had seen a Chinaman on the property brandishing a bloody machete?" Jer says.

"Sort of."

"Let me refresh your memory me hearty or prepare to walk the plank," he says as he ties the scarf around his head pirate style and brandishes the machete.

His pirate portrayal triggers my recall of one of my storytelling embellishments to the Chinaman's Story.

The Chinaman's Story grew with my every telling. I aimed to portray the cabin as an even scarier place. The Chinaman wore pantaloons and a red and black plaid kerchief tied around his head. To show how menacing a character he was, I always described him as barefoot as he chopped firewood with the machete that was soon dripping with blood.

"Harrrh!" Jer says as he doffs his shoes and socks.

Even with the cold snow and ice on the ground, the Chinaman went barefoot in my telling.

"That was a delicate touch, me boyo," Jer says, "Uncle Paul taught you well."

"Building more fear into the story backfired," Jer says. "I remember when your friend Essie became curious about who lived in the cabin. She called the police when she saw a bloody machete stuck in the chopping block behind the woodshed."

The Chinaman had chopped the head off a chicken for dinner and left the knife in the tree stump.

"I never knew it was Essie," I say as I recollect that all the increased activity made mom nervous when the police visited the farm.

Why would the local police make mom nervous?

Jer and I continue to thrust and parry over the spirits that are leading us as we scavenge on. It's apparent that we are in the presence of a collective of ghosts. But I'm convinced that Connie's spirit is the ringleader, and he's adamant that it's Charlee's specter.

I realize that my memories of my mom are ghost-like. There are no photos of her in the albums. It's the curse of being the family photographer. Jer opens an album marked 'Christmas Feast' in 1940. The cover photo is of everyone awaiting grandma's entrance to start dinner. Another series of images shows grandma entering the dining room, untying her flour and food-stained apron, folding it, and setting it on the counter. Everyone else stands behind their chairs, waiting for her to take her seat, the closest to the kitchen.

"That was everyone's signal to sit down," Jer says.

Helping grandma take her seat is Jer. Great Uncle Ernest is at the head of the adult table with his hands held out for everybody to join in a circle. He offers a brief prayer which Mom has written on the back of the photograph.

"We thank thee, Lord, for these blessings and for thy bounty and for another fine crop of potatoes, apples, and a year of safety. And we welcome Charlee, Franklin, and Tinya to our family."

A snapshot of "The children's table" features a circle of children. Timmy, Stella, Tinya, Franklin, Clifton, Clara, Sandy, Millicent, Helen, Herbie, Jer and I. We are all seated and holding hands at a separate table. Charlee is taking a seat with us. Could have sat with the adults.

"That's the full cast of children at Paul's telling of *The Chinaman's Story*," Jer says.

I nod. Essie wasn't there and I wanted her to hear Uncle Paul's story.

My excitement rises when we discover an album that contains a list of Grandma's delicious dishes. Mashed potatoes, sweet peas and beans, cornbread, ham and lima beans, bowls of lettuce heads, potato-leek soup, brown sugared sweet potatoes, and beef pot pie. But no recipe book.

The list of dishes reminds me of the game, Uncle Paul often played with us when he started one of his scary stories; but before I can mention it, Jer cuts in..."My favorite is grandma's st- stew."

I spoke with Timmy Nordling a few years later before moving to St. Louis. He was overcoming his stuttering. The last time I saw him was in the flickering firelight atop Big Black Rock when I retold the Chinaman's story to Claire.

My mood is too dark for laughing.

The remark leads me to recall that the pièce de résistance is yet to come. There isn't anything but empty bowls and plates and platters on the table as the kids helped with the dishes. Images show the children clearing both tables, taking the plates and utensils to the kitchen sink for rinsing and washing, then helping with the drying. Grandma puts on her glasses to supervise the restacking in the cupboards of her best china. These precious cups and saucers survived the journey by ship and rail from Sweden to Spokane.

"I already put grandma's porcelain in the garage with the stuff headed for storage."

"Maybe Grandma ghost is here now," I say. "I can smell warm rhubarb and strawberries, in the fresh-baked pies."

Jer nods in agreement, and we join in laughter, recalling once more how lucky we were that Uncle Paul had kept our secret that day.

"I'm guessing that both grandma and mom knew all along that you and I stole the strawberry-rhubarb pie," Jer says.

"But it sure was delicious. We need to recover her recipe book."

Jer closes the footlocker and refastens the leather straps, slides it under the kitchen table.

I call and make flight arrangements for Seattle and our meeting at Red Square. Can't wait to find out what Father L's decryptions of Connie's journals and Charlee's last letter revealed.

CHAPTER 22

J er and I are at the Pacific Air ticket counter at Spokane's Intermodal Airport, when we get a pleasant surprise. We settle into our first-class seats aboard Pacific Air flight 224. I wonder how Claire managed these premium seats. Maybe she knows the CEO of Pacific Airlines or has beaucoup frequent flyer miles. Regardless, I enjoy being spoiled.

A perky flight attendant wearing a pale blue cap and matching uniform asks, "May I serve you, gentlemen, a beverage of your choice?"

"I'll take a Rainier."

"Make that two."

We clinked our bottles and toasted Claire and Uncle Paul.

On our flight to Seattle, Jer sees how tense I am.

"Relax brother," he says, "drink the Rainier. We'll soon find some answers to this mystery when we get Father L's decoding of Connie's journals."

I can't relax, my head is spinning and sending logs that are distracting. The cloud of guilt hangs over my head, and I need to think backwards to find more of the missing clues relevant to the secret behind The

Chinaman's Story.

Pausing to tie my shoelace in Boeing's busy International terminal, I manage to avoid colliding with a cart full of baggage. I double knot the laces and rise from my kneeling position.

A stunning lady dressed in a striking cream-colored business suit is trying to get Jer's and my attention from the adjacent luggage carousel.

She waves and says, "Hi Jer and Daniel, you big, beautiful men!"

Jer gives her a hug, collects his luggage, and disappears into a line of passengers waiting for taxi rides into town. He'll meet us at the meeting at Red Square in the morning. He doesn't care for crowds, and he wants to give us some private time. My guess is he's having a sugar low.

"Love the suit," I say as Claire and I embrace, "love the hairdo."

Claire takes the dual compliments in stride, as I intend, and as she expects.

"Needed a change," she says, flicking the orange highlights in her blonde hair.

I prefer her as a redhead but I'm not stupid.

"You seem more depressed than when I left you in Spokane, what's up?"

I struggle to come up with a satisfactory reply.

"I've run into some real memory blocks," I say. "Jer's memories are filling in some gaps, don't know if we're making much progress."

"Let's stop at Soo Wong's on the road home, we can get takeout."

Well over an hour later, buried under a thick warm comforter, Claire snuggles close. When I come up for air, she says, "Isn't it peculiar how one can miss someone they talk to daily."

"Telephones are so inadequate for intimate communication," I say, "I hope someone invents a more social means of connection."

"I'm in favor of physical contact. I believe we have been testing that proposition for some time in a variety of exotic world settings."

Claire slides out from under the comforter, heading for the shower. I admire.

"Don't forget to remove the wire handles from the Chinese food boxes before you put them in the microwave."

I'm still grinning ten minutes later. We dine on re-warmed Szechuan and Cantonese dishes; moo goo gai pan, fried rice, mixed vegetables, wontons, spring rolls, a pot of green tea, and a bag of fortune cookies. All for less than a Hamilton. She snaps open a fortune cookie and hands it to me.

"Are we supposed to keep these little gems of wisdom a secret?" she says. "You know, the same as making a wish on a shooting star."

"I'm not sure what the Chinese, Japanese, or American tradition is, let's share."

"Mine reads, eat more and enjoy more."

"Doesn't sound like Chinese wisdom to me, more of an American fast-food TV ad," I say, "besides, I believe they have that backwards."

I crack my fortune cookie open and take a bite.

"What's the attraction?" I say. "Not the taste."

"My fortune reads, a member of your family is trying to contact you with an important message."

"You're making that up."

◆ ◆ ◆

Ten minutes into our morning run, we near the entrance to the oriental gardens. We follow a winding path past stone lanterns and going over and arched bridge in Seattle's Washington Park Arboretum. Claire bumps me as we run side by side. She challenges me to a quarter-mile sprint, which she wins; then, she glares at me with a look of accusation. I shrug. She gets angry if I let her win. Sometimes I don't, but let's keep that secret.

There is no one else alive in this serene setting, I can hear her heartbeats, and my guilt is taking a rare recess.

"I forgot to mention that Dawselle sent me a telegram. She qualified for the RSA Olympic marathon team."

"Fabulous!" Claire says, "I'll call her tonight and congratulate her."

The serenity ceases. A large vehicle rumbles down a side street, brakes squealing on the wet pavement. Empty cans clanking. It rolls to a stop near us. Then the same sounds repeat, squeal... clank... clank... squeal... clank, getting louder as a second Seattle City Maintenance truck makes its appearance. The first garbage truck turns down 32nd Street along the edge of the park and continues its path, destroying the serenity for the rest of the neighborhood. The second heads northwest towards the lake.

A lean figure appears out of the shadows, glides alongside, and matches our pace.

"Watch out for the slugs, they're slippery after a shower," a deep, resonant voice says. "Mind if I join you, citizens, on this fine misty morning?"

"We only share our runs with Olympic caliber runners from Africa," Claire says.

"What a splendid coincidence," he says.

"Good to see you my friend."

We run three abreast, varying our pace at one-mile intervals. It's six miles across the Arboretum's length from south to north to the Montlake Cut Bridge. We slow to a walk, cross the bridge, and confront the magnificent Gothic structure of the Suzzallo Library. Mount Rainier's majestic snow-covered peak shrouded by a halo of cumulus clouds looms in the distance as the morning mist dissipates and the skies clear.

In the manner of long-distance runners everywhere, the three of us check and synchronize our wristwatches as we finish our run at Red Square.

"Time hack 1:25:09 mark!" Father L says.

"An hour and thirty minutes for the ten miles," I say, glancing at my watch, "Translates to a pace of 8 minutes and 10 seconds per mile. Not up to our usual standards. Any run is a run well taken."

CHAPTER 23

Jer is waiting for us at a table in the Suzzallo Library' espresso house.

"Greetings, Claire!" he says, getting up to give her a hug, "Sorry, I was so rude at the airport."

"No need to apologize, I forgot how much you dislike crowds."

"Father L, so good to see you," Jer says, "I ordered a two-quart jug of Cascadian Mountain for you runners."

The barista arrives with a pitcher of ice and the bottle of spring water, pouring us each a glass.

"Double espressos all around coming up next."

"Are you psychic?"

"It's Father L's standing order," the barista says.

Father L taps a spoon on his water glass and says, "May I offer a toast to friendships past and present and the success of this investigation."

Clinking glasses all around. I sense optimism in Father L's voice. Jer has also predicted we'll get some answers at this meeting. Claire noted whatever else happened to them, Franklin and Tinya would remain together.

"At first, I followed the theme Franklin and Tinya were inseparable," Claire says, "now I'm wavering on that."

"My apologies for continuing to call her Tinya instead of Opa."

"A bright spot came when I checked the Pierce County adoption records. I found Toho Yoshino's name on an adoption record as she said I would."

"Most of my digging into King County Records was for naught."

Meanwhile, Samuel is digging into his storage locker for the Captain's log. But Franklin's Japanese heritage still made him a target for EO9066 internment, as she noted in her report. Claire got the idea to search the DOD records further. Military service was one way to avoid internment, according to Major Nutting. Franklin turned 18 in the spring of 1943, and if he served, his military records should verify his American citizenship, when and where he was born, at sea or otherwise.

"Hence you concluded in your earlier report, Franklin would never desert Tinya under any circumstance," Jer says.

"It still perplexes me," Claire says.

"Why?" I ask.

"I'll explain after Father L shares a segment from Connie's journal."

Connie's Journal #1: Franklin's heritage
(Christmas 1940) A sadness overtook Franklin

as I interviewed him, and we discussed his heritage and the mother he never knew. The baby's surname is in doubt, as is his citizenship.

If Franklin was born on an American ship at sea, doesn't that make him an American citizen? If we can provide proof in the ship's logbook.

◆ ◆ ◆

"Sorry to interrupt," Claire says, "but all this means I've been on the wrong track with my investigations into Franklin's heritage, please carry on."

Reading a segment about Franklin's heritage, Father L says, "This part was easy to decrypt."

The ship's Captain knew the mother was Japanese. He placed the baby in a basket and put him on the steps of the orphanage in Tacoma. The Yoshino couple who ran the orphanage named him Franklin. Western first names were popular with Asian immigrants, as they hoped to blend in better with the locals.

"But there is no DOD record of a Franklin Yoshino enlisting in 1943," Claire says.

"Let me read another part of Connie's journal about Franklin," Father L says. "It suggests Claire and Samuel are on the right track. The ship's Captain entered the birth and death in his log."

Father L reads another segment of Connie's notes attributed to Charlee Sang.

Franklin's American citizenship was in doubt

until Paul asked a UW law student to investigate. The law student discovered Franklin's mother had given birth to him somewhere between Honolulu and Seattle, in the summer of 1925. He noted that Hawaii became a US protectorate in 1894. The ship was a Matson Lines cargo ship, an old steamer named the SS Manulani registered out of San Diego, making it American.

◆ ◆ ◆

"Let's hear more about Franklin's military service."

"I'll get to those DOD military service records from Major Nutting later," Claire says.

She explains that the DOD records confirm Franklin's American citizenship, but they also state he wasn't exempt from internment as laid out in EO 9066. Meaning we still need an answer about what happened to Franklin in the spring of 1943.

Father L thanks Claire for her historical context report and turns our attention to our changed mission. Our next task is to turn to the recent developments posed by these journals from Connie and decide on an alternative course of action.

A vehicle with a broken muffler comes coughing into the square, disrupting the tranquility and silence befitting a Gothic library. A Vespa motor-scooter trailing smoke screeches to a halt below the entrance to the espresso house.

"That beast needs to see a mechanic," I say.

Shelia, Father L's graduate assistant, has arrived. Without turning off the engine, she hops off. Unties a bundle from the scooter, dropping a stack of folders on the steps.

"Be right back!" she says as she parks the Vespa in a nearby bike rack, and the sanctity of quiet once more prevails.

"Sorry I'm late. The department copier needs a tune-up."

Shelia passes us copies of the first transcribed journal.

"The courier arrived the day before yesterday," Father L says, as the barista brings us our espressos.

"The letters you sent us with samples of Connie's handwriting aided our transcribing," Father L says.

Connie took great pride in being articulate on paper and when speaking. She taught her two sons well, but Jer and I lapsed into handwriting which resembles a doctor's illegible prescriptions. It threw us off when we couldn't make sense of her journals.

"Shelia and I completed decoding all, but the last segment of the second journal entitled 'The Plan'," Father L says. "We have some exciting news and some surprises."

"Wow! You already broke the code?" Claire says, "I love surprises."

"Well, yes, and no!" Father L says, "I'll let Shelia fill you in on our code-breaking efforts."

Father L explains there are several gaps in Connie's journals.

Before we get into the details of Shelia's and

my transcriptions, Father L states he's assuming Sara Swenson filled us in on Connie's lengthy struggles with dementia. These journals represent Connie's valiant attempt at documenting the events of 1940 to 1943.

"Connie's journals end in the spring of 1943," Father L says. "Now there is an even greater mystery to solve. Franklin and Tinya disappeared for the second time."

Father L reports that as soon as Shelia decoded the first of Connie's journals, it was apparent we face a challenging mission.

After Franklin and Tinya escaped from the Camp Harmony Relocation Center buses in March 1942, they disappeared for a second time in April 1943. Put it another way. We can't reunite the extended family as Paul wished until we first find out what happened to them during that year.

Is there more about Charlee Sang in Connie's Journals?

"Shelia and I finished the first half of Connie's 'The Plan'."

"Restoring Charlee Sang's last letter is proving a challenge," Father L says, "but I'm working on having it done before the auction."

It's deflating at this point to hear this news.

After an espresso break, Shelia passes out copies of the first segment from Connie's second journal entitled, 'The Plan'.

Father L returns to narrating while we read along, turning our attention to discovering if what Claire has suspected all along is true. Claire and Jer sit on the edge of our stools, at attention, with espressos going cold, waiting for Father L to reveal the surprise in 'The Plan'. And the secret we pursue. I'm fidgeting on my barstool. Claire's clutching my hand.

"Patience, my friend," Father L says. "I believe you once told me that after the war, your mom took you, boys, back east to St. Louis, where she found work."

Jer and I both nod in agreement, but with a puzzled look. Where is he going?

"The family left your grandma to care for the farm?" Father L says.

I nod.

He explains further. When she came back home to care for your grandmother, she entrusted the notes and other items to her friend and lawyer, Sara Swenson.

"You're correct!" Jer says, "Sara informed us two days ago."

"Here comes the surprising part of our decryption," Father L says, "Connie told Sara she was afraid she was losing her memory. She was frightened when she learned she no longer knew how to decode her own shorthand notes."

"Shorthand!" Jer says with a tone of incredulity. "Did you say shorthand?"

"I couldn't make much sense of Connie's scribbling," Father L says with a chuckle.

"Father L's just teasing about my breaking the code," Shelia says. "Connie's shorthand was easy to decipher once we compared the journals with the sample of her handwriting."

"Some secret code," Jer says. "we needed a linguistics expert to decode shorthand?"

Everyone is laughing at our oversight. Mom, being a secretary, had used shorthand all her life.

CHAPTER 24

"**M**y next surprise contains the answer we seek most," Father L says at last. "Connie has been leading her boys to a secret she kept for all those years to protect members of her family."

Connie's second journal provides us with a solution to the critical piece of our puzzle. 'The Plan' elaborates on a clue Claire and I have discussed and shared with Father L and Jer. Which lad in the 3 lads' photo is Japanese, and which one is Chinese? The answer to this lies in Charlee Sang's comments about all Asians looking alike to westerners.

Father L says, "Check the second page, the third paragraph of Connie's 2d journal.

"Claire and Daniel assumed that the planning and scheming at the Cut and at Red Square back in 1940 was about Asians looking alike. It was about the personal safety of two Japanese Americans, Franklin and Tinya," Father L says. "Their safety was the mission."

"The secret lies within Connie's 'The Plan'," Father L says, "that comes next."

I'm so excited, no, make that thrilled, but what's

the punch line?

Claire is strangling my hand.

Jer's been silent since the meeting began.

"Now take a gander at page seventeen," Father L says.

But he's interrupted by the barista bringing another round.

I can't hold it back any longer, and I'm about to ask Father L what that secret is when Jer gives me an icy stare.

Reacting once more to how my wandering ways had left mom alone to agonize over her lost memories. The mention of Connie has him visibly upset.

"You were in Asia and Africa, and lord knows where else for the past few decades," Jer says. "You didn't see mom's daily deterioration and loss of memory. She left notes everywhere to remind herself to do this and to do that. Check the calendar on the fridge. Near the end, she didn't even know me."

Jer's remarks send me plunging deep into my guilt and self-pity over my neglect of family responsibility and caring for mom.

The barista arrives with a tray of espressos while Jer and I are at a standoff.

"The second round of espressos is on the house," she says.

"Great timing!" Claire says.

Claire tries to get us back on the subject, to distract Jer and me.

"Whatever else we find," Claire says. "I'm certain of one thing, Franklin would have wanted to stay with Tinya no matter what happened to them between Camp Harmony and the end of Connie's journals in April

1943."

Jer's and my setback has me too depressed to care. We are on the verge of solving the mystery, but the underlying problem remains. We have yet to determine the secret behind Uncle Paul's story.

"Bear with me," Father L says, attempting to restore order. "We need to turn our full attention to Shelia's decoding of the first segment of 'The Plan'. That gap between 1942 and the spring of 1943 is our ultimate focus."

Jer and I are still sulking as we try to return our attention to Connie's second journal.

Connie's Journal #2: The Plan.

The discussion that began on the library steps remained only a plan in the making. Until February 19, 1942. EO 9066 hit the news and posters all over Seattle and Tacoma. People of Japanese heritage prepare for relocation. On March 7, 1942, the authorities rounded up the dozens of Japanese American orphans at the JLS and Children's Home in Tacoma. They loaded them in buses for the ride to the relocation center in Puyallup, Camp Harmony. Then it was on to inland camps.

Connie enclosed a copy of a Seattle-Times newspaper clipping in her journal.

Bainbridge Island (March 4, 1942): General DeWitt issued Civilian Exclusion Orders for specific areas within Military Area No. 1. Japanese Americans here on the island are the first in the USA to be subject to an exclusion order, due to the island's proximity to naval bases. He stated, I give them until March 30 to prepare themselves for removal from the island.

I'm reminded of the taunts and newspaper headlines that Jer and I read while at Suzzallo Library the day we toured the UW campus in 1940.

◆ ◆ ◆

As our meeting is about to break up or fall apart, Major Nutting at the DOD calls Claire with details about the service records of all three lads.

"Connie and the lads feared for the safety of Japanese Americans two years earlier than EO 9066," Claire says. "Major Nutting and I are looking into the DOD records to see if Franklin enlisted."

A problem remains. As Claire had put it earlier, Franklin would not desert Tinya even if he was an American citizen. Would it matter if they got married?

Major Nutting reports on the EO9066 guidelines. Relocation is mandatory for all Japanese. Japanese Americans included. Military service was one way that they could avoid going to the camps, but while Franklin a citizen, Tinya was not. There is no record of a Franklin Yoshino ever enlisting. It's a dead end.

I'm puzzled by what Father L has decrypted. Connie's journals end in April 1943, well before the end of the war in the Pacific in the summer of 1945.

"Here's the surprise," Father L says, "The rest of 'The Plan' provides the answer to the secret we have been searching for."

As he reads the following segment, I fight to set aside my feelings of guilt, but my excitement returns.

Connie's Journal #2 Continues

Step 1: We need to keep trespassers away from Franklin and Tinya while staying in the cabin just in case someone recognizes them as Japanese. Spokane should be far enough inland so that no one will suspect a Chinese couple.

Connie calls this part of the plan, double insurance: distance and deception.

Paul has created a scary tale about a Chinaman and his fierce protective bear. He lives in the cabin with his wife. He has tasked Daniel to be his storytelling apprentice and to spread his scary story at school and in the community. The story is intended to warn off strangers. But also, to inform everyone, including the authorities, that the couple living in the cabin are Chinese from Manchukuo, not Japanese.

Step 2: The plan is for Franklin and Tinya to live in the cabin in the woods and keep the fireplace stoked. A trail of smoke warns that the Chinese sentry and his fierce bear are in residence.

For them to get married, they needed false identities. Age 16 is the Washington State marriage minimum. Tinya is 16, and Franklin is almost 17. We need to convince the SPOKANE County Marriage License Office that both Franklin and Tinya are Chinese, not Japanese.

This disguise needs to hold until this war in the Pacific ends. Charlee's proposition has me convinced, and I don't expect the clerks at the Spokane County Court Marriage Office to give Franklin and Tinya any problems.

He will get some contacts in the Chinese community in Spokane to swear they are both descendants of parents killed in the war with Japan. They will provide false identity papers.

He will work out the details for a small Confucian ceremony in Spokane's Chinatown District.

Step 3: Franklin finished building the cabin in the woods for Tinya and him to live in. Caveat: if Grandma gives her approval, they can move in. Grandma is the reason they need to get married before they move in, she's old-fashioned.

Step 4: We must keep Franklin and Tinya safe. We will hide them in plain sight. So, the authorities won't move them to an inland camp. Grandma will supply food to Franklin and Tinya after they get to the cabin, so they won't need to go to town. They must be as invisible as possible is the way Paul puts it. The police came last week to investigate a rumor about the Chinaman. That reminded me that the authorities include our sheriff.

◆ ◆ ◆

Her 2d journal ends in the spring of 1943, and so does the smoke from the cabin. We now know why Charlee Sang wasn't at Bremerton enlisting in the Navy with Paul. But where did he disappear to? We hope Father L's restoration of Charlee's last letter will provide an answer.

"What a simple yet brilliant plan," Claire says, being the first to voice the excitement we are all feeling.

My reaction to The Plan is almost as ebullient as Claire's. I sit fidgeting and trying to make sense of it all, the ruse, and the fake Chinese identities. I'm feeling troubled by all the secrecy.

"What's bothering you?" Claire says, picking up on the worry lines that crease my forehead.

Two things," I say. "First, it was a spring day in 1943 when I told the machete story which brought the police to the farm, and I saw smoke coming from the cabin. Second, I'm bewildered why Jer, and I were part of the plan but kept out of the secret."

"Me too," Jer says, breaking his silence, "Heck, you and I are Swedes, and we can keep a secret with the best of the Jonson's."

"Such childish petulance," Claire says. "Perhaps not being in on the secret plan made your telling of the Chinaman's story more real.

"If 'The Chinaman's Story' was to be effective in keeping Franklin and Tinya safe from the authorities, then the smoke had to be real," Jer says.

"We did as Uncle Paul instructed, staying away when the smoke was rising from the cabin. But you convinced yourself and your audience of children that there was a dangerous person in the cabin."

She explains that there was a scary bear on guard and a fierce Chinaman. If the children saw smoke coming from the cabin, they knew to keep their distance. Essie got too close once. Best of all, if you were right there telling the story, you couldn't be the one who set the fire that caused the smoke.

"The smoke!" I say. "Now that I think about it, the smoke from the cabin ended in April 1943. April was also the only time I revealed that embellishment, and it was atop Big Black Rock."

The Chinaman's Story is no longer fiction, it takes on reality. Uncle Paul's stories had that effect on the children and me. Besides, I had promised Uncle Paul that I would stay away whenever I saw smoke coming from the cabin. If I had known that Franklin and Tinya stoked the fires in the cabin, I would have wanted to help with the ruse. I'd have been less convincing in my storytelling. That would have spoiled everything.

"I thought the smoke bit was my embellishment."

We now know the answer to Uncle Paul's secret reason for creating "The Chinaman's Story".

Paul, Connie, and Charlee wanted to keep Franklin and Tinya safe from the taunts and the negative news and public attitudes towards the Japanese. What continues to amaze me is that they began their plan over a year before the attacks on Pearl Harbor and 15 months before EO 9066 came out.

"I'm impressed by their foresight," I say. "And their ability to keep their secret, hiding Franklin and Tinya in plain sight."

"Claire is right," Jer says, "your belief in the story lent credibility and authenticity to your story."

Is he praising my storytelling skills, is the ice breaking between us once more?

The guilt came but it faded with his words.

"Charlee Sang's all Asians look alike proposition was the premise for their plan all along," Claire says. "Good for you Daniel, you deduced the same early on when we did our reenactment at the Cut."

"We were sitting on these steps," I say. "When Charlee first illuminated us with his Asian's all appear the same to whites' proposition. It was in response to the taunts. And Uncle Paul revealed that he had a new scary story to tell at the family gathering."

They established the ruse of a Chinese couple living in the cabin. When the authorities came searching for Japanese Americans; they would find a Chinese couple. Charlee assumed that these authorities couldn't tell Asians apart.

"Thank Sherlock, not me," I say, "just thinking backwards."

"We put that proposition of Charlee's to bed too early," Claire says.

"Connie's journals end in the spring of 1943, and Franklin and Tinya vanish for a second time," Father L says, adding, "What happened to them next?"

"Could it be that Connie became worried about the local police?" Jer says. "You know, after they came to check about the Chinaman with the bloody machete. Franklin and Tinya could have moved to another location?"

"That's it," I say, "but..."

"But why have we never heard from them?" Jer says, finishing my sentence.

Is there a problem with Daniel and Jer not seeing Franklin and Tinya during these years and months from March 1942 when they disappeared to Spring 1943? What about after Spring 1943 to Spring 1945? Is the problem an event?

"The dates hold the clue."

"My sentiments too," Father L says, "That is the prime reason we need to refocus our investigation."

"Find and reunite family," I say, as a huge emotional burden seems to float away down the sluice.

Now I realize more fully how Connie and Jer shared the responsibility while I repressed it and went wandering.

The meeting breaks up after Claire and Father L establish our new mission. Our immediate focus is twofold, first to find out what happened to Franklin and Tinya in April 1943. And second, discover what happened to Charlee Sang after the wedding?

"I'll check in with Major Nutting and we'll investigate what happened to Charlee Sang and we'll do another search for Franklin within the context of the time," Claire says.

Meanwhile, Jer and I will return to the farm and continue to scavenge away. Our first task is to put any treasures we want to keep in a rental locker at Speke's. I'm hoping we can store Black Beauty and grandma's precious china in one of the larger storage sheds. The auction becomes our immediate concern.

"Love you!" I say with a laugh and a wave as Father L and Shelia leave Red Square and return to classes at Seattle University.

Claire drops Jer off at his hotel, and we drive to her place.

Our new mission has challenging tasks for all of us. Father L and Shelia decode the last part of Connie's 2d journal and finish restoring Charlee Sang's last letter. Claire is digging into Spokane marriage records and more DOD stuff on the 3 lads. Jer and I need to overcome our latest setback and return to scavenging and preparing for the auction.

CHAPTER 25

"Locating lost relatives to put on her mailing list for the auction has been Sara's task and I wonder if she has been successful."

"Did you keep in touch with the children that heard Uncle Paul tell The Chinaman's Story?" Claire says.

"No!"

"How about you, Jer?"

"Cousin Stella Nordling got married and has two daughters, they live in Minnesota. Timmy was KIA in the Korean War," Jer says with a cloud of doom hanging over him.

The twins moved with their father to Saudi Arabia. He worked for ARAMCO with Great Uncle Ernest until he retired, and then I lost track of them. Everyone else vanished or died.

"Mom keeps an address book she's good at sending out Christmas cards," I say, it comes out before I realize mom's not with us anymore.

I cut myself off, but it's too late. The old can of worms reopens with my slip. Jer and my estrangement has always been about my failure to attend to family responsibilities and my wandering ways.

"I know you've been reliving a traumatic time in your childhood and our reenactments are taxing your energy, but we have more to do," Claire says.

"After the reenactments," I say. "I understand that the childhood trauma drove me to a career of wandering the world."

"It's called escapism, ties to repressed memories."

Jer gets distracted when the conversation refocuses on mom.

My thoughts shift to Jer and I being the only ones still living who heard Uncle Paul's scary story that night on Big Black Rock. This revelation has a sad connotation. My guilt surges.

"At least Jer tried to stay in touch with some extended family, I did not."

"Dropping the self-pity might help," Claire says. "I'm looking forward to returning to the farm, so you and I can test that lovely featherdown bed I saw upstairs."

"That's Grandma Jonson's bed," Jer says. "See you both in the morning."

"Why is he so snippy?" Claire asks as Jer stalks off to his hotel.

"Just a spat between brothers."

Claire points out that Jer is also feeling guilt. It's soaking in that Connie and Jer shared in that second promise and that I do not bear the failure and responsibility alone.

"You both need to vent," Claire says, "but I'm also sensing and hearing a lot of joy in your childhood memories, don't lose sight of those precious moments."

So lovely and so insightful.

Back at Claire's home, we get ready for bed.

"I'm still looking forward to cuddling in that big featherbed."

I put a Brother's Four album on her record player, and we join in a warm embrace. Listening to the sounds of my favorite song.

"Come to my bedside my darling... lay your body soft and close beside me and drop your petticoat upon the floor".

"I love you doll," I say, transfixed by her silhouette as she turns out the light and her bathrobe glides to the floor.

I leave the warmth of Claire's bed, but with a smile on my face. It's raining heavily as my taxi drops me off at Seattle's Boeing Airport for the 6 am PST flight back to Spokane. She wanted to drive me but driving in hazardous slippery conditions is not her forte.

Jer strides across the airport lounge and hands me my flight ticket.

"These were waiting for us at the PSA counter."

"What's that strange smile all about?" he says, "must be Claire's influence."

Aboard the aircraft a flight attendant says, "Care for a beverage?"

"I'll take a Rainier," Jer says.

"Make that two."

He leans across the elderly lady seated next to

him as we settle into our first-class seats for the flight to Spokane.

"I've been a bit of an ass little brother," Jer says.

"Excuse my language!" he says to the lady.

"I need to apologize for snipping at Claire about grandma's bed," Jer says, "I wasn't around as much as I should have been when mom needed help."

Logs are loosening, sending a cascade of childhood memories into my consciousness at an incredible pace. I find this astonishing and confusing, as if someone is sweeping out the cobwebs and clutter before I can digest what they mean. It's up to me to sort through it all before it disappears into the dustbin.

Connie was on the right track, forcing Jer and me to be together when we opened her package. The key to understanding the family secret lies in her boys' reconciling. Now we must combine again. Break the barrier between two brothers that has existed for decades and has once more resurfaced.

The ice melts between Jer and me as we talk about how Connie's plan and our two escapees from Camp Harmony.

But the mystery remains even though we now know about the ruse, the secret reason behind Uncle Paul's Chinaman's Story. The second promise to Uncle Paul remains unfulfilled, and 50-year-old cold cases will not prove easy to solve. There are still loose ends to tie off if we are to keep the second promise. What happened to Franklin and Tinya in April 1943? Did Charlee Sang disappear after they got married, or was he killed in the war? Maybe Claire will find something from her DOD contacts.

My feelings of failure and guilt remain. But tempered and mixed with frustration as Jer and I head back to the farm to continue our scavenger hunt. We pursue clues to complete our new mission, with the added urgency of the auction being only two days away.

We fly the rest of the way back to Spokane in near silence. It helps that we are sitting across the aisle from each other.

Neither of us is in a favorable mood towards the task at hand of preparing for the auction on August 16. Mom's efforts to bring Jer and me together as a critical step in reuniting our shattered family have suffered a setback. Claire thinks we're petulant children. But her reminder to me when I left to remember all the childhood joys has uplifted me. I share it with Jer as we buckle up for landing.

CHAPTER 26

*August 14, 1992, Spokane
(Auction August 16)*

We walk from the baggage claim at Spokane Intermodal to the long-term parking lot.
Ironically, the same problem that created our tiff, shirking my family responsibility, is providing a resolution to our brotherly spat.

We pick up Black Beauty at the Cadillac dealer.

"Dibs on driving," Jer says.

We flip a coin. Jer gets in the driver's seat with an enormous smile on his face.

To gamble and win is easy, to live with loss is hard. Something Paul told us.

Jer fumbles with the ignition.

Reaching across the top of the steering column, I pump the choke twice. He grinds the gears, but I know better than to ask if he remembers how to drive a stick shift.

Sulking over Jer's admonishment for my wandering persists. I'm not over my disappointment at not being privileged to the secret details of 'the plan'. I tell

Jer that I feel that they duped me into playing my story-telling role. Not being included in the secret plan bugs him and me. Besides, as he has reminded me, he is a year older than me. The adults should have trusted him, if not me. Our not being let in on the family secret is what breaks the chill between us, and soon we agree to pursue our new mission.

Connie meant to tell her boys, but that was decades later. Her journals and the parcel she left for us with Sara Swenson was all about the family secret. But why didn't mom tell Jer and me about all this intrigue after the war was over, since all the Japanese prisoners left the internment camps?

We have our answer. Connie put together the package of tools for organizing us in our quest to discover what happened to our extended family. Then dementia intervened. Did she intend to share the family secret with us?

Grandma's crocheted tablecloth is on the kitchen table adorned by a vase of wilted flowers. I drop them in the trash bin under the kitchen sink.

I sit in silence, sipping a cup of French press, with my elbows propped on Grandma's kitchen table.

"Daniel Matthew mind your manners and remove your elbows from my table while eating!"

I jerk my elbows off the table.

Imitating grandma's voice is Jer's specialty. A chuckle follows, which soon turns into our sharing a moment of joyful laughter.

Vanishing with the warm biscuits is half a jar of delicious apricot marmalade from grandma's pantry.

My sense of family is being restored as Jer, and I restart our scavenger hunt in the attic.

"Mom always was smarter than either of us."

I smile and nod my agreement, adding, "Grandma too!"

"The Jonson's know how to keep a secret."

Reconciled for the moment, we return to scavenging. The auction begins in less than 48 hours, giving us a sense of urgency. Confronted by stacks of boxes and sundry memorabilia. We haul some of this stuff to Speke's Corner Store and put it in storage.

Claire calls from Seattle, and Jer puts her on speaker so I can join in.

"I'm sorry for my outburst at the airport," Jer says. "Daniel and I have Grandma Jonson's old feather bed ready for you."

Claire laughs and says, "Thanks, Jer. Father L, and I will arrive in Spokane the day before the auction."

"Somewhere between Puyallup and Spokane 'The Plan' went askew," Claire says, "That little factoid has been gnawing at me ever since our meeting."

She explains that it's the together part that just might lead us in the right direction. By thinking of Franklin and Tinya as a couple, Claire tells us it forced her to recognize that they would stay together no matter what happened. Franklin enlisting doesn't work. He wouldn't leave Tinya. Connie's 'The Plan' tells us they must have gotten married in early March 1942 after they disappeared from Camp Harmony. Further evidence that they would stick together.

"I called the Spokane County Courthouse Records Office, and they verified that they issued Opa Zhang and Franklin Sang a marriage license in March 1942," Claire says.

Something must have gone wrong with 'The Plan', between then and Spring 1943.

"Wait a minute," Jer says. "The timing is off. 'The Plan' was first hatched at the races in 1940. Escape from the authorities was in March 1942. So, why April 1943?"

There's no way Connie and the others knew of EO 9066 in late 1940 when they first discussed 'The Plan'. The authorities plastered posters all over Seattle and Tacoma, but not until February 1942. They ordered all Japanese people living on the Pacific coast to prepare to leave their homes and businesses.

It was the taunts at Red Square and in the community in 1940 that inspired 'The Plan', not the posters and the official relocation announcement.

The relocation posters confirmed their worst fears for their Japanese friends and caused them to put their plan into operation before they had their marriage license and fake identities established.

"EO 9066 came on February 19, 1942," Claire says. "That forced Franklin and Tinya to act on The Plan sooner than they may have expected. They had to escape from the relocation bus somewhere between Puyallup and Spokane if they were to get married."

"I'm okay with that," Jer says. "Connie could have revised the plan after EO 9066 and or after seeing the

Bainbridge News item."

"Something else went awry," Claire says.

The rest of the plan as laid out by Connie tells us that Franklin and Tinya were to get married in Spokane. Then pose as a Chinese couple living in the cabin for the duration. But they needed Charlee Sang's help to pull this off.

"I get it," Jer says. "That's why Charlee didn't show up in Bremerton to join Uncle Paul in enlisting in the Navy."

"That's true, and you and Daniel both told us that the smoke stopped in the spring of 1943," Claire says.

"The last time I saw smoke rising from the cabin was in the Spring of 1943 when I told the machete story, and the police came."

"My point," Claire says, "the pieces don't fit together."

Franklin and Tinya vanished after jumping off the relocation buses at Puyallup in March 1942. Assuming they got married in Spokane, they moved into the cabin for the duration, which we now know to be in Spring 1945.

Claire is right. It makes little sense. Franklin and Tinya disappeared a second time a year later when the smoke stopped, in April 1943.

"Check! Check! and Check!" Jer says, with a quizzical look. "So, what happened next to Charlee and to Franklin and Tinya?"

Our attention returns to finding out what happened to Charlee Sang. He disappeared after the marriage in March 1942.

Franklin Sang and Opa Zhang vanished again in April 1943.

"I called Major Nutting and asked him to search the DOD service records for Charlee Sang enlisting early in 1942 and for Franklin Sang enlisting in Spring 1943."

"So, you separated Franklin and Tinya?" I ask, "Why?"

"Meanwhile, something else is confounding me," Claire says. "The war wasn't over when Uncle Paul returned to Bremerton, so why did you continue to spread the tale of the Chinaman? You said you were spreading and embellishing even after the smoke ceased in Spring 1943 until Spring 1945."

"What's confusing about that?"

"Why didn't Uncle Paul ask Connie about Franklin and Tinya?" Claire says. "I don't recall him mentioning them at Bremerton. And why didn't he tell you to cease spreading the Chinaman's story?"

"Good questions."

"When he died, you blocked things out."

"If they left the cabin in the spring of 1943," Claire says, "why continue the ruse?"

"I see your dilemma."

"A ghost or ghosts seems to be our best alternative," Jer says. "Since Connie's been leading us all along, she's a prime candidate."

"I agree," Claire says, "Connie must have had something to do with the second disappearance of Franklin and Tinya, but what?"

I resist declaring victory. There is over one ghost operating in this mystery.

Franklin and Tinya moved into the woods in March 1942 and were not in the cabin after April 1943 when the smoke stopped.

"Could it be that Connie changed 'The Plan' and

moved them after the police officer came to the cabin?"

"Your proposition is that Connie may have moved the couple after the police visit."

"That would make it my turn to find an answer," Claire says.

I close my eyes, envisioning Claire's fabulous silhouette and feeling her warmth.

"There's that strange smile again," Jer says, shattering the mood.

Jer heads upstairs to take a shower, and I carry a load of stuff headed for storage out to the garage.

The kitchen wall phone is ringing with some urgency when I return from the garage.

"I restored Charlee Sang's last letter," Father L says in a deep, subdued tone. "It will be necessary to meet again and refocus our investigations on a completely new secret."

"Okay, my friend," I say, "What is this new secret from Charlee's letter that has you so upset?"

"Not over an unsecured line," Father L says, his tone ominous. "It must wait until I see you at the auction the day after tomorrow."

Father L's call lifts me out of the remnants of my self-pity state. Why is he worried about security? Now there's a new secret that he won't even talk about on an insecure phone line. He'll be arriving with Claire in less than 48 hours, I need to contain my curiosity. I turn my attention to the stack of storage items and the auction.

Jer stumbles down the stairs, rubbing his hair with a towel. He pours himself a cup of French press and says, "Who called?"

"Father L called to tell us he and Claire are arriving tomorrow and won't need a ride from the airport."

I assume that Father L doesn't want me to mention the new secret to anyone, not even Jer or Claire.

We continue reminiscing about our heritage as we trek back and forth to the garage with loads headed for storage.

Our game of ghosts resumes. One remaining mystery is a 'who done it' of a unique kind, and Jer and I attack it with gusto.

I read aloud a passage from Connie's journal about the Jonson's farm:

> After arriving by ship at Ellis Island, the Jonson's and Nordling's boarded the Great Northern and headed west. The Nordling's eldest son, Alex and his brother Dom found work in the logging industry north of Spokane. After a few months, they had a bit of cash saved up, which they shared with grandpa to help build the big barn, then the farmhouse. They were all excellent carpenters. First, they build a barn, then the farmhouse. They paint both in Falu red, mixed using grandpa's secret formula.

"I remember helping Uncle Paul with the refreshing of the house and barn with the Falu red paint," Jer says, "Christmas of 1940."

He explained how to restore the luster of the Falu red paint.

"Brush the surface and then add fresh paint."

"Uncle Paul told us that Grandpa kept the secret formula for mixing Falu red paint written on a piece of old parchment in his toolbox in the barn," Jer says. "Do you remember that too?"

"It's right here in Connie's last set of notes," Jer says. There is a secret recipe that comes from the Falun copper mine in the Dalarna region north of Stockholm. It's the only paint of its kind.

"This information tells us that whoever the ghost is that restored the paint on the farmhouse and the barn."

"They knew about the secret properties of Falu red paint," Jer says, completing my sentence.

"The mystery is about who did the recent brush-work."

Jer recalls how he and I helped the three lads built the cabins and refresh the Falu red paint on the farm-house and the barn in 1941.

"I'm considering Charlee as my candidate for the ghost who repainted the farm buildings," Jer says with a grin.

"A very astute observation," I say, "not a Swede, but he may have had the knowledge of the secret for-mula."

"I'm still curious about who was rummaging around in the attic and who oiled the ladder."

"Secrets abounded in our family," I say.

These ghosts and secrets still aren't providing an answer to Claire's dilemma. What happened to Franklin and Tinya in April 1943? Returning to family secrets has me refocusing on what happened to Charlee Sang.

"Charlee told us that all Asians look alike."

"White folks can't tell the difference between a Chinese and a Japanese."

"Uncle Paul told us not to pay any attention to

the newspapers and others that spread the bile and lies about the 'Yellow Peril'," I say.

"Always remember Charlee, Franklin, and Tinya are family and loyal Americans," Jer says.

"That's the same promise we made to Uncle Paul," I say. "That's no coincidence."

Connie's journal also mentions a fight Jer, and I had with Fat Teddy at the time of the Christmas family gatherings when Franklin, Tinya, and Charlee visited the farm.

"My dad says that 'Japs are Japs'. You Swedes are Jap lovers," Fat Teddy said with a sneer as he pedaled past our house with his gang every school day.

"Japs are Japs!" another boy says.

"The Jonson's are Jap lovers!"

The taunts echoed over and over from Fat Teddy and his gang as they rode by on their bicycles, hurling their ugly words.

"Fat Teddy must have seen the yellow ribbons on the ancient oak," I say to Jer. "He knew he was disrespecting our family."

"We shouldn't have knick-named him, Fat Teddy," Jer says.

"I shouldn't have defeated him at marbles," I say, and we both laugh.

One Friday, when the two of us came home from Grant Park with cuts and scrapes, I had a dandy of a shiner, and Jer's upper jaw was bleeding. Grandma knew what happened without asking. She told Jer to hold an ice pack on his swollen lip before taking a needle and thread and stitching the cut closed.

"Hold that beefsteak on your eye, Daniel," Grandma said, "and remember what your Uncle Paul taught you, sometimes you have to fight; but pick your fights."

Grandma, Uncle Paul, and Connie were right. Our extended family members are all proud to be Americans.

"So are we, my brother," Jer says, "So are we."

CHAPTER 27

Entering Grandma's kitchen in the darkness before dawn. We plan to get an early start on the Falu paint ghost and check out the barn for grandpa's secret formula before preparing for the auction.

Getting us back on speaking terms is step one. Claire interceded in our spat. Making it possible to move ahead. My admiration for Claire will never be adequate.

Looking through another of mom's photo albums, I eat my fill of warm biscuits and finish off the apricot marmalade. Now we need to find out what happened to Franklin and Tinya after they got married. While we await Father L's restoration of Charlee Sang's last letter and the new secret, we need to cooperate on the task at hand.

I thought more on fact-finding Sherlock Holmes's style, 'thinking backwards', realizing how backtracking and reenacting events led us to clues as to the whereabouts of lost family.

Critical to his investigative approach is an organized memory-attic. Not my forte.

Mom archived the happenings at family holiday

gatherings. An album entitled "Jonson Family Farm" is full of photos of every building and acre of the farm.

My respect for Connie is taking on a unique perspective since Jer agrees with me she may be the ghost.

Her snapshots of the Falu red farmhouse and barn, Big Black Rock, Uncle Paul's cabin, the Chinaman's cabin, family members, and neighbors. It's as if she knew things were changing, and she wanted a record of the way people were before the war.

"Are we being led by the rings in our noses?" I say to Jer as he pokes his head down through the attic opening.

"What was that you just said?" he says. "I found two double-sized crates marked 'Xmas decorations'. Want to keep them?"

Sliding the boxes down one at a time, I carry them into the garage for storage.

"Claire told me we were being led by a ghost at the start of this quest," I say. "I thought she was teasing me."

"Sounds reasonable to me," Jer says as he navigates his way down the slippery rungs with some difficulty. He misses a rung while climbing down.

"Damn!" He mutters, "This shaky old ladder won't hold up under my bulk much longer."

"Tsk and pshaw!" I say.

Cinching the belt on his trousers, he steps off the shaking ladder.

Dementia had upset Connie's efforts to devise a way to deliver the story and details of the secret plan to her two sons. But it hadn't deterred her. Jer and I can benefit from her example. We now know that mom was the planner. For me, that proves she is the prime candidate for being the ghost.

"My legs are cramping, and my back is killing me from all the bending over and lifting," Jer says. "What say we stretch our limbs and go on a ghost hunt?"

Connie may be my choice, but we still have multiple candidates for ghostly activities. The oiled ladder hinges add to the earlier evidence that someone rummaged around up here before we arrived. And there's the unresolved Falu red paint mystery.

"A ghost hunt," I say. "What a marvelous idea."

I'm looking at a photo of the barn in the 'Jonson's Farm' album. An excellent place to start our trek about the property in search of ghosts and answers.

"Let's assume that the ghost who refreshed the paint knew of the secret recipe for Falu red paint," I say. "I wonder if grandpa's old toolbox with the parchment is still in the barn."

"My money is still on Charlee's ghost as the culprit who refreshed the paint?" Jer says with a chuckle.

I put the 'Jonson's Farm' album in my backpack. We can use the pictures as our guide for our ghost hunt and trek around the farm. We are both laughing as we start our trek out of grandma's kitchen on the trail at the base of Big Black Rock. On our way to the barn, we pass the woodshed where we first saw a stack of cut firewood a few days ago, another ghost. This time, it sparks a memory in Jer.

"Connie's journals started me recalling how Grandpa dealt out punishment at the woodshed behind the barn."

He points at a five-foot willow switch hanging from a hook.

I can't believe it's still there.

Another not so secret family secret. We sense

that grandpa's specter is likely watching. Discipline was Grandpa Jonson's domain, and outsiders don't get to discipline a Jonson child, not even a church elder. Elder Thomas from our church came by the barn to get some baskets of apples. Jer and I were chopping wood and stacking it when I got a splinter. I swore and the Elder admonished me and reached for the willow switch. Jer stepped in, took the switch away from him.

Grandpa saw us and he came over and said to Elder Thomas, "Don't you ever lay hands on my boys."

What I'm feeling most is a memory of how close Jer and I once were.

We trek on to the barn. In the colder months, children and guests use the facilities in the barn. It's the source of many smells. Oats and hay for feeding the livestock, the cow dung and chicken poop needed cleaning daily, all familiar smells. On the top of the pile is wood with a fresh cut, green odor. The lower pile smells of rotting wood full of silverfish, termites, and earwigs. My chore is bringing in the right firewood, bug-free, into the house for grandma's potbelly kitchen stove.

The album has a picture of the outhouse; it comes to life as we approach the barn. As we step into the shed through the broken door, the toxic odor of lye and human excrement is overwhelming. The image is of two holes in a bench, hinged cover board and a loose shingle propped against the wall. A small shelf holds a stack of cut strips of newsprint and a peg with a soiled rag towel hangs on a wooden dowel next to the bench. The photo alerts Jer.

"Did mom ever tell you what happened to her in the outhouse?" Jer says.

"No!" I say, thinking another family secret and

wondering if he is about to reveal more evidence that mom's ghost has been leading us all along.

"The bathroom in the barn is the setting for Connie's worst nightmare, one that haunted her all her life," Jer says.

The stench remains, but it's not as strong today as the outhouse got replaced by modern toilets in the house and cabins a few years ago. In years past, in the Winter, everyone used the outhouse next to the firewood shed. It's closer to the farmhouse, so no one noticed Connie was missing from after supper until breakfast. She fell into the foul smelling and slimy pit and screamed until she had no energy left. Paul pulled her from the sludge the next morning.

"I can't imagine spending twelve hours in a smelly pit of excrement," I say. "What an incredible trauma that must have been."

Grandpa had wanted to punish her for being out overnight, reckoning she was misbehaving. She sometimes took a delightful storybook and a lantern up into the barn loft and fell asleep reading. That meant the willow switch; but Paul came to her rescue. She was 12 years old.

As small as he was at age 7, Paul couldn't tolerate his big sister receiving a switching after having been through such a horrible experience. He spread his legs and stood his ground in front of Grandpa, expecting the willow switch would be his fate.

"I wish we had a photo of that," Jer says. "Mom only told me her story a few weeks before dying."

In a rare lucid moment, mom told Jer she was too embarrassed to share her story and kept it secret all her life. I now understand why she developed a compulsion with being clean, taking baths, and changing clothes at every opportunity. I wonder why she told Jer after all these years and not me. Our family is rife with secrets.

"Mom also told me that one can keep a secret to a point where it ceases to be relevant."

"I get it," I say. "She was telling you the essence of a secret. If no one ever finds out, and you take a secret to your grave, is it a secret?"

"Claire thinks it took Connie a lifetime to uncover that horrid event," Jer says.

Once Connie recognized the source of her trauma, it became her deepest darkest secret until she could get beyond it and remember other things.

"Connie tried every day to remember what happened during the war," Jer says. "She was getting ready to tell you and I about the secret plan, but dementia got worse and stopped her."

He pauses for several seconds, then says, "Claire told me Connie may have been calling you in Africa the night she died, for the same reason."

I'm trying to reconcile why Claire never mentioned this to me. Claire has years of experience at keeping her client's cases confidential.

The difference between Connie's psychological trauma case and mine is that I have Claire helping me reenact the events that triggered my trauma while mom suffered in silence all her life until near the end when she gave the package to Sara Swenson and swore her to secrecy.

Connie's fear that she forgot things overwhelmed her in her last months. I'm glad Sara and Jer were there to share her story.

Connie's outhouse story has thrown me off as

regards one of our original objectives for searching the barn. Before leaving the barn, I glance at an object in the corner by the door. It stands out because they have brushed aside the hay and dust that covered it. It's grandpa's old toolbox, and it's unlocked. I lift out the tool tray and find the oilskin parchment. I unfold it and spread it on a wooden bench. It lists the secret ingredients for mixing Falu red paint along with a note on how to refresh the pigment.

"Charlee's ghost beat us here!" Jer says with an enormous grin.

"At least he or she left the parchment."

Apply the paint correctly the first time. Brush it every several years instead of having to add primer. Add fresh paint to restore the luster.

The mystery of the ghost who refreshed the Falu red paint remains unresolved. We leave the barn and trek through the crabapple and golden delicious apple orchards and past grandma's vegetable patch. The sickly-sweet stench of rotting apples and vegetables prevails. We trek on, past a few acres of Idaho potatoes that went unpicked, and another of grandma's vegetable patches, located near the farmhouse in a treeless patch to get the most sunlight.

The smells of the outhouse and the ever-present odor of rotting compost permeates our clothes. I recall the many times grandma said for us to wash up and change into clean clothes, leaving our dirty boots on the back porch before we came into her clean kitchen after doing chores.

Jer winks at me and points at a bed of strawberries and rhubarb in several rows at the base of the back porch. The squirrels are the only ones attending to them in recent times.

We grab an apple crate from a stack under the porch and fill it with what remains of the strawberries, rhubarb, and winter squashes. We did the same for grandma many mornings. Sometimes she left a handwritten list stuck to the refrigerator door of what she needed for her baking and meals for the day. Mom had taken a photo of one of grandma's records, stuck to the fridge. It listed strawberries and rhubarb stalks, the last of the season. This may be the closest we'll come to finding another lost secret, grandma's pie recipe.

"Grandma's strawberry-rhubarb pies were to die for," I say as we left our boots on the back porch.

Jer and I wash up with an old bar of '99 and 44/100 percent pure' Ivory soap and rinse off in the ice-chilly water in the galvanized sink next to the ringer washer.

I list all the secrets we Jonson's had. Secret red Falu paint formula, secret recipes for strawberry-rhubarb pie and the pie escapade, Connie's personal disaster at the outhouse in the barn ... and many more. I'm proud of Uncle Paul, Connie, Charlee Sang, and Grandma. They devised a secret plan that kept Franklin and Tinya safe from the authorities after EO 9066. All our extended family thrives on secrets.

Connie or her ghost has been leading us on our quest to investigate what happened to our extended family members during the Pacific war. Maybe she had intended all along to share the secret plan. But her sons had drifted apart, and one had wandered off to Africa. She didn't want us involved if the authorities discovered the ruse. That's where the police came in. She didn't want to share the secret plan until Jer, and I joined forces and rediscovered our love of family.

Maybe she couldn't share the outhouse secret. Not until the moment came when the repressed memory of that horrible event revealed itself before her dementia took over. She, too, had suffered from trauma and repression. She wandered to St. Louis and Chicago and Denver, distancing herself from the scene of her trauma, but unlike me, she never shirked her responsibility to her family.

Connie got frightened and challenged by diminishing capacity in her later years. I now realize that Claire was right from the outset of our investigation when she said someone is leading us.

Jer is also right. Where was I when most needed?

As I mull over Uncle Paul's last words about soliciting our promise to reunite the extended family after the war ends, Jer puts a fresh twist on my feelings of who's ghost is leading us.

Jer and I look at and revisit every photo in the album when we sit down at the kitchen table to take a break before continuing our trek around the farm. Another image shows Grandma and me, age 7, standing in the kitchen in front of her sink. It's labelled, 'Lesson learned'.

Grandma Jonson was a firm but gentle disciplinarian. She never raised her voice in anger. I remember what she was saying to me at that very moment. It came after I had made a smart-aleck remark that included the word damn. She did not tolerate profanity.

"Oh pshaw, Daniel Matthew," Jer says, mimicking grandma, "Get to the back porch sink and wash out your mouth with soap."

"The same bar of Ivory we just washed up with," I

say. "Damn, I never knew mom took that picture."

"Watch those damns!" Jer says with a laugh, "I think 'oh pshaw' was the harshest thing I ever heard from grandma."

"Grandma's punishments were more effective than the willow stick."

"Amen to that!" Jer says.

While waiting for a pause in the rain, I thumb through the last few pages of the 'Jonson's Family Farm' album. A photo marked 'All present, Christmas 1941' catches my interest. It depicts the adults in our extended family. Jer and I must guess who some people are. The faces are small and often turned sideways, laughing, drinking eggnog, and hanging ornaments on the Christmas tree.

"The only family member not in that photo is the family photographer," Jer says.

He's right, Connie's ghost is everywhere but not seen in any of these photos. She has been with us all along.

Now we know that Uncle Paul's aimed his secret at keeping Franklin and Tinya hidden from the authorities. He and Connie wanted them to live in peace and escape the horrid prospect of being sent to an internment camp. Claire has figured out that in April 1943, the smoke from the cabin ceased. This leaves us with the mystery, the second disappearance of Franklin and Tinya.

I turn the last page on the 'Jonson Family' album and fixate on a photo depicting a curling trail of smoke coming from the camp in the woods. The snapshot dated April 3, 1943, shows the ground covered in snow. Uncle Paul told the children not to be pestering the Chinaman whenever there was smoke, so we didn't. It was a matter of obeying our elders.

"The rain is easing, and we've still got an hour of daylight, what say we check out the Cabin in the woods for more ghosts?"

We put our boots and jackets on and return to the cool that comes with twilight in the spring months in these parts. We continue our ghost hunt from where we left off, behind the barn, at the fork in the trail that leads from Big Black Rock to the Chinaman's cabin.

"I smell smoke," Jer says.

"Stop with the jokes!"

"No joke!" he says, pointing in the cabin's direction. "Look, there's a faint trail of smoke rising over the woodlands, I can smell it, and see it."

Then, I, too, see it.

Even though curious, I hesitate.

"The smoke was a warning signal, telling trespassers to stay away," Jer says. "Now, I'm suggesting that you had the same first instinct regarding smoke and fire."

My hesitance to track the smoke through the woods to the cabin lent believability to my telling of the Chinaman's scary tale. Jer is suggesting that my hesitation is what Uncle Paul intended.

All the children in our neighborhood grew up

with billboards featuring Smokey the Bear pointing at us and warning us not to play with matches.

"Only you can prevent forest fires," I say, pointing at Jer.

Uncle Paul completed his cabin with the help of Charlee and Franklin during Fall 1941. The Chinaman's cabin remained unfinished when Paul and Charlee returned to university after the Japanese attacked Pearl Harbor. Uncle Paul then enlisted in the Navy soon after Christmas 1941. Charlee Sang disappeared. Franklin stayed behind to put the finishing touches on the cabin in the woods behind Big Black Rock. Then he returned to the JLS in Tacoma to be with Tinya. The first smoke rising from the Chinaman's cabin came in the Winter of 1942.

"Okay!" I say.

"Bear with me," Jer says with a grin. "Smoke in the forests of the Rocky Mountains has always been a sign of danger."

Together we remember watching the 'smoke jumpers' near Uncle Alex's ranch in Montana. They jumped out of an old twin-engine airplane and knifed through the cirrus clouds before their chutes opened and rescued them from certain death. Vultures circling over the mountain range, they slowly glided down, before steering for the nearby hangars at the Missoula airstrip.

"I get it," I say. "Our general fear of forest fires. Make that my fear. It was why Uncle Paul ended the Chinaman's story with a warning to stay away from the Chinaman's cabin if we saw any smoke trailing over the trees."

Jer explains that Uncle Paul was taking advantage

of an engrained fear children around here are all taught at an early age. Be careful with matches and campfires and all that Smokey the Bear stuff.

"Wouldn't it follow that if the children saw smoke, they'd report it to the fire department or police?" I say. "That's what Essie did after I told the machete story."

"It was Essie who called the police?" Jer says, "I never knew that."

"Yes," I say, "she told me later that she thought the smoke was from a campfire, so some kids went to investigate."

All this talk of family heritage and values, outhouse secrets and promises, ghosts, and red Falu paint recipes, Smokey the Bear, and now the smoke has me on full alert.

"Avast me hearty," Jer says, returning to his pirate character. "Let's check out who's stoking the fire at the Chinaman's cabin."

I remain hesitant but we continue our trek down the trail with the curl of smoke overhead.

"You're falling for your own story," Jer says with a grin. "That's what Uncle Paul wanted you to do."

CHAPTER 28

Continuing our trek down the path past the woodshed, we enter the south woods to investigate the source of the fire; Jer takes the lead. A ribbon of gray crowns the tops of the dense pines and spruces.

Fresh deep tracks from a drag sled run down the trail from the shed into the trees, toward the Chinaman's cabin. I'm expecting to run into a machete-wielding Chinaman and his fierce moon bear. They are real to me. Jer's laughter contrasts with my hesitance.

Drifting out of the chimney is smoke, coming from the open front door is a familiar tune.

"That's Benny Goodman's *'How High the Moon'*," Jer says as we get close.

The gas canister missing from the garage is on the steps. I pick up an axe propped against a tree and bury in a stump that serves as a chopping block. A Puyallup style drag sled is against the side of the house, still loaded with firewood. A shovel sticks out of a fresh mound of dirt next to a pit. Next to the hole lies a small coffin and headstone.

I feel as if I'm straddling a rolling log, trying to stay upright and keep from falling into the water, or in this case, the grave.

I've never been this to the Chinaman's cabin. I'm expecting an attack from a fierce protective moon bear.

"Anyone home!" Jer says.

"Be right out," a voice says, "I'm brewing some ho-jicha tea, care for a cup?"

"Make that two cups."

A ghostly figure comes out of the cabin's interior shadows stepping into the light of the doorway. He's carrying a tray with a pot and three teacups. He sets the platter down on the front steps. Steam rises from the pot, and he lets it steep.

He's an Asian man in his forties, fit, and about my height. Dressed in a plaid shirt with the sleeves rolled up to his elbows and a leather carpenter's apron. He's wearing knickers and knee-length socks and unlaced work boots, and he has a red and black bandana tied around his neck.

He smiles with a set of perfect white teeth as he hands us each a cup.

"Good morning, gentlemen," he says with a slight bow. "My name is Reggie Sang. You must be the Jonson brothers."

Duplicating his traditional Japanese bow, I say, "Sang is an unusual surname for someone of Japanese heritage."

He looks at me.

"The bowing part of your greeting," I say, "it's a sure giveaway that you're Japanese and not Chinese."

"Nice to meet you, Reggie Sang," Jer says. "Whatever your heritage, I'm Jer, and he's Daniel."

"My middle name is Yoshino," Reggie says.

My thoughts drift to Franklin, Tinya, and Samuel

Yoshino.

"You must be the only person in the world with that mixture of Japanese manners and a combined Japanese and Chinese name," Jer says.

"I believe you knew my father, Franklin," Reggie says. "He helped build this cabin many years ago with his friends, Charlee Sang and Paul Jonson."

"Are you related to a Charlee Sang?"

"Sort of!"

He has Charlee's looks, but he could pass for Franklin.

"I wasn't sure when you would arrive at the farm," Reggie says. "Perhaps not until the auction. I called several times to let you know when I was arriving, but the phone line was inoperative."

"I weeded the gardens and refreshed the paint on the house and barn so prospective buyers would find the property in good repair," he says. "Then I went to Lake Coeur d'Alene for three days."

Noticing he says refreshed, we know we are in the presence of one of our ghosts.

"Okay by me," I say, "but who taught you how to refresh Falu red paint?"

"I found an old parchment with the recipe for mixing Falu red paint and how to refresh it in a toolbox in the barn."

"Did you also rummage through the attic and leave the boxes in disarray?" Jer asks.

"I'm not the one who made a mess in the attic," Reggie says, "But I could use a hand to repair that rickety attic ladder, oiling it didn't fix it."

"Who told you about the house key over the rear door, or was that just a lucky guess?"

"My father told me to use the key above the back door to get into the house."

I'm stunned. Could Reggie's father be alive?

He explains that his goal was to do some cleaning, spruce the place up a bit. The electric power is off. But he thought he heard something up in the attic, and the ladder was down. He grabbed a flashlight out of his truck and climbed up and poked around. That's when he found an open box with a crocheted tablecloth.

"I thought the tablecloth would dress up the kitchen."

We are certain Connie was a key player in planning the secret, and I'm not yet ready to give up my version of the ghost theory in its entirety. One ghost to go. Who was rummaging in the attic?

I'm still in a state of surprise, stuck on my father told me.

Jer and I glance at each other. This Reggie guy is Franklin's son, he's for real, not the ghost we've been speculating about. Dare I ask if Franklin is alive?

"You said your father Franklin told you about the house key," I say, almost afraid of the answer, "Is he still alive?"

I focus on finding out about Franklin and Tinya in 1943 at the cabin and after the war.

"We've been looking for evidence of what happened to Charlee Sang and to Franklin and Tinya for several months," I say. "Our investigation ends abruptly in April 1943 when they all vanished."

"My father spent Christmas 1940 and 1941 at the Jonson family gatherings. Tinya was my father's nickname for my mother," Reggie says, "her actual name was Opa."

We knew this. So, I just wait while he gathers his thoughts. Franklin was 16, and Opa was 15 when they got married. Charlee Sang helped them get some forged birth certificates using Chinese surnames, Sang and Zhang. They got married in a Chinese ceremony in Spokane, then they moved into and lived in this cabin for almost a year.

"Tell us about 1943."

"I was born here in this cabin in the spring of 1943," Reggie says. "Franklin told me that Connie Jonson assisted him by purchasing tickets to take us on the Great Northern Railroad Line to Chicago and then transfer on to Boston."

Reggie explains how Charlee Sang went to Boston in early 1942 after the wedding to search for a man who might be his last living relative from Manchuria. Charlee called him Uncle Rabbit.

"I call him Uncle Zhang," Reggie says, "He owns the house and store in Boston I grew up in."

Charlee enlisted in the Navy while in Boston and shipped out to the European front in the Spring of 1942. When Charlee called Connie to tell him. There began a series of communications between her and the Zhangs. Later, when I was born, she figured that Franklin and I, being Japanese, would be safer back east living with a Chinese family, rather than here at the cabin.

Franklin turned 18, left me in Uncle Zhang's care, then he too joined the Navy.

"Wait a minute," I say, "Why would Franklin leave his baby and Tinya?"

"Excuse me I need to turn off the record player."

Reggie withdraws, reluctant to continue his story.

The Benny Goodman mood music has stopped, and the sound that comes from the old phonograph repeats ... the moon ... the moon ... the moon.

"Come inside and check out this beauty while I reset the needle on the record," Reggie says a few moments later. "I found a box of big band and swing era jazz vinyls in the attic and I took a few. Also found this classic old RCA Victor hand-cranked phonograph with a black bell horn."

"She's a beaut," Jer says. "I'll bet that horn is rhino."

He got the phonograph working with a few dozen cranks and some three-in-one oil. The sound was scratchy; he tells us he's played and replayed the Benny Goodman "*How High the Moon*" tune all morning.

I wondered why we hadn't heard it as sound carries from the woods to the farmhouse. But that must have been when the winds shifted, and we caught the smell of smoke and the sound of the music.

Jer glances at me with a told you so smirk on his face.

"When Daniel and I arrived, we noticed that someone's burying a box near the cabin," Jer says.

"On the day after I arrived," Reggie says, "No one was at home in the farmhouse, so I walked around the grounds. While passing the cemetery on the way to the cabin, I noticed a new urn and gravestone. The encryption read Connie Jonson, "*Loving daughter of Matilda and Charles Jonson. May she find peace!*"

Reggie tells us of the friendship between Franklin, Uncle Paul, Connie, and the Jonson family. Then he recalls they were also friends of his mother, Opa.

He goes silent, overwhelmed with grief for a second time.

"I have grave markers for Franklin's and Opa's stones," Reggie says. "Step outside and see them."

"Check this inscription under Opa's name," Jer says, "*Loving wife of Franklin, may our family reunite in paradise.*"

Etched into the stone marker with the name Franklin is the epitaph, "*Devoted husband of Opa and father of Reggie, Americans All.*"

"Thought it best to omit the surnames."

"Now, with your permission," Reggie says, "I need to keep a promise I made to my father to bury his and Opa's ashes here."

A third grave marker is leaning against a small coffin next to the hole in front of the cabin. It has a crescent moon carved into it, no name.

"Will you help me rebury Moonbear's remains next to Franklin and Opa?" Reggie says. "She will watch over my parents and protect them in the next life."

I want to ask about Tinya being Opa, but something stops me.

"Wait!" I say, "We can't do this, the auction conflicts with these burials."

It's the same problem that confronted Jer and me when we interred mom's urn in the family cemetery earlier. The law may require us to move the graves after we sell the estate.

"Altering the resting place of the spirits of any person or creature unnerves me," I say.

"Moonbear's not just a creature," Reggie says as he nods his agreement, and a tear flows down his cheek.

"I was born here in this cabin on April 3, 1943,"

he says so softly I can barely hear him. "My mother Opa died giving me life, right in this room."

April 3, 1943, coincides with the date when Connie's journals ended.

He recovers his composure and continues with his story.

Reggie's father often spoke to him of the farm and the Jonson family that adopted him and his best friend Paul, who died in the war. Franklin returned to Boston after the war with shell shock that damaged his memories.

He died a few months ago, and with his last breath, he said, "Promise me you'll bury Opa and me next to Moonbear."

"Paul used to say, a promise made is a promise kept."

"I dug up Moonbear's coffin this morning," Reggie says.

"We'll make these sacred burials happen," Jer says.
**

Now we know why Reggie returned to the family farm. Well, most of the story.

"Before he passed, he had a rare lucid moment this past Christmas," Reggie says. "Franklin and I were watching the Boston TV news about the President's apology to Japanese Americans interned during WWII."

He figured it was time to come out of hiding, to end our Chinese disguises.

Something we should have done long before. But I always followed my father's wishes. We both feared the authorities would punish the Jonson's for hiding him and Opa. The president's apology in the news canceled that fear.

"Uncle Zhang showed me a letter from a Ms. Sara Swenson, attorney at law," Reggie says. "The message announced that Connie Jonson had died, and the Jonson homestead in Spokane was coming up for sale at auction in August."

"It's my duty to fulfill my father's last wish," Reggie says. "But I suppose I can wait to bury their ashes until after the auction. At least that gives me time to contact a Shinto priest from town to bless the graves."

If we sell the property, will he be able to keep his sacred promise?

CHAPTER 29

The last albums from the attic comprise photographs of the gatherings of children at Speke's Country Store. While the kids bought nickel Cokes and licorice sticks, I elaborated on The Chinaman's Story. The girls preferred the red, the boys the brown or black.

"Licorice isn't licorice unless it's black," Jer says.

"The same smell as the anise oil grandma gave us when we had colds. That stink is why I prefer brown."

At every opportunity, I spread the tales of the mystery of the Chinaman, even at church after Sunday school.

"That's Uncle Al's Lutheran chapel in that picture," Jer says. "One Sunday, we were out behind the woodpile at the back of his church telling tales, chewing on our licorice sticks from Speke's Country Store. The church choirmaster caught us suspecting we were smoking cigarettes."

The elder asked what we were doing.

"You told him we're eating licorice and catching up on the neighborhood gossip," Jer says, "That reply almost got you a lashing, gossip is a sin and all. And I think he said licorice and chewing gum were also sins."

"What I recall best," I say, " is what you said that church elder, not to be laying a switch on my brother Danny."

"The skinny kid in this photo is Jimmy Lee Speke," Jer says as he points at another photo.

Jimmy Lee is holding a book of Audubon's bird drawings open to a picture.

"What's your interest in a sketch of a red-headed woodpecker?"

Jimmy Lee told us that his dad changed the family name from Wang. It happened after visiting a Chinese takeout restaurant in the village of Speke. It's on the Mersey River near Liverpool, England. Travelling from Shanghai to America, that was Poppa's first stop.

I asked him what Speke means, suspecting it was a proper name. It means woodpecker in Gaelic or Anglo-Saxon lore.

"The taller lad next to Jimmy Lee in the photo is his brother, Joshua," Jer says. "Reading and talking about airplanes and flying was all he did from as early as I can recall. He helped you and I build a replica of Captain Eddie Rickenbacker's WWI Spad XIII biplane."

"We hung it from the ceiling in our room."

We are in synch, both wondering the same thing.

"It won't appear by magic or find itself," Jer says as he cinches up his belt and climbs up the attic ladder.

An hour of banging around up there, and dozens of bumps and curses later, he makes another less than a graceful trip down the rickety rungs to the kitchen. He has the grin of a Cheshire cat.

In the loft, he found more photos of the Speke's in a box labeled 'Christmas's Past'. One picture is of old man Speke standing in front of his country store, with Joshua standing to his left wearing the uniform of the Royal Canadian Air Force. Another photo is of Private Jimmy Lee dressed in Army greens.

"That was the last time we saw Joshua before his RCAF wing went to Dover," Jer says. "His Mosquito got shot down over the English Channel."

Wrapped in tissue paper is the old Spad model. It's in excellent condition.

"That same weekend Grandma finished canning a large batch of her apricot and strawberry preserves. And you and I took three dozen Mason jars to Speke's country store."

We made that five-block journey nearly every day. Riding the dirt road to the intersection with the closest paved street. It was a bumpy trip for a beat-up red wagon or bicycle. We traded with Old Man Speke for Cokes and root beers and licorice sticks.

"When a Western Union boy wheeled up on a bicycle, word of Joshua's fate came in the form of a telegram," Jer says in a reverent tone.

Jer and I are thinking we need to visit the 'Wall of Honor'.

"I'll drive," Jer says.

"Let's walk. I saw the red wagon in the garage," I say, "A few squirts of 3 in1 oil and it should be good to roll."

"Let's pack a box of these photos and the Spad model and cart them up to Speke's in the wagon," I say.

We hope Oldman Speke will add these photographs and the Spad to the memorial wall.

An elderly man stands grinning as Jer and I pull our wagon into the parking lot. It's as if he's expecting us. I would estimate he was in his 90s, with thick spectacles and several strands of overlong hair on his chin, his version of a beard. He still stands straight and appears much the same as when I last saw him fifty years ago. He offers us tea, and we sit at a small round table next to the 'wall of honor'.

Our visit to Speke's turns into a reenactment. The photographs on the wall bring back reminiscences, including when Uncle Paul said, "If you want to learn who an actual hero is, check out 'the wall of honor' at Speke's and talk to the whole family."

A picture of a Mosquito in flight with RCAF markings on the wings hangs over the cash register. It depicts the pilot in an oval; next to the photo are several RACF medals, including the Distinguished Flying Cross. There is a star-shaped gold medal with a tiny silver star in the center, several campaign ribbons, and insignias, the highest rank being Flight Lieutenant. These decorate the south wall of Speke's store, a shrine to Flight Lieutenant Joshua Lee Speke. Joshua served as a pilot with the RCAF for two years before the Americans entered the war against the Nazis. They never recovered his body from the channel waters.

A second photograph depicts a young 17-year-old Army Private. He stands at attention with a fixed bayonet on his rifle and with an American flag draped over his shoulders. Backdropped by a beach littered with bodies tangled in rolls of barbed wire, burned-out half-tracks, somewhere far away from the fertile lands along the Spokane River valley.

I was twelve when I first asked Oldman Speke about the medal in the glass case. At the center of the exhibit, there is an official letter with a USA Presidential Seal and the signature of Franklin Delano Roosevelt. The words tell of "extraordinary heroism under enemy fire and valor".

Oldman Speke read the letter aloud, "PFC Jimmy Lee Speke ... saved the lives of his platoon when he displayed extraordinary courage braving heavy enemy mortar and machinegun fire without regard for his personal safety."

He paused, unable to continue as tears welled up in his eyes.

"Jimmy Lee's Congressional Medal of Honor."

Today as Jer and I visit Speke's Country Store re-enacting those memories, I think about that Medal of Honor and the tributes on the wall. I'm thinking to myself how brave old man Speke was to have suffered and survived the loss of their sons while caring for his invalid wife and raising a daughter. How courageous they all were, to endure insults and humiliation, as they maintained their loyalty to America. Only to have the Japanese attack Pearl Harbor and extend their land grab from China, the Speke's former homeland. War took an enormous toll on this family of Americans years before we heard President Roosevelt's speech on the radio at the Jonson farm on December 7 of 1941. They are Asians, but they are of Chinese heritage, not Japanese. All Asians look alike flashes into my brain once more.

Jer and I don't say a word to each other, but our thoughts are in synch. How unjust and agonizing those taunts of disloyalty must have felt to the Speke's. In the lower right corner of the wall of honor is a yellowed and aged tintype, a black-and-white wedding picture of Old-man Speke and his wife. I thought to myself, that was one memory likely never to change for him. The Speke's survived and escaped from the same horrors as Charlee Sang. They were also of Manchurian heritage, never threats to America, they are proud Americans.

My thoughts return to Charlee Sang's family, slaughtered by the Japanese occupiers in Manchukuo years before Pearl Harbor. No wall of honor for Charlee, hell, no family. He was an orphan until he came to the farm for our Christmas gathering in 1940. We still have unfinished business. I'm glad Reggie informed us that Charlee was not an orphan and he reunited with his Uncle Rabbit.

We give Oldman Speke the photos Connie took of his sons from Christmases past. Then Jer gives him the replica of the Spad that Joshua made for us.

"These are for your 'Wall of Honor'," Jer says.

"The auction starts at noon today," I say to Mr. Speke as we are leaving the store, "Please come and bring Angie and the kids."

We walk out of the parking lot at the country store, pulling our wagon of supplies.
Oldman Speke's stories of his sons Joshua and Jimmy and their medals of valor and Uncle Paul's Purple Heart Medal soon couple in our memories, and we realize the wisdom Uncle Paul had shown at Bremerton.

"That was when mom smiled, and Uncle Paul put the medal back in his footlocker and said, heroes do not need medals," Jer says.

This marks a near end to our scavenger hunt, and we soon turn our full attention to family and guests for the auction.

CHAPTER 30

I'm still wrestling with the dilemma of the auction versus relocating graves and a home for Reggie's family. Reggie joins Jer and I in the farmhouse as we unload the supplies from the wagon and store them in the pantry.

Sharing photos with Reggie, we find some with relevance to the mystery of the Chinaman and the mysterious disappearances of Charlee Sang, Franklin, and Tinya. Reggie fluctuates between excitement and bursts of tears as we go through an album labeled, 'Franklin Yoshino'.

Reggie tells us how his father Franklin, at age 13 or 14, first met Paul in Seattle at the Japanese Language School, where he taught English as a second language. He points out the JLS sign in the background of the image.

Reggie might shed some light on what happened in April 1943 when smoke last rose from the cabin until when the war ended in 1945 after Uncle Paul died. Our quest to learn the fates of extended family after they disappeared for the second time in April 1943 is still incomplete.

"Franklin was too frail to travel even though he wanted to come home to the farm. But that presidential apology drove me to fulfill my father's last request. He hoped for a burial beside Opa and Moonbear at the Jonson farm."

"Let's head for the living room," I say.

Hanging over the fireplace is the 3 lads painting Jer, and I had quibbled over. Reggie recognizes his father. Franklin is the lad to the left of Uncle Paul on the Montlake Cut Bridge. What I notice is the strong family resemblance between Franklin and Reggie, the same broad toothy smile. One minor mystery solved.

"I'll bet that painting is from when Charlee and Paul made the freshman crew team at UW," Reggie says. "See the scull crew rowing in the water beneath the bridge."

Reggie tells of a day he sat with Franklin on the south bank of the Charles River near Boston University and Harvard. He got excited as they watched a race between coxed 8-man shells. Franklin said he had only one genuine regret in life, that he had never crewed for the Washington Huskies.

"He admired and envied Paul and Charlee," Reggie says.

I unwrap another of Father L's restorations. A photo of Opa and Moonbear. The smile leaves Reggie's face. He touches the cheek of his mother, seeing her image for the first time.

"Opa died giving birth to me," Reggie says, fighting back his emotions. "You must tell me everything you know of my mother."

"You have my promise."

Interrupting our reminiscing over memories and photos is the infernal ringing.

"The Department of Defense calling for a Professor Daniel Jonson."

"Professor Jonson here."

"Please hold one moment for Major Nutting."

"Professor Jonson," a crisp voice says, "Major Nutting of the DOD, I have Doctor Parsons with me on speaker in my office."

"Daniel, Samuel called me this morning," Claire says, "he found the Captain's logbook page in a box of memorabilia he hadn't opened since Mikki's death."

She describes it as a lined sheet dated May 15, 1925, most likely a duplicate traced from the captain's log of an American steamship run by the Matson Lines. In the margin of the page is a hand-written note, "I am an orphan, please take care of me."

"Samuel says he'll bring the log page with him to the auction," Claire says. "Meanwhile, I'll read to you from the copy he sent me of the Captain's Log of the SS Manulani.

1) Day 2 out from Honolulu. Steamed east, leaving the big island of Hawaii in our wake. 10 km east of the island of Hawaii.
2) A passenger, Mrs. T. Hito, gave birth to a baby boy an hour after sunrise, 0605 hours on May 17, 1925.
3) Mrs. T. Hito died of complications. Burial at sea at noon on May 18, 1925. Three hours east of Honolulu. No boy should be without a name, I shall call him Franklin.

"No wonder you found nothing in the DOD ser-vice records under Franklin Yoshino or Franklin Sang," I say.

"Major Nutting and I went back into the DOD records this morning and did another search of 1943 enlistment."

"Petty Officer Franklin Hito is an American citi-zen," Major Nutting says. "He was born aboard an American ship at sea within the 12 nautical mile limit of the USA territory known as the Hawaiian Islands."

"When I was very young, I remember seeing the name Hito stitched on his fatigues when he came home to Boston," Reggie says. "When I asked him about it, he told me that was a story for another day."

"Wouldn't that mean that your actual name is Reggie Hito?"

"No," Reggie says.

Franklin never told him about his Japanese heri-tage until President Bush's apology. I had assumed that Franklin, being an American citizen at birth, would have been exempt from being sent to a Japanese intern-ment camp until Claire informed me otherwise.

"Besides, as Claire put it in her report," Jer says, "Franklin would not have deserted Tinya under any cir-cumstance."

"Franklin Hito's military service records verified his American citizenship," Claire says. "But his Japanese heritage would still have made him a target for EO9066 internment, as I noted in my report."

Major Nutting informs us that the DOD records reveal that artillery rounds sank PO Franklin Hito's ship off the coast of Italy. As the war ended in Europe in

1945, they evacuated him to Bethesda Naval Hospital in Maryland with a severe head wound that impaired his memory.

"PO Franklin Hito's records list an Uncle R. Zhang of Boston and a son Reggie Sang as his next of kin when he enlisted in the Navy," Major Nutting says. "Those surnames were proof enough that we had the right records for Franklin."

"Reggie's been telling us about his father Franklin for the past few hours," Jer says. "He's with us here at the farm in Spokane and listening."

"Reggie Sang, Franklin's son, is with you in Grandma Jonson's kitchen," Claire says, pausing. "I'm so excited. May I speak to him?"

"Hello, Doctor Parsons," Reggie says, "I heard from Daniel and Jer that you've been crucial to their investigations."

"We will meet at the auction," Claire says. "Meanwhile, may I welcome you to what I too call my family."

Her family, I thought. Yes.

Then I thought, I know little of the Parsons, only that she had a brother. I must remedy that.

"See you all at the farm for the auction, " Claire says. "I can't wait to meet you."

CHAPTER 31

March 1942

After escaping from Camp Harmony, Opa and Franklin found a local Spokane judge who married them. Reggie shows us his copy of the Spokane County marriage license, which reads Franklin Sang and Opa Zhang, listing their race as Manchurian. Did the marriage judge's benevolence prevail, or was their deception that good?

Moving into the Chinaman's Cabin with Opa, Franklin remained there until April 1943. After they escaped from the authorities, they did not dare to contact the Yoshino's or the other orphans for fear of being caught. This fits with why Franklin never told Reggie about the Hito surname.

"Opa became pregnant, and in early Spring of 1943, she gave birth," Reggie says.

"I believe a local doctor delivered me," Reggie says, "Here in the cabin, but he could not save my mother's life."

Connie's journal ending in the spring of 1943 and the smoke ceasing to come from the cabin in the woods are no longer a mystery.

"Wow! You're on edge," Jer says, as he reaches the phone before me.

"It's for you, Reggie."

Who knows Reggie is at the farm?

"Hello!" Reggie says as he cups his hand over the phone, turns to me. "It's Winnie, my wife."

"Winnie's arriving with our twins tomorrow," Reggie says. "She won't take my word for it, wants to hear you say it's okay for them to move into the cabin with me."

"Greetings, Mrs. Sang, I'm Daniel Jonson," I say. "The Chinaman's cabin is as much Reggie's as anyone else's. There's a lot of his father Franklin in every log. I look forward to meeting you and your children."

Sara Swenson and her staff have made calls and sent letters to everyone in the family. She also has a list of potential buyers for the auction on August 16, 1992. She includes directions to the Jonson farm on 9th Street in Southeast Spokane, two miles from Grant Park. Property Description: Large 5-bedroom two-story house, full barn fresh paint, two log cabins on 200+ acres of rock cleared farmland suitable for apple orchard, potatoes, and other crops. Local schools are excellent and shopping nearby.

"This farm is the hub of our childhoods," I say to

Jer. "Big Black Rock, the Falu red farmhouse, the cabins. Plus, all the memories are irreplaceable, ghosts and all."

"So, why are we selling the place?"

"I don't have an excellent reason," I say, adding, "But the Sang family poses a fresh twist. What about the cemetery? Where will they live after the auction?"

"Maybe they're only planning on visiting," Jer says.

"This farm is a spiritual venue to you and me," I say.

"And to Reggie," Jer says. "He's bringing his family all the way from Boston to fulfill his father's dying wish and to reunite with his extended family at the place of his birth."

Reenacting much of my childhood and in the process discovering the secret reason for the Chinaman's Story. Claire has led us as much as Connie. These restored memories have increased the importance for Jer and I, of keeping our promises and reuniting our family. When we sell the farm, there will be no hub for the next generation no place for a family gathering for Christmas.

CHAPTER 32

Auction Day

August 16, 1992

A dorning the ancient oak tree with yellow ribbons as proud symbols of Uncle Paul and Charlee Sang serving their nation has a different meaning for Jer and I this morning. The postman drives up with his white light flashing on the roof of his red, white, and blue Jeep.

"This could be my last deliveries to the Jonson farm," he says as he walks across the front lawn and hands me a package.

I sit on the front porch swing and stare at the unopened parcel. Pondering whether the ghosts have a say in what happens next. I imagine that mom is on the porch swing with me, and I'm flashing back to the spring of 1945. Many deliveries came to this location. I'm still thinking about what I told Jer, this homestead is a spiritual venue.

Tearing down the Hunt Realtor's sign, AUCTION TODAY, crosses my thoughts. Instead, I straighten it and pound it further into the ground by the gigantic oak. I pause and glare at it. The sign symbolizes what troubles me, it's about selling the farmhouse, barn, cabins, and orchards. I'm surrounded by sad and happy visions.

During our scavenger hunt, we have checked one photo after another, recalling most of the children we grew up with and what we remembered best about them.

My childhood once more competes with other memories for space in my conscious mind.

Then it comes to me why I had first objected to the sight of the auction sign in the front yard.

Staring at the ancient oak as depicted in the photo, I fixate on the yellow ribbons, with the ice truck parked close by. I recover it from the kitchen.

Mail, ice, ice cream, milk, and book deliveries were all made right here by the ancient oak.

Grandma and mom had tied the big yellow ribbons around the oak when Paul and Charlee shipped out for the Pacific War. I remember that mom untied one of the yellow ribbons from the oak tree the morning she got the official envelope from the Navy.

"No wonder the auction sign is so offensive."

"It's sacrilege!" Jer says. "Two yellow ribbons, I can't look at the venerable oak and not see them."

We share a second glimpse at the image on the cover of mom's 'Deliveries' album. It features the enormous oak tree in our front yard, which has two ribbons tied around its trunk. Children's bikes lie sprawling all over the front lawn, a tangle of wreckage.

"Yellow ribbons appear gray in a black-and-white photo," Jer says.

Thinking once more about the mailman delivering the official letter from the Navy, informing grandma and mom of CPO Paul Jonson's return home. Connie is untying a single ribbon from the old oak tree. There is no caption, but I remember seeing her cry the day after CPO Paul Jonson died. Who took the photograph?

"I don't recall when mom took Charlee Sang's ribbon down, do you?" I ask Jer as I show him the photo.

Jer shakes his head.

Uncle Paul's face is shimmering in the firelight atop Big Black Rock in the photo on the cover of a thick scrapbook labeled 'Paul'.

I have assumed that CPO Paul Jonson contracted a virulent form of malaria while in Subic Bay in the Philippines.

A news clipping in the scrapbook reads: Gen. Douglas MacArthur had a predicament in May 1943.

> "This will be a long war if for every division I have facing the enemy I must count on a second division in the hospital with malaria and a third division convalescing from this debilitating disease!" MacArthur was less worried about defeating the Japanese, than about failing to beat the Anopheles mosquito.
> 60,000 US troops died in Africa and the South Pacific from malaria. US Forces could succeed only after organizing a successful attack on malaria. 500,000 cases in US Army; over 110,000 and 90 deaths in Navy and Marines. Dependency on quinine as the only antimalarial later gave way to chloroquine.

Several more faded newspaper articles are pasted onto pages in the album.

A Spokesman-Review obit reads, "CPO Paul Jonson, 1938 graduate and track star from Spokane H.S., member of UW freshman skull team, Navy veteran and purple heart recipient, dies at Bremerton Naval Hospital."

The clippings and that General MacArthur quote reinforce what I had sensed back in 1945 and reenacted when Claire and I visited Bremerton. A solution to the mystery of Uncle Paul's illness. I hand the articles to Jer.

"Mom knew all along that he was dying when we visited him at Bremerton," Jer says.

In genuine Swedish tradition, no family member spoke of Uncle Paul's illness. I think to myself the world knows nothing of this man who was so important to our extended family and to Jer's and my childhood. I may write a story about him.

Peeling away the onion layers of the mystery of his illness, I lapse into my feelings of guilt as I recall the two yellow ribbons, one for Uncle Paul, one for Charlee Sang.

We know CPO Jonson died but until now not what killed him. My recall returns me to Bremerton when Uncle Paul said that Charlee Sang's last letter will help us find Charlee after the war. We don't know what happened to Charlee Sang, and his last message is still missing.

Jer and I return to our scavenger hunt. Photo albums continue to slow our progress to a crawl. Albums of music enliven our pursuit, but boxes of books slow our efforts. We search on. The auction nears.

We discovered the two yellow ribbons we had found earlier and tied them around the old oak. Back on the porch, we sit and front swing and admire our handiwork. That brings a smile to Jer's and my faces.

"Better?"

"Much better," Jer says, adding, "What's in the package?"

CHAPTER 33

August 16, 1992,

approaching high noon

J er and I are still on the porch swing admiring our handiwork when a white Lincoln sedan crunches into the driveway and skids to a halt. The first arrival for the auction is Father L, who walks around the car to hold the passenger door open. Stepping out of car is an elegant lady, one very shapely leg at a time. Her immaculate white suit shouts class and wealth. She shakes out her long auburn locks with fresh light blue highlights with a flick of her head. Adjusts her huge, blue-rimmed sunglasses and the single strand of pearls around her neck.

Jer looks at her, and without taking his eyes off her, he says loud enough for her to hear, "This elegant lady knows how to make a theatric entrance."

Claire is laughing as she glides up to Jer, embraces him, and gives him a royal buss on the cheek.

"Why doesn't your brother Daniel have the fine level of appreciation you have."

"I love the blue," I say, sensing that my compliment is too little too late.

Brushing aside my late accolade, she says,"Remind me Daniel, why are you selling this fabulous estate?"

I can't come up with a plausible reason now any more than when Jer asked, but she knows what I'm thinking.

"This venue is sacred," I say.

She points at the parcel which the postman delivered as if she knows something I don't know. I notice the return address on the box, Heidi Pitre, New Orleans, LA.."

Now that's eerie.

"Open it," she says.

Jer glances over my shoulder as I unwrap the parcel. It contains a portrait of Connie Jonson holding the copy of "*Black Beauty*" in her lap.

Who took Connie's photo?

A card enclosed in the package reads, "A gift for my sons. Think backwards and never stop telling stories. Love Mom!"

"Nothing ghostly about that," Jer says with a laugh.

"The portrait is fabulous," Father L says as he makes his reappearance after parking the Lincoln in the driveway.

"Surprise!" Claire says, "Jer told me you didn't find any photos of Connie during your scavenger hunt. Father L and I found a copy of Connie's driver's license when I checked into the Spokane County Records Office."

The next person to arrive for the auction is Clem

Clawson, the auctioneer. He drives up and gets out of his mint 1957 Chevy station wagon. He's an antique car buff and has coveted the old La Salle for years.

I greet him and introduce him to Claire, Father L, and Reggie.

"Damn, you look familiar," Clem says as he shakes Reggie's hand. "A ghost from the past."

Reggie, taking no offense, responds, "I'm Franklin Yoshino's son, Reggie."

"I recall a Franklin," Clem says. "Let me see, he was one of Paul's friends who visited December 1941 when the Japs attacked."

Clem Clawson is a distant relative whose parents immigrated to America around when the Nordling's and Jonson's arrived. Clem is a balding little man with the look of an accountant. Eyeglasses propped halfway down his significant nose. A total introvert when not talking at machinegun speed while rattling off bids at auctions. He is the only auctioneer on the south side of the Spokane River.

A few onlookers are parking across the Street, one being Mr. Speke from the corner store and his family, and two men in suits from Hunt Realtors Agency. Sara Swenson, our family lawyer, arrives with one of her junior partners to check out the paperwork for the sale once they consummate it. She hands Clem a list of 7 potential buyers. Father L, Reggie, and I assist Clem with the setting up of two dozen folding chairs and a small auctioneer's podium and table on the front lawn under the oak tree. Clem pulls his silver gavel out of a briefcase and places it next to the podium. It's the tool of his trade.

"Before the real bidders get here," Father L says.

"Let's get some of that delicious Kenya AA and find a quiet place to talk."

He gestures for Claire, Jer, and me to join him, then he includes Reggie.

"I have an urgent matter to discuss with you all before the auction."

We gather around Grandma Jonson's kitchen table.

Father L explains how he cleaned off the mold and used a new laser tool to restore the damaged segments of Charlee Sang's last letter.

"Charlee Sang's heritage has a disconcerting element we must speak about in strictest confidence," Father L says, glancing around before continuing. I'm thinking this man knows how to set up a story and raise my blood pressure.

"I'll read you the letter," Father L says as he lays out the photo-enlargement copy he has made.

"The first part of the letter affirms a lot of what we already know about Charlee Sang's heritage, but the rest reveals a story about something he has likely hidden somewhere on the farm."

Why doesn't he just hand us copies?

"As I read the restored letter aloud, you'll see what alarms me."

To: Paul & Connie
From: Charlee Sang, March 24, 1942
To Paul, I need to apologize for not being able to join you in Bremerton at the Navy enlistment post; however, I hope you will understand. I've only this morning received news of my Uncle

Zhang. I thought the Japanese Army killed him at Marco Polo Bridge. My Uncle Rabbit survived the toxic gases inflicted on the populace by the Japanese occupation forces and is living in Boston. I'm headed back east to visit him and intend to enlist in the Navy in Boston.

It looks as though my orphan days are over. But I will always be a Jonson.

To Connie: I fear that by the time this letter catches up with Paul in the Pacific, I will be back east, so I'm also writing to you. Please convey the contents to Paul when you get his Fleet Post Office (FPO) address.

I'm entrusting you with a secret letter my father gave me as I will soon enlist and don't have a safe place to hide it. Franklin and Paul helped me translate the letter written in Japanese. It's an authorization by Japanese Emperor Hirohito to use chemical weapons against the people of Manchukuo. If I'm unable to recover it after the war, you will find it hidden under a protecting moon. Do whatever your conscience dictates with the letter. I trust you.

Hope to visit next Christmas for the family gathering. Your friend and brother, Charlee."

Signed, Oar #7.

"Wonderful," Claire says.

Reuniting with his Uncle Zhang, means Charlee isn't an orphan. He enlisted in the Navy in Boston; he left Connie a secret letter and a parable. It's a lot to take in.

"We all need to proceed with caution about this Emperor's secret letter," Father L says. "Claire, be careful with how you deal with the DOD."

Father L adds that we should make no calls to each other about the letter and no mail couriers.

"The Emperor's secret letter suggests horrific war crimes by the Emperor and his officers in Manchukuo, including Colonel Chō in the 1930s," Father L says.

"The part about a secret Japanese letter hidden under the protection of moon," I say, adding, "That parable is the 'new secret' you mentioned."

Father L nods.

"Under the protection of moon," Claire says. "Who's good at allegory?"

Father L informs us of his historical research on Manchukuo and the Japanese occupation during the 2nd Sino-Japanese War. He confirms some details about Charlee's escape in the 1930s. He also learned the names of Emperor Hirohito and the Japanese Army officers in command in Manchukuo, a Prince Asaka, and a Lt. Colonel Chō.

"I just looked at the list Sara Swenson gave to Clem," Father L says, "the surname Chō is on her bidder's list for today's auction."

Learning of the earlier alert, we now have a full-blown danger signal. This can't be mere coincidence.

"Meanwhile," Father L says, "I've started a contact with a colleague to do some further investigating into the Chō's and to check into that intrusion at the Jonson's farmhouse attic."

Jer and I swap glances.

The Emperor's secret letter is a startling revelation.

Father L has clarified that it has dangerous implications for the safety of our extended family. He states with confidence there is a link between the break in at the farmhouse and the Chō's wanting the Emperor's Secret Letter. They think it's hidden on the Jonson's farm, the last known whereabouts of Charlee Sang, son of Sang Lee Chuyen.

"I knew that intrusion was relevant," I say, "you're telling me it wasn't a ghost?"

The auction takes on new significance.

Ten minutes before the auction starts, a twenty-something woman wearing a badge around her neck that reads PRESS shows up with a cameraman weighted down with equipment.

"Hi Professor Jonson," the reporter says, as she runs her fingers through her blonde hair. She adjusts her Ray-Ban wire-rim spectacles. "I'm Sammie Danish of the Spokesman-Review."

"May I take ten minutes of your time before the auction? I wish to ask you some questions about how long the farm has been in your family and about your Swedish ancestry."

I'm still trying to get a grip on the new secret and Father L's warning of the danger it poses, so I'm nervous about the press and her interest in the farm.

Before I can answer, she pops another question. It reveals her real interest for which she seeks an answer.

"I have a source who informs me they used the cabins on the Jonson farm as part of what they describe as an underground railroad for Japanese hiding and escaping the authorities and EO 9066 back in the 1940s," Sammie says.

Sticking a hand-held recorder close to my face, she says, "Care to comment?"

The press is here to get a story that ties in to the 50th anniversary of Pearl Harbor and the Presidential apology to Japanese Americans. This aroused Sammie's attention, and she's tracking down a rumor, hoping to uncover a story that might make the headlines.

I envision the headline, "Spokane family part of 1940s underground railroad".

I rise from my seat on the front porch swing; but get distracted by the crunch of tires on the gravel driveway. A long black Cadillac limousine with the name Chō Enterprises in gold letters on the side glides to a stop.

"Chō, isn't that the Japanese Colonel's name you just mentioned?" I say as I look around to find Father L, but he is nowhere in sight.

A uniformed chauffeur adjusts his hat as he walks around the limo. The right rear window powers down, an arm gestures for the chauffeur to wait, then the window closes. I assume the passenger is talking to someone else in the rear seat he doesn't want me to see.

Jer stands beside me on the porch as more cars arrive and deposit people for the auction.

"Care to comment?" Sammie says returning and brandishing her recorder.

Interceding, Jer says, "Comment about what?"

Sammie restates her rumor to Jer as I slip away.

CHAPTER 34

August 16. 1992 at noon

B reaking through the cirrus clouds, the sun de-
buts for the first time in days. Clem bangs his
gavel twice on the podium set atop the small
wooden table we worker bees arranged in front of the
rows of folding chairs. The auction is underway. Clem
sets forth the rules for the bidding. The minimum starting bid is 200,000, and bids will be in 10k intervals, payment by cashier's check at the close.

Reggie surprises me as he raises his bidder's paddle, #14, and makes the first bid.
"$200,000."

"The opening bid of 200k from #14," Clem says as
his clerk notates the bid, "who will bid 210k?"

An elderly man in a tan cloth suit doffs his straw
fedora and wipes his forehead with a large red bandana.
He raises a bidder's paddle numbered 11.

"I have 210,000 from #11, the man in the straw
hat, do I get a 220?"

A tall, thin man with a cowboy hat is filling his
curved pipe with tobacco and tamping it down. He

closes the tobacco pouch and puts it in his vest pocket. He scratches a match across the sandpaper side and lights up, drawing in and puffing out with a satisfied grin. The aroma of vanilla drifts towards me. He has a familiar look. He removes the cowboy hat, and I see his white hair and his sharp jawline. I know that he is a Nordling. He must be 90.

Lifting his cowboy hat in his right hand, he says, "230,000".

"It must be a hat day," Clem says. "Please use your numbered paddle. The cowboy hat with the pipe holds up # 18 and bids 230,000, may I have 240,000? "

After he makes his bid, the old man approaches me.

"Hello Daniel," he says. "I'm your great uncle Ernest, Alexander Nordling's brother, do you remember me?"

"I know you're a Nordling."

"I saw you Christmas 1941," he says, gesturing chest high, "you were only about so tall."

He takes a long pull on his pipe before tapping out the tobacco grounds on the heel of his cowboy boot. The aroma of vanilla lingers. He tells me he has spent three decades in the oil fields of Saudi Arabia teaching Arabian American Oil Company (ARAMCO) employees how to operate heavy equipment. He later built a home in southern California.

I dig deep. Remembering the last time, I saw him I was 10 years old.

When the bidding reaches $300,000, I look at Claire.

"Jer and I are having second thoughts, misgivings if you prefer, about selling the old place."

Claire shrugs her shoulders and says, "Go figure."

"I noticed that the old gentleman with the cowboy hat has stopped bidding," Reggie says as he takes the seat next to me.

"How do you know he's no longer bidding?"

"Just a hunch," Reggie says. "I've taken part in dozens of auctions for my Uncle Zhang's real estate firm back in Boston, and you get an instinct for these things."

Turning to introduce the two, I say, "This old dude with the cowboy hat is my Great Uncle Ernest."

"Pleased to meet you," Great Uncle Ernest says. "Sorry I can't bid more my funds are tied up in a land deal in Beverly Hills."

"Damn!" I say when it hits me that Uncle Ernest, being family, shouldn't be bidding.

I wonder if it's legal for me to bid on property owned by my family.

I need to check with the junior lawyer Sara Swenson's law firm sent over.

"Wait here, I'll be right back."

A young lady dressed in a grey three-piece suit and smiling with so many teeth I swear the sun reflects off them, is Ginger Curtis, attorney-at-law, Sara's junior partner. She offers her hand and gestures for me to take a seat.

"I need to know, is it legal for me to contribute to someone else's bid on my family-owned farm?"

Ginger says, "Since Sara Swenson is your lawyer and you and your brother are the executors of your mother's estate, the simple answer is NO."

"Can we call off the auction?"

"No way, not since the opening bid met the minimum."

The bidding has reached 400k by the time I return.

"Damn!" I repeat once more, handing each of them a refreshing glass of lemonade I picked up from the kitchen.

I take a seat next to Reggie and Uncle Ernest. Uncle Ernest nods a thank you and taps out his pipe on his boot sole before taking a sip.

"Got anything stronger to put in this lemon drink?"

"Check out the top right cupboard in the kitchen," Jer says. "should be a bottle of vodka in there."

"What's the law on digging up private cemeteries?" Reggie says.

"No can do," I say.

"I have another idea," Reggie says. "I have $230,000 in savings, so the bidding has exceeded my ceiling. How much can each of you afford to bid?"

"I get it," I say."You can still make the bid, you're not family, or are you?"

"To my way of thinking, you are as much family as anyone," I say to Reggie. "But I get what you are saying. Where do we get another 230k?"

Uncle Ernest comes back from the kitchen, stirring his lemon aid with his finger and taking a sip.

"Much better."

Uncle Ernest whispers something to Reggie about an old gentleman being at the back porch asking for him.

Reggie steps out to see who is there.

The bidding turns into a bidding war between two parties. An agent for Hunt Realtors and a representative of Chō Enterprises raise the bid price to $470,000,

$480,000, $490,000, and then to $500,000.

"Any more bids?" Clem says pausing, and adding, "If there are no more bids, I will close the bidding at $500K. Going once, going twice...."

Before he could say the words "sold for five hundred thousand" and bang his gavel, Reggie raises his paddle.

"$510k," he says, raising his paddle and adding, "That's as high as I can go."

The Hunt Real Estate man has the grin of a barn cat about to catch a cornered mouse as he raises his #3 paddle and says, "520,000."

Reggie slumps down into his folding chair between Uncle Ernest, Father L, Claire, Jer, and I, exhaling a dramatic groan of defeat.

Uncle Ernest jabs Reggie and says loud enough for the Chō Enterprises rep and the Hunt RE man to overhear.

"Let him have it," he says his shoulders sagging while exhaling in a manner resigned to defeat.

Once more, Clem, the auctioneer, starts his routine about closing the bids.

"I have a bid of 520,000 from #3," Clem says, "if no one bids 530,000... going once, going twice..."

The Real Estate man looks smug and self-satisfied, he is brandishing his checkbook and rising from his folding chair.

"Will you take a company check for $520,000?" he says to Clem before the gavel falls.

At that precise moment, I notice the Chō rep did not make a counter bid, and he too is smiling a similar smile.

They've been in collusion all along.

Before I could warn Reggie, Clem says, "One last chance, who will bid $530,000?"

"530k!" Reggie says, pouncing eagerly and trembling a bit as he waves his #14 paddle, then adds with a theatrical flair, "I don't care if it breaks me."

"Going once for 530k, going twice, SOLD for 530k to the bidder with paddle #14," Clem says as he raps the podium with his gavel signifying the bidding is over.

This time the faces of the Hunt RE man and the Chō rep show shock. They are caught off guard and don't react.

"Please make payment to the gentleman to my right," Clem says, pointing at Reggie with his gavel while turning and grinning at me.

Uncle Ernest leans over and says to Reggie, "You played possum, best I've ever seen."

"What's a possum?" Reggie asks.

They shake all over with laughter. Reggie grins and points to a familiar figure who has just arrived.

"Meet Mr. Yoshino," Reggie says.

Samuel Yoshino arrived unnoticed at the auction. He sought Reggie and spoke to him on the back porch with Uncle Ernest. Then he wrote a check for $70k and gave it to Reggie to add to his 230k and Ernest's 230k.

"Neat how they pulled that off," Jer says.

"How does it feel to be the owner of this fine estate?" I ask Reggie.

"I've never written a bank draft for such a sizeable amount," Reggie says as he heads for the front table to pay Clem's banker.

The Jonson farm is still family owned. It occurs to me that I won't need to ask Sara Swenson about local burial laws. We can go ahead with Reggie's plans for a

Shinto ceremony and for his family from Boston. And Winnie and the twins can stay in the cabin as long as they want.

As the auction ends, Sammie Danish approaches me one more time. I reckon all reporters are persistent; however, Sammie takes the cake.

"Please comment on or at least tell me some history of the Jonson's and their farm for my news column," she says, once more wielding her recorder.

"I'll tell you a bit about the ancestral history of Jonson's farm," I say. "But you must wait a few days for 'the rest of the story'."

"Paul Harvey!" Sammie says, beaming as she adjusts her spectacles, flips open her notepad, and licks her pencil.

At the turn of the century, the Jonson's and the Nordling's traveled by ship and by rail to escape the famine in Sweden. They settled on the fertile lands of the Spokane River Valley and grew potatoes and pursued a better life.

The Jonson's farm was the hub of extended family gatherings for Christmas every year until the Pacific War broke out in1941. After the war, we counted and honored our dead and went about the tasks of the living. Soon we were being absorbed into the beginnings of the nuclear family era of the late 1940s to the 1980s.

Instead of gathering the family together for Christmas holidays, we live enormous distances apart, across the states and even in different nations, in Africa, Saudi Arabia, and Canada.

After Uncle Paul's death, the war in the Pacific ended. Paul was the storyteller in our family, and it passed to me as his apprentice to carry on the tradition.

The Jonson's and Nordling's began a series of family relocations motivated by the need for work and income. With the war ended and the war machine was shutting down, hundreds of thousands of returning veterans sought work. When work opportunities for women dried up, Connie Jonson and her sons moved back east.

The Nordling's and the Jonson's spread out in two directions, west and south. Charlee Sang moved to Boston, and we lost touch. Franklin and Tinya Yoshino disappeared amidst the government's internment of Japanese Americans. My Great Uncle Ernest was working for ARAMCO in Saudi Arabia. When grandma took ill, Connie returned to the farm to care for her. Connie died a few weeks ago. And here we are at the auction.

"The rest of the story," Sammie says, "the part you're not telling me. Does it have to do with the Japanese American members of your extended family?"

I laugh and wag my finger. I don't tell her that I couldn't have told her this much a few months ago before all the reenactments.

"A girl has to try," she says.

I'm developing a fondness for this persistent young lady, and she's the best listener of the reporters I've known. Besides, if she knows who Paul Harvey is, Connie and Claire would approve of her, and so would Connie and Uncle Paul.

"When I finish writing up my notes on "*The Chinaman's Story*," I promise to give you an exclusive."

"Fair enough," Sammie says as she gives me a hug,

closes her notepad, and tucks her pencil behind her ear.

"There's another rumor about a Christmas family gathering floating around, held here at the Jonson's farm in December," Sammie says, "any chance I can wangle an invitation?"

"I might know someone, perhaps we could arrange a swap for the source of the rumor."

She laughs and wags her finger back at me as she hops in her yellow VW Beetle, the next to last to leave the auction. I noticed that the Chō's limousine departed as soon as the bidding closed. Clem and his stack of folding chairs are the only remaining signs that an auction occurred. I crunch across the driveway to the front lawn and lend him a hand, putting the folding chairs in his pickup.

CHAPTER 35

The morning after the auction

A pale-yellow sun adorns Big Black Rock. Claire and I stayed the night in Uncle Paul's cabin, and I hustle out to the old oak tree in the front yard. I can't wait another minute to pull out the auction sign and toss it in the incinerator. Jer strides up to me and we crunch across the gravel to the oil drum we use for burning trash.

"What's that you're burning, Daniel?"

"Burning that ugly auction sign."

He erupts in one of his belly-laughs as he joins me.

Jer makes a carafe of French press, and we head for the front-porch swing.

"Front lawn looks a lot lovelier without that ugly sign," Jer says in between sips.

The newspaper boy bicycles down 9th Street, flings the morning Spokane-Times up on the porch.

"Nice shot!" Jer and I say and wave in unison. We must let the boy know to continue his deliveries. Ours is just about the last neighborhood in America, where we still get our newspapers delivered.

Sitting on the swing, smelling the robust aroma, and sipping my Kenya AA, I remove the rubber band from the rolled-up newspaper. Straightening the paper, I fold it in half for easier reading and hand Jer the sports and comics sections.

Page 1 features a column by Sammie Danish entitled, "A traditional family gathering gets restored."

The pale yellow morning light gives way to daylight as I read Sammie's editorial.

The Chō Enterprises limousine glides to a stop in front of the house on 9th Street. These people get up early. Perhaps they lost something at the auction. No pun intended. The driver dons his cap as he walks around the limo and the rear window on the passenger side motors down. The passenger's arm extends and gestures for me to come over.

"If you please," the chauffeur says, "Mr. Chō asks to have a word with you."

Colonel Chō would be ancient, so this must be a relative with the same surname as the Japanese Colonel that Father L is investigating concerning the Emperor's Secret Letter.

I can't make out his face, but he has long black hair tied in a ponytail.

Speaking to me without leaving the darkness and comfort of his seat in the limousine, he says,"I've tried to contact the new owners to whom I wish to present a most generous offer of $600,000 for the Jonson property."

"My lawyer has been in touch with Ms. Swenson, but she does not represent the new owner, do you know his phone or address?"

The Chō's had lost the bidding at the auction; they had not given up. Their persistence confirms or at least supports Father L's proposition that Chō Enterprises has an ulterior motive for owning Jonson's farm.

Was Chō Enterprises behind the intruder and the mess in the attic? Are they still searching for the Emperor's Letter?

No way I'm taking any more chances. Father L has warned us of the seriousness of the matter and that has me on guard. I never saw his shadow man at the auction, but I sense he is close.

The limousine departs for the second time down 9th Street. The auction sign is smouldering in the trash barrel. It soaks in that the Jonson's in the collective still own the farm. It comes to me we need to celebrate. What better than a family gathering at Christmas.

I call Sammie Danish. Tell her thanks for the editorial and extend an official invitation to our Christmas gathering.

Then I dial Sara Swenson and ask her to mail out invites to everyone she has on her list except Chō Enterprises.

For the first time in weeks, I think of Dawselle and her adopted daughter in South Africa. I need to call her to find out about the Olympics. And invite her and Tracy to visit us at the farm for the holidays now that the family still owns it.

The Barcelona Olympics closing ceremony was on August 9, 1992. The next morning, I draw up a postal money order sufficient for her to purchase two airfares to Spokane for the Christmas gathering. I tear up the check and add adequate funds for first class tickets. Claire is having an influence on me in so many ways.

Reading the remainder of the Spokesman-Review article under the byline of Sammie Danish. On page 2, left column, she concludes with "A traditional family gathering: May it continue forever."

Reggie's brief interview follows wherein he tells Sammie the story of his father Franklin Yoshino and his friendship with Paul Jonson. He says that was his motivation for buying the property and that he planned to renovate and farm a section of the land. Sammie concludes her article with, "I'll tell you the rest of this remarkable family's story soon."

Father L's dire warning returns with the name Yoshino.

My fear for our family's safety grows. I wonder if the Chō's have seen this article and found that Reggie is Japanese and not the son of Charlee Sang. The name Yoshino would surely have tipped them off.

Would that be enough to get them to back off and leave his family alone? Not likely, if they will cough up $600,000 for the farm, they appear certain about the secret letter being hidden on the farm, but it's worth a try.

An editorial below Sammie's article reads, "It's too bad that foreigners are buying up our country," attributes to anonymous.

I can never prove it, but I tell Claire that I suspect that Hunt Realtors and Chō Enterprises are the ones behind that editorial. Maybe I'm paranoid, but Father L's warning rings in my head.

CHAPTER 36

Jonson's farm, November-
December 1992

After all our research and reenactments, Claire is pleased that Jer and I have learned that we never fell out of love with the old Jonson homestead. It's a spiritual venue. Our extended family is reuniting.

I failed to make these connections during the war when I was a boy of 10 to 14. But I realize, as we plan for the first family gathering in over fifty years, that my nightmare in Africa was a wake-up call sent to me by my mom.

My trauma over Uncle Paul's grave caused me to block out my childhood. Then I wandered the world, unaware that I have repressed painful childhood memories. Mom's death led me to a renewed sense of guilt over failing to keep my promise to reunite the family.

But Claire is right. Many joyful memories now flood my memory-attic.

Clustering around grandma's kitchen table, I

sense friendly family ghosts. We draw up plans for where to house our extended family and guests. A family gathering of twenty adults and ten children will arrive at the hub from scattered locations around the world for the renewal of a family Christmas tradition. Those numbers are according to the list of acceptances to Sara Swenson's invitation letters.

"How did we get 40 relatives into this place in the forties?" Jer says. "We hadn't built the cabins."

"Speaking of building cabins, back to work," Reggie says as he straps on his carpentry belt and hands me mine, which I sling over my shoulder.

At ten past noon, Reggie declares the Chinaman's cabin ready for the first family arrivals. His wife Winnie and their 10-year-old twins, Conrad, and Paula are arriving at Spokane Intermodal in two hours.

I hang my tool belt on the coat rack by the front door and sidle up to Reggie.

"Thank goodness we won't have to move the family graves."

Reggie grins and reminds me we have some burials to attend to as a Shinto priest is coming to sanctify Opa's and Franklin's graves later today. First, he's headed for town and promises to return with Winnie and the twins.

"Don't let the priest start the ceremony without us," Reggie says. "I have one last favor to ask. May we rebury Moonbear next to Franklin and Opa, so she can watch over them in the next life?"

An hour later, the sound of gravel crunches in the driveway as Reggie drives past in a rental Chevy pickup truck, headed for town and the airport. Winnie and the twins are the initial family to arrive for our first family gathering in 50 years. Guests and clan members will arrive the week before Christmas.

Claire, Father L, Jer, and I are on the front porch to greet Reggie's family when they arrive at the farm.

"Wow! Is that barn ever red?" Conrad says.

"No, that's the Jonson's house," Reggie says, "I'll show you the barn later."

"Can we climb up on that big black rock?" Paula says.

"Do you enjoy scary stories?"

"Oh, very much," Paula says.

"When all the family and children have arrived," I say, "on Christmas Eve, we'll climb up on Big Black Rock. I'll tell you a scary tale that features the cabin you'll be living in."

Reggie cuts in and asks, "Does anyone want to see the cabin?"

"I was wondering where we'll be staying," Winnie says with a smile.

We all climb aboard Reggie's truck. The twins and I hang our feet over the tailgate as we bounce along down the trail to the Chinaman's cabin. Nestled in the forest and isolated from view, it's a private place. Reggie and I tack a huge holly wreath to the front door and hang a banner that reads, "Welcome Home!"

"Welcome to your new home!" I say, "I know you'll be happy living here."

After dropping off their luggage and getting them settled in at the cabin, we all return to grandma's kitchen for a snack while awaiting the Shinto priest.

Someone's knocking on the front door.

"Please see who that is?" I say to the twins.

Paula and Conrad drop the popcorn they are stringing for the Christmas tree and scramble to the door.

The twins stare at the stranger, a short, stout man with a thinning goatee.

"Who is it?"

The twins act puzzled.

"Welcome to casa Jonson," I say as I step forward to greet him.

"He's your godfather, Samuel," I say.

Conrad and Paula each grab a hand and drag Samuel into the living room to see the tree they are decorating.

It was not clear when or if Samuel was coming to our family gathering, so we haven't planned for him.

"I need to trek over to the cabin and tell Reggie and Winnie that Samuel Yoshino is here," I say to Claire. "He can stay in their cabin."

Meanwhile, another vehicle crunches through the gravel in the driveway.

"The Shinto priest has arrived," Reggie says. "He'll bless the cabin first, and then we'll rebury Moonbear next to Franklin and Opa in the family cemetery before sunset."

"Please join us," Reggie says to Samuel.

A vintage VW bus with hippie peace symbols and colorful flowers painted on the sides, parks in the gravel driveway. He first performs a Shinto ceremony at the Chinaman's cabin to free it of evil.

Then we all assemble behind Uncle Paul's cabin near the base of Big Black Rock at the family cemetery, where he performs a second traditional ritual over the graves. He places sticks around the circumference of the cemetery. Burning incense fills the air, purifying the grounds of all evil spirits. The Shinto priest wears a ghostlike white garment. He holds up a silver decanter. It hangs from a chain that spreads smoke as he shakes and swings it while doing his dance and incantations.

"In Japan, they call it a Kumikō ceremony, " Samuel says.

Participants sit near one another and take turns drawing in the aroma from a censer they pass around. We play games to guess the incense material. Samuel wins.

Reggie has fulfilled his father's last request and reburied Moonbear's ashes next to Franklin's and Opa's.

Friends and relatives of our extended family continue arriving all week, right up to Christmas Eve. Jer's wife Amanda and Lilly are settling in upstairs in the farmhouse.

Mrs. Yamasaki and her granddaughter Cayla arrive and reunite with Samuel Yoshino.

Everyone hurries into the house after the Shinto priest departs, it's getting cold. There's a soft knock on the front door.

A small child stands in the doorway, shivering and clinging to her mother's leg.

"Come in!" I say, "Warm yourselves by the fire."

"How about some hot apple cider with cinnamon?" Claire says.

"Thank you!" the tiny woman says as she unbundles the oversized fur-lined parka that consumes the child.

"Is Father Kibet here?"

At the sound of his name, Father L comes to the front door. He has been so quiet that I swear he is on sentry duty.

"Greetings, Mrs. Yamazaki," Father L says, "I'm so pleased you are here."

Samuel Yoshino rises from next to the fireplace. He is weeping tears of joy.

"Tanti, it is you, and this must be my great-granddaughter?"

"Yes, Cayla was five last month."

They embrace, and while the old man and Tanti cry tears of happiness, Cayla smiles. Samuel lifts her to look into her eyes and see into her soul.

Tanti, the woman I know as Ms. Yamasaki, is one of Samuel and Mikki Yoshino's adopted children, and they will soon share many memories.

Samuel looks up at me and says, "This is the best Christmas present of all."

Dawselle calls, "We are at the airport in Amsterdam."

Tracy cuts in, "Mom got a medal for you."

After Dawselle rings off, I join Claire on the front porch swing enjoying the crisp winter air and leave the diner dishes to Jer and Father L.

A taxi pulls up next to the gigantic oak, and the driver honks twice. A man carries himself with athletic grace as he walks up to the porch, leading a child in each hand.

"I can't tell if he's Chinese or Japanese, all Asians look alike to white people," I say to Claire.

"Is this the Jonson place?"

Claire and I rise and greet them as they reach the porch steps.

"I'm Daniel Jonson."

"Curt Sang," the man says. "These are my grand-children, Juniper and Eric. I'm Charlee's son."

Claire says, "What a fantastic surprise."

"Excuse us for not sending you a message that we will come," Curt says.

They have just arrived from their home in Ha-waii. It was only the day before yesterday when they got the invite from Sara Swenson about the family gather-ing.

"My wife is taking care of our other two grand-children at our home in Hawaii, and she sends her bless-ings."

When Curt tells us of his father Charlee's passing, I feel a unique mix of sadness and joy; I have long im-agined him as still missing in action. It seemed right.

My joy is over Charlee having a son and grandchil-dren; but I feel for their safety.

And what of Curt? He will be the actual target of the Chō's if they find out he is alive and at the farm.

The day before Christmas, 1992

The extended family has gathered for the first

time in five decades. At sunset, a crescent moon creeps in and out of the clouds. I have something important to do on this hallowed eve. It's not about either of my promises to my Uncle Paul, or is it?

We left the two yellow ribbons tied to the ancient oak tree after the auction. Jer and I bundle up the children in winter coats and scarves and we head out front to tell them the story behind our family heroes.

Then we summon everyone to gather around the old oak as Father L says a prayer for the spirits and souls of those who went before us.

A renewal of a tradition is taking place, not a reenactment, a reality, 50 years after our last family gathering.

"Maybe this gathering makes all the reenactments worthwhile," Claire says, "But I sense that you are far away somewhere in that memory-attic of yours."

"I have yet another promise to keep," I say. "An unspoken one, more about family responsibility. I am the family storyteller."

Claire solicits Winnie's help with the cooking duties, and by evening familiar aromas fill the kitchen and the entire house. Pies are baking in the big oven. I wait for the timer to ding, signaling that the strawberry-rhubarb pies are ready to take from the oven and cool on the kitchen windowsill. Soon the mouthwatering aroma reaches as far away as the cabins.

I swear that within 5 minutes, Reggie's twins are at the kitchen door asking their mom and Claire, "What's baking?"

"Strawberry rhubarb pie," Claire says, adding, "the pies are for dessert after Christmas supper this evening. But first run and tell all the children to meet Uncle Daniel atop Big Black Rock, and he will tell them Uncle Paul's favorite scary story."

As Claire places the last of the pies on the kitchen windowsill to cool in the night air, she hears a ghostly voice.

"Now, don't you children be spoiling this evening's supper?"

◆ ◆ ◆

7 pm PST, December 24, 1992

Big Black Rock

The evening sky turns into a painter's canvas of reds and yellows, dark blue, and then black. I gather an armload of firewood and leave the cemetery and climb atop Big Black Rock. I asked Claire and Father L to lead the children up before dark. Seated around a crackling fire to stay warm, with a carpet of stars overhead, I wait for the children to settle in and for one of them to spot the crescent moon in a parting of the clouds.

Winnie points up.

"Thank you, Winnie."

Then I introduce a new generation to the storytelling part of our family gathering tradition.

A crescent moon appears as we depart the cemetery. As I start the fire, I'm thinking serendipity.

Conrad and Paula are the first to join me atop Big Black Rock, eager to learn the legend of The Chinaman's Story. Claire and Father L arrive with Samuel, Tanti and Cayla, Dawselle with Tracy, Curt with Juniper and Eric.

Jer and Amanda with granddaughter Lilly, and Great Uncle Ernest and Reggie and Winnie bring up the rear.

I offer a silent prayer for those not with us. Grandpa and Grandma, Connie, Uncle Paul, Charlee Sang, Franklin and Opa, Mikki, and Moonbear. The full report from Major Nutting and the DOD confirms that Corporal Timmy Nordling was KIA in North Africa in the summer of 1942. I see all their eager faces in the flickering firelight.

As dark settles in around us, I motion for the children to move in close to the fire.
I repeat Uncle Paul's tale of the history of Big Black Rock, and then I say, "Does anyone want to play a game?"

We play grandma's food game.

Then I say, "Do you want to hear a scary story?"

I point up, and the children all look up just as the clouds pass by and part, revealing a bright shining crescent moon overhead.

'The Chinaman's Story' is part of our family heritage. Soon, I must select an apprentice storyteller on whom will fall the duty of spreading past legends, to keep our ancestors alive for another generation.

Grandma Jonson's Strawberry-Rhubarb Pie:
Pie crust, woven top, as per all my pies.
Filling:
Sweet strawberries (6 cups sliced, not diced)
Tart rhubarb (3 cups cooked in fruit juice)
Orange juice with tiny slices of peel
Light brown sugar on top (optional)
(With Grandma's Permission)

The kitchen phone is ringing. I let it go to the answering machine.

A sexy gravelly voice says, "It's after hours, please call back."

The End

AUTHOR'S NOTES

The Japanese American Repository (JAR) is a fictitious name; however, an important and wonderful archive is maintained by Densho, a nonprofit organization started in 1996.

Densho is a Japanese term meaning to pass on to the next generation, or to leave a legacy.

The legacy of the United States government incarceration of innocent people for the duration of World War II, solely because of their ancestry. Testimonials and artifacts are archived on the Densho website.

David Marshall Hunt

Visit the author's website and join no obligation mailing list and receive a FREE essay and occasional newsletters:

https://www.davidmarshallhunt.com

Check out his Amazon author page at:

http://amazon.com/author/dhunt

Other novels by David :

The Star Stone, The Chair, & The Dog Book1: Secrets of the Star Stone Society. The Pilgrimage Book 2.

Flower Girl: A Burton Family Mystery.

"Under the Protection of Moon," continues the family gathering mystery series with the Emperor's Secret Letter introduced in "Strawberry Rhubarb Pie" ... the family is in real danger when family secrets collide ... COMING SOON!